PLAGUE SAINT

Rory North

Chapter One
As Red as Roses

Everyone who said hell was fire and flames was wrong. Hell was the biting cold and dark skies that came with the season Winter Pierce was named for.

"You're brooding," River said as he walked by, mug of coffee in hand.

Winter didn't stop trying to glare the icy street below the window out of existence. "Of course I am. It's dark and it's cold."

River stopped, then backed up until he was at her side. "Can't you sign up for afternoon shifts?"

Not anymore. But River couldn't know about that. "Then it would be dark when I leave work instead." Winter sighed. "This place really is hell."

Her brother took another sip of his coffee, undoubtedly coming up with a polite way to tell her she was being ridiculous. "And what exactly do you think you're being punished for?"

Two weeks ago, Winter wouldn't have had an answer. But killing someone and impersonating them probably left some kind of mark on your soul. Even if the death was an accident. Even if it was to save your mother.

"Come on, Winter," River pressed. "Snow's just snow. Seasons are just seasons."

"And Devil's Pass is just a city built too far north for my taste." Winter finally turned around, sick of staring at the dark street outside their apartment building. The hallway River had been headed for branched off to her left. The space in front of her was the family's dining and living room. The wooden floors were always cold, the white walls could do with a fresh coat of paint, and the sparse furniture had been there for as long as Winter could remember.

River reached into the pocket of his coat and pulled out a golden locket. *The* golden locket. "Would it cheer you up if I let you win this back?"

Winter snorted. "Let me win? Yeah, right." Her gaze flickered to the old grandfather clock on the other side of the dining table. "But we don't have time for a card game." Last time Dad had caught them playing cards before work, he'd warned them that he'd confiscate the deck for a month if they were late.

"Lucky draw, then?" River raised an eyebrow. "Come on. You have nothing to lose."

"Fine."

Winter followed River through the dining room into the kitchen, where Mom was packing up her own bag to go to work at the bank near City Hall. Her long hair, the same shade of dark brown as River's, hung in a thick braid down her back.

River's hair had almost grown long enough to be pulled back, too. Dad would probably tell him to go get a trim soon.

Mom slid on one of her gloves. "You two leaving now?" she asked as she reached for the other.

"In a minute." River opened a drawer and pulled out the card deck. He shuffled the stack a few times, then fanned them out across the counter facedown and gestured for Winter to pick one. After she made her choice, he selected his own card.

Winter held up hers. "Six of roses."

"Damn." River revealed his. Two of suns.

Winter laughed and held out her hand. Despite losing, River grinned as he dropped the locket into her palm. "Enjoy it while it lasts," he told her. "After dinner tonight, I'm beating you at devil's bridge."

"Keep telling yourself that." Winter slid the locket into her coat.

Still smiling, River asked, "You walking out with Mom and I?"

"I have to get my bag from my room," Winter replied. "And if I leave now, I'll be early, anyway." She nodded to the cards spread out on the counter. "I can put those away."

"That's the winner's job, anyway."

Winter rolled her eyes. "Sure."

"We'll see you tonight, then," Mom said as she finished buttoning her coat and picked up her bag. "Your father said he's making casserole, so be back by six. Both of you."

Winter nodded. "See you tonight."

While Mom and River headed out, Winter gathered up the cards. The last one she picked up was her winning card, and she took a moment to run her thumb along the edge, to study the white roses printed on the front. It had been a couple of weeks since she and River had made time to play a real game. It would be nice to take her mind off of things for an hour or so.

She returned the cards to the drawer and walked to her room. Pausing in her doorway, she took the locket back out. Her thumb pressed the button on top and it popped open, revealing the photograph of Daisy—the Saint Bernard they'd lost to old age three years ago—with Winter and River on either side of her.

So sentimental this morning. Winter shook her head. Maybe she was getting sick. She crossed the room to her window and pushed it open. A blast of frigid wind greeted her, making her wince. Jaw clenched, hand shivering, she grabbed her black bag off the dark tiled roof below and yanked it inside.

Cold as it was, this rear roof was the best hiding place. Her family wouldn't stumble across the bag accidentally, and the high stone wall behind their building made it impossible to access or even see the roof from anywhere but Winter's window.

She slung the bag over her shoulder and returned to the kitchen. Dad was up now, reading the newspaper at the counter. He looked up as she entered. "Off to the station?"

Winter nodded and set her bag on the counter. As she pulled her long white-blonde hair up into a ponytail—lighter than even Dad's blonde—she noticed his gaze linger on the black bag a little too long for comfort.

"Mom said you're making casserole tonight?" Winter asked, hoping to distract him.

It worked. His pale blue eyes flitted to her. "That's the plan. You'll be back by six?"

"I should be." Winter picked her bag back up. "See you tonight."

"See you tonight."

Winter pulled her hood over her head and stepped out into the darkness. It was already seven a.m., but there wasn't even a hint of sun on the horizon. Only dull streetlights and the glow from apartment windows offered a glimpse of the snowflakes drifting through the air.

She hurried down the icy metal stairs as fast as she dared, sparing a quick glance at the drawn curtains of the apartment below hers. Rumor had it the Fischers were getting sick, but she had yet to see them come into the hospital.

They probably couldn't afford it.

Winter waited for the trolley under the streetlight that flickered more and more each day. She kept a gloved hand wrapped around the knife in her pocket. She'd yet to hear of any trouble on this block, but enough mugging victims came into the hospital each week to keep her on her toes. Of course, that wasn't her department.

The trolley finally came rolling up the tracks, bell ringing and loose parts rattling, a little more of its yellow paint chipped off than the day before. Winter nodded a greeting at the conductor as she climbed in and made her way to the back.

The new routine was becoming familiar: passing the city guard station where she used to organize files, getting off the trolley at a restaurant across the street from the hospital, changing into her stolen uniform in the bathroom, and sneaking out the window.

Winter paused outside the restaurant to stare across the street at the hospital. The building sat at the very edge of the city's north side, its back facing the forest beyond. Besides the restaurant, there were also a few shops and apartments on this street, but it was clear that this area bordered on wilderness. The dark forest loomed in the gaps between buildings. Some mornings, Winter could hear the cries of animals. Occasional howls that chilled her blood.

The snow began to fall faster. Still, she turned to gaze at the rest of Devil's Pass. The land sloped down from here, and from the right angle, she could see the trolley tracks snaking down the pass. Then there were the sections of stone wall around the city, the warm glow of streetlights scattered in the darkness, and even the gleaming bronze dome of City Hall.

Mountains loomed over it all, icy and jagged, towering in every direction. Apparently, they made most people feel protected. Winter just felt trapped.

Unable to stand the suffocating view any longer, she went inside.

The smell of coffee and cooking sausages followed Winter as she hurried past the front counter and into the bathroom before any employees could notice her. In one of the stalls, she shrugged off her coat and kicked off her boots. The black long-sleeved shirt and pants she wore underneath were too thin to keep out the cold, but they were perfect to wear with the Plague Saint's uniform.

The uniform was mostly black leather—the coat, the hat, the boots, the gloves. The exception was the beaked bronze mask that attached to an upper faceplate. It covered the front of Winter's head and hid her eyes under dark lenses. It was apparently a simpler, sleeker version of something from the old world, according to the texts she'd found in the real Plague Saint's office. Something even older than the rare pieces of technology in the hospital labs.

She ran a finger along the curved metal beak. This mask had always struck her as unnecessary. The other doctors wore simple surgical masks and managed to avoid catching their patients' illnesses. Winter didn't know much about the man whose place she'd taken, but she suspected he had a flair for the dramatic. After all, he'd quickly embraced the title of Saint when people first began whispering it years ago.

Or maybe he'd simply hoped the strange outfit would distract from the fact that he was on the shorter side. It certainly worked to Winter's advantage. She was just tall enough to make the uniform fit.

This wasn't the only uniform. The Saint had several more in his office, all identical. And of course, there was the one still on his body, somewhere. Winter shuddered at the thought.

The uniform's coat buttoned up and its thin hood went underneath the hat. Winter put the mask on last, threw her bag over her shoulder, and pressed an ear to the stall door. The bathroom was usually empty this time of morning—even with the restaurant already serving breakfast—but she couldn't be too careful.

Nothing. She slipped out of the stall, made her way to the window, and climbed into the alley behind the building.

Winter had known when she started all this that she wouldn't be able to keep it up forever. She also had no idea what to do about it. She could simply stop showing up to the hospital and get a job somewhere else. Maybe even try going back to the guard station. But the sudden disappearance of the most important person in the city would surely launch an investigation.

And if she stopped, people would die. Well, more than were already dying. She couldn't save everyone.

It was so much brighter inside the hospital, and the light was only intensified by how white everything was: white floors, white walls, white ceilings. Winter squinted as she headed for her office, grateful for the fact that her face was hidden.

Her office. How long had she thought of the place as hers? She'd felt like a stranger in someone else's home, at first. Afraid to touch anything. Afraid one misplaced item would give her away as an imposter.

Light spilled out from under the office door. Phoebe was already here, then. Winter turned the handle and stepped inside.

The office was a welcome reprieve from the sterile white of the hallways behind her. The floors were dark wood, the wallpaper patterned gray and green, and the shelves lining the walls were packed with a variety of books. Chairs upholstered with red fabric sat on either side of a large desk. In fact, the door to the laboratory was the only significant patch of white in the space.

Phoebe was on her feet in an instant, moving so fast she nearly knocked over her chair. "Finally! You're late."

The Plague Saint was two minutes later than usual, and Phoebe was panicking. Not surprising. Winter eyed the papers in her assistant's hands. "I hope those are patient files and not doodles."

In her time working at the city guard station, she'd learned a valuable piece of information: guard helmets had built-in voice modifiers that made the guards sound more intimidating by deepening their voices. Swiping one had been no easy task, even before she'd quit, and fitting it into the plague mask was a challenge. But it had been worth it. Winter's voice was unrecognizable.

"Uh—" Phoebe shuffled through the pages, a hint of a flush showing on the warm, golden tones of her face. "Of course. Oh, the hospital director stopped by! He brought this week's payment." She nodded to the envelope on Winter's desk.

"Great." Winter moved toward the desk.

"That's not all." Phoebe tucked one of her dark shoulder-length curls behind her ear. "He asked for a follow-up on Andersen's bill."

"Jacob Andersen?" Winter picked up a piece of paper left under her payment. It was the bill in question. "He died."

"Director says money's still owed." Phoebe shrugged. "Said to contact his family."

"He didn't have any immediate family." Winter sighed. She'd have to deal with that later. The other stack of papers that had been left on the desk, her patient files for the morning, went into her bag. "I'm starting my rounds. The rest of yesterday's evaluations still need to be sorted."

"Will do, sir."

Winter picked up her bag—which contained, among other things, the book that stood between her and failure—and the unusually heavy black staff that was topped with a pair of carved bronze wings. She hated the damn thing. The old Plague Saint had carried it around and made it clear he'd use it to keep people away from him without hesitation. So far, Winter hadn't had to do more than carry it, but she worried someone might force her hand.

You've already killed someone, genius.

But that was an accident. Mostly. And regardless, there was a difference between the powerful man she'd killed and the desperate, dying people that filled the hospital.

The book, on the other hand, was the most valuable thing the Plague Saint had left behind. The Plague Bible, as he'd titled it, had all of the information Winter needed to help people. Help enough of them to avoid suspicion, at least.

In addition to notes on identifying plagues and checklists to run through for new patients, the Plague Bible was full of formulas for medications. Winter found all of the ingredients mentioned in the Saint's lab, and the equipment involved was easy enough to figure out with his instructions.

But medicine was only part of the equation. The real doctor had years of experience to back him up. Sometimes decisions had to be made, sometimes unusual symptoms popped up, and Winter could only make her best guess on how to respond based on old patient notes.

Winter entered her first patient's room. The woman had been checked in an hour before her arrival, and while other doctors had started treatment, she'd been asked to consult.

"Has she been diagnosed, yet?" Winter asked the nurse standing over the unconscious woman.

The nurse shook his head. "All we've done so far is get her hydrated." He held out a clipboard. "Here are Dr. Morrison's notes. He was thinking green or blue, because of the eye infection."

The plagues that had sprung up in the northern cities were just one of the many consequences of a damaged Earth. Devil's Pass was safe from heat waves and floods, but it was infested with diseases that lingered even centuries after its founding, said to have emerged from thawed glaciers. Nearly a dozen illnesses were considered common, and at some point, someone decided to slap the name "plague" on the five worst ones, along with a random color to differentiate them.

Green plague was the easiest to treat. Blue would be a bit trickier. Winter dismissed the nurse with a nod of her head and moved to examine the woman, scanning Dr. Morrison's notes as she did. It would be tough to determine which of the two plagues the woman had by sight alone. She'd have to run a sample test, another procedure outlined in the Plague Bible.

The worst thing she'd learned from reading the Plague Bible wasn't the descriptions of awful symptoms that couldn't be treated, nor was it the countless documented cases that ended in death. It was the surprising amount of useful information that only the Saint had known. He'd detailed a dozen different tricks to identify diseases that were otherwise indistinguishable from each other. He had cures for many, and treatments for most others. And for the ones that he'd yet to find a way to fight, he had remedies for the symptoms to keep patients comfortable until they were either lucky enough to recover or faced the more likely outcome: death.

And he'd kept it all to himself.

Other doctors thought the Plague Saint was a miracle worker, but he wasn't even a real doctor. He was a scientist who refused to share. Winter initially assumed it was so he could have all the glory, but knowing what she'd learned before killing him, she supposed he might have had even more sinister reasons. Power. Leverage. The entire city, government included, under his control.

She'd begun revealing his secrets to the other doctors, but she could only share so much at once. Dumping the entire Plague Bible's wealth of knowledge in a single day would raise questions she couldn't answer without revealing herself.

Winter took a sample of the sick woman's saliva to test and moved on to the next patient. Once she finished her first round of check-ins, she'd show a few of the other doctors the chemical test that would reveal whether the woman had green or blue plague.

Of course, what should have been an hour's work was interrupted by questions from other doctors, Phoebe popping up to ask for signatures on paperwork, and new patients coming in. But nearly four hours after arriving at the hospital, Winter was finally in the lab connected to her office, setting up the test.

Phoebe knocked on the open door frame. "May I enter, oh great Plague Saint?"

Winter sighed. "Sure."

Phoebe had started working as Winter's assistant two days after she'd replaced the real Saint, and at first, she'd thought it another bit of good luck that the Saint's request for an assistant had been filled so late. She interacted with Phoebe more than anyone else at the hospital, and replicating whatever interactions her and the Saint would have had prior to Winter taking his place would have been impossible.

The downside was that Phoebe was unfamiliar with how harsh the Saint had been to people around him, and Winter apparently wasn't enough of an asshole to scare Phoebe into avoiding sarcasm and the occasional quip. Phoebe was the only person in the hospital who didn't fear her to some degree.

Well, Phoebe, and the hospital director.

"There's a new patient you should see," Phoebe said, snapping Winter from her thoughts. "His coworkers said he was fine this morning but got really sick in just a few hours."

Winter frowned. "A few hours? Why didn't they bring him in as soon as he started showing symptoms?"

"His supervisor threatened to fire him if he left, until it was clear he was on the verge of dropping dead. And everyone who did help get him here is getting their pay slashed for the day."

Great. Not only had this poor guy's chances of survival gone down, but he'd probably spread whatever he had to his coworkers. Maybe Winter could persuade the director to let her bill the factory instead of the patient. She'd had the idea for a couple of weeks, and this was the perfect opportunity to try it.

"If he got sick that quickly, it's probably red plague," she said to Phoebe. Even red plague didn't typically come on quite that fast, but Winter had to assume the guy had been hiding his symptoms at first in hopes of getting a few more hours of work in. "What room?"

"Seven-oh-four," Phoebe answered.

The tower. That part of the hospital had the strictest quarantine protocols. Winter grabbed her bag. "I'll go get his treatment started. I should be back in about fifteen minutes. Could you get word to any available doctors that I'm going to run a demonstration?"

"Yessir." Phoebe did a mock salute as Winter passed her. "Say, you think maybe this guy could have the white plague?"

"That's not real."

"You sure about that, doc?" Phoebe asked. "Because I'm hearing more and more nurses say that some of the red plague deaths aren't quite like the rest—"

"Everyone's body reacts differently," Winter interrupted, pausing in the doorway. "And it's not your job to worry about it."

There was no white plague. There couldn't be. The Plague Saint had never mentioned anything like it in his notes.

Which meant if it was real, Winter would have nothing to fight it with.

She shook her head as she left the lab behind. Green, blue, violet, yellow, red. Those were the five major plagues, the same five that had been around since Devil's Pass was little more than a mining settlement. Various mayors over the past century or so had built their campaigns on getting rid of the damn things once and for all, but none had succeeded. Some tried quarantines that the city failed to commit to well enough to do any good. Trade with nearby communities only complicated matters.

There had also been attempts to distribute masks to the general population, which helped, though there had never been enough money funneled into their production to make a real difference.

Other mayors had paid scientists exorbitantly to find permanent cures that would impart immunity on the population, but nothing stuck. Even current treatments occasionally had to be modified as the plagues evolved. Slowly, but surely, they were getting tougher to fight. And they were strangely persistent. Even the Saint had made notes in the Bible about their unusual nature, though he'd never made any real conclusions about why that was.

In addition to eye infections, green and blue plagues caused bruising all over the body. Violet plague was a more serious illness characterized mainly by frequent vomiting, while yellow affected the liver and produced extreme jaundice. And red plague, the worst of them all, caused patients to cough up blood.

Winter rode the elevator up to the seventh floor alone. It was such a creaky, rickety thing that she usually preferred the stairs, but red plague cases were time sensitive.

Five nurses were already in the room when she arrived, blocking the patient from view. Winter sighed. "Coming through. Give him some space, please."

"We started the stabilization process," one nurse said as she took a step back.

Winter's mouth opened to thank her, but the words caught in her throat. The rest of the nurses moved out of the way, leaving her to stare at the young man lying unconscious in the hospital bed.

Another nurse spoke up. "Here's the patient's file." He handed Winter a clipboard, and she took it, barely processing the action. "Need anything else from us?"

She didn't answer. Couldn't answer. All she could do was move her gaze back and forth between the familiar name on the file and her unconscious brother.

Chapter Two
In Sight and Mind

Three hours. River had started showing symptoms three hours before he was brought in.

Could he have infected Mom? Dad? Winter? And where did he catch it? Someone else at the factory? The Plague Saint had noted that red plague exposure could lead to symptoms in half a day or less in many patients; the five plagues all had unusually short incubation periods compared to other illnesses, which the Saint had repeatedly commented on as bizarre.

But what if Phoebe was right? What if this was something worse than red plague? Something that didn't have a standard treatment, let alone a cure?

"Plague Saint?" the closest nurse pressed, his tone laced with concern. "Is something wrong?"

Focus. Winter sucked in a deep breath. She couldn't save River if she was panicking. "You gave him a starter dose of Red-X?"

"Of course."

"He waited three hours to come in." Winter scanned the notes the nurses had made. "Let's put him on a level five schedule. Keep him hydrated. I'm going to bring him a new supplemental treatment I've been working on." The Saint had "supplemental treatments" for all five plagues. And he'd had some of them for months, based on his notes. "Has his family been contacted?"

One of the other nurses shook her head. "Not yet."

"Well, get on it." Dad had nowhere else to be today, and company would be good for River. They'd make him wear a mask and stay ten feet away, but it was better than nothing. Winter handed the clipboard back to one of the nurses. "I'll be back soon."

Her gaze lingered on River for a moment before she forced her legs to take her out of the room. His light skin had paled to near white, and the sheen of sweat on his forehead indicated fever.

No need to panic yet. The Saint's medicine still had a decent chance of helping him. It would do far more than Red-X alone, at least.

Red-X was one of the drugs developed by the hospital. Each plague had a corresponding drug, but the treatments the Saint had created were more effective. In the two weeks since Winter had taken over and begun using the Saint's treatments more...*liberally* than he had, the red plague survival rate had gone up from nine percent to fifty-two percent. Winter claimed a recent breakthrough, but the treatment had existed for nearly a month prior. And the Saint's notes even stated that he'd used it on some patients.

But why not all of them?

Fifty-two percent. But there were a dozen factors she had to take into account. River was only twenty-one and had a healthy immune system, but he'd waited so long to come in. *Idiot.* How many of his coworkers had he spread it to? His supervisor had better pray Winter didn't retaliate. Was there someone she could file a complaint to? Would they care?

Not now. Winter needed to focus on getting him stable. Retaliation—or, God forbid, revenge for her brother's life—would have to wait.

Winter threw open the door to the Saint's office and froze. Again. As if this day couldn't get any worse.

The tall, thin man standing in the center of the office turned to face Winter as she entered. The gray in his hair and wrinkles in his pale skin put him in his late fifties. The dark blue suit he wore suggested he was important.

"Plague Saint," Director Adams greeted her without a hint of warmth. "We need to discuss a few matters."

"Now's not a good time." Winter fought to keep her voice cool. "I have a red plague patient I need to get treatment to."

"That's part of why I'm here, actually." Adams sank into the chair opposite Winter's desk, the same chair Phoebe usually sat in. Winter frowned, wondering where Phoebe was.

Apparently guessing her question, Adams said, "I told your assistant to take a lunch break. We'll have some time to ourselves." He nodded toward the door.

Winter pulled it shut behind her and crossed the room to her desk.

"As I'm sure you know, I've been incredibly busy the past couple of weeks," Adams said as she sat down. "Mayor Atherton's been dealing with complaints about the city budget, particularly in relation to the hospital." He leaned forward and clasped his hands together. "Of course, it's not your job to worry about that. It's your job to heal the sick, isn't it, Plague Saint?"

Winter's heart hammered against its cage. Was he accusing her of something?

"So, you understand why I haven't been around much," Adams continued after a moment. "And why I've only been able to communicate with you through letters. Which can easily fall into the wrong hands."

Winter needed to say something. Anything. "Of course."

"That being said, I do find it interesting that survival rates have increased so...*dramatically* over the past couple of weeks."

Winter's hands tightened into fists in her lap. This is what she'd been afraid of. There was a status quo, and no matter how many entries she read in the Saint's journals, there were things she couldn't replicate: relationships, habits, and all the little details of whatever agreement he had with the hospital director.

"I've made some rapid progress in my treatments," she said, internally wincing at how flimsy the statement sounded.

Adams leaned forward. "I understand that being mysterious and aloof is your thing, but don't forget that I'm the one paying you. I also understand that I haven't been able to communicate my desires for our patients. But I'm back now." His voice lowered. "And I am very close friends with the owner of the factory River Pierce works at. This whole incident is a lawsuit waiting to happen, if he survives. Or worse, protests. Louder and harder to fight."

Winter's jaw clenched. The fact that Adams was laying this out so plainly to her only made it clearer what kind of man the Plague Saint had been.

Adams rose to his feet. "Medicine is expensive," he continued. "I think we should keep Pierce on Red-X for now. That should do just fine, don't you think?"

A Red-X-only treatment schedule would likely kill River. Winter stood up, mirroring Adams. "I agree."

So much for Winter's plan of billing the factory and saving her family from even more debt. She watched the back of Adam's head as he approached the door. Her best option was to sneak the better treatment to River, right? Blame his recovery on pure luck? Pray Adams didn't question her further?

Adam paused. "Oh, and if I don't receive an update on Andersen's payment by the end of the day, I'm sending the bill to the city guard. If you have time, maybe track down his next of kin and give them a warning. But no need to concern yourself with it if you're busy."

Winter swallowed and nodded. She knew from her time working in the guard office exactly what would happen: the city guard would track down whatever poor soul was Andersen's closest living relative, and if they couldn't pay the bill—or afford a sufficient payment plan—they'd be thrown in jail. Or at the very least, lose their home.

Winter couldn't let that happen. But she was on thin ice as it was. Apparently, the Plague Saint had been picking and choosing who to save based on Adams's requests.

Monsters. Both of them. And the factory owner, as well. Winter paced back and forth across the office. With Adams back, she'd probably have to stop sharing new information with the other doctors, too.

Well, Winter had already killed one man...

By accident, she reminded herself. She dismissed the idea as soon as it entered her mind. It was ridiculous. She couldn't just kill the hospital director.

The door opened, and Winter braced herself for the director to reappear with even worse news, but it wasn't him. It was Phoebe. Phoebe, with tears streaming down her face and a folded piece of paper in one of her clenched fists.

Oh, boy. What was Winter supposed to say here? "Is something wrong?" she asked, heart pounding. Did she sound concerned enough? Or did she sound too concerned, for someone as supposedly mysterious and aloof as the Plague Saint?

Phoebe sniffed. "Director came by earlier. Said the hospital's budget is being slashed, and he has to cut my pay in half."

That was rather absurd, considering the recent pay raises noted in the Saint's records. Adams hadn't said anything to Winter about cutting her pay. "I'm sorry," she said lamely.

"I'm not going to be able to pay my tuition!"

"Tuition?" Winter's brow furrowed. "What tuition?"

"I'm taking night classes at St. Minerva's College." Phoebe sniffed again and wiped an arm across her face. "Nursing classes. I applied for this assistant job to get my foot in the door, you know? But now it might not even matter."

Winter had a dozen other problems to deal with. But seeing Phoebe like this was oddly disheartening, even if Winter usually found her upbeat attitude a little overwhelming. "I'll talk to the director," Winter told her. "I'm sure there's money somewhere."

Phoebe looked up. "Really? You think he'd change his mind?"

"I think I can convince him." *Definitely not.* But Winter was being paid three times the amount she'd made at the guard station, and she'd simply been stashing it away in case of emergency. What she had now was far from covering River's hospital bills, anyway, so sparing a little for Phoebe wouldn't make much of a difference. "How much more do you need?"

"Two hundred pieces a week."

Okay. That was doable. Winter nodded. "I'll talk to him later today." She paused, a question crossing her mind. She really didn't need the answer, but she was curious. "I thought you were only seventeen."

"The college lets you start classes as young as sixteen, if you pass a bunch of tests," Phoebe explained.

"Oh." It had been a little weird, taking Phoebe on as an assistant when Winter was secretly the same age as her. Winter moved toward the lab door. "Well, I'll let you know what Adams says later. But I have a few things to take care of first."

She entered the lab and began poking around. She swore she had some red plague treatment left over from the last time she'd made it but couldn't remember where she'd put it. It wasn't much, but it would at least give River a boost while she made more.

She tried a few cabinets. Most were kept empty, but sometimes she threw random bottles and tools in them to deal with later. This row, however, was proving fruitless. She reached the corner of the room and pulled open the last door.

The final cabinet was occupied by a few cobwebs and a dusty brown book leaning against the back wall. Frowning, Winter reached for it. She must not have opened this door before, because she didn't recognize the book.

She grabbed the book and realized it was stuck in place. What the hell? Was it nailed to the cabinet? She pulled harder. The book tipped forward half an inch, and something clicked.

The wall to Winter's right groaned. A vertical gap appeared, and then a section of the wall swung open. A hidden door.

Seriously? That had been there the entire time? Winter stepped back from the cabinet. She'd been here two weeks and failed to find the Plague Saint's secret...dungeon?

She darted to the lab door, checked that it was locked, then returned to the newly opened gap in the wall. A set of stairs took her down a level and into a long, narrow hallway that took nearly ten minutes to traverse. Just as she was considering turning back, she took a sharp corner and found herself facing a heavy iron door.

It was unlocked. Winter eased it open and stepped into—

A lab. Another lab. What did the Plague Saint need a second lab for?

A *secret* second lab, Winter reminded herself as she entered the space. Did anyone else know about this? Despite the Saint's agreement with Director Adams, maybe there were things he'd been keeping from his boss.

A quick sweep of the room revealed several things of note. The most interesting find was a black notebook similar to the Plague Bible, which at a glance appeared to have completely different entries and notes. There were also more than a dozen vials and bottles that were seemingly older versions of treatments for the plagues. Beyond that, the drawers and cabinets mostly held mundane stationery, such as the black pens with gold bands near the tips that matched the pens scattered throughout the Saint's office.

The strangest thing, though, was the empty cages.

Winter poked around the cages. Whatever they'd held must have been small. But besides those, the lab had most of the same equipment as the one upstairs. Some of it was basic stuff that Winter knew how to use: microscopes and pipettes and centrifuges and the like. There was even a camera and some film. Everything else was more advanced machinery that the Saint had been using in his research, but nothing Winter needed to mix serums and make medicine.

Winter tucked the notebook under her arm and, after one last sweep of the room, headed back to the hospital lab. She wanted to conduct a more thorough investigation of the space, but that would have to wait until she knew no one would come looking for her. And a look through the notebook might give her a better idea of what the Saint had been doing down here.

The notebook's introductory pages explained how the secret laboratory had come to exist. The hospital had originally been built with plenty of underground rooms and access to tunnels under the city, primarily for carrying out bodies during the height of the worst plague waves. The entrance passage between this lab and the hospital had been blocked off during a phase of reconstruction, and the Plague Saint had uncovered it during a round of more recent renovations. He'd had the hidden door and switch installed by bribing a few of the workers. And, according to his notes, Director Adams had no idea it existed.

Unfortunately, a few pages in, the Saint had switched to writing his entries in code. Winter spent five minutes trying to decipher the jumble of letters before tossing the book onto a table in frustration. She didn't have time for this during a busy shift.

But even as she went back to her usual work and turned her focus to saving River, she couldn't help mulling over the notebook in the back of her mind. The secret lab. The empty cages.

What the hell had the Plague Saint been working on?

Chapter Three
Sinner in Saint's Clothing

Two weeks earlier, Winter had made a trip to the hospital to visit her mother. Alone.

Mom had been there a week already with the blue plague, and while she didn't seem to be getting worse, she wasn't getting better, either.

It was late when Winter arrived, but technically still visiting hours. The Plague Saint must not have expected anyone else to come tonight, though. When Winter reached the open doorway to Mom's room, he was in the process of putting a pale blue liquid in her IV line. The lights in the room were dimmed.

Winter was just about to ask the Saint how her mother was doing when another man spoke.

"I'll be in a lot of meetings at City Hall the next couple of weeks," the man said from the corner of the room. "Won't be around much. But I think you can figure out who to treat with what. I'll send a message if anything changes."

The Plague Saint nodded. The low light gleamed off his mask's bronze beak.

Winter wasn't sure why her instincts drove her to move back from the doorway, but she did. Neither of the two men took notice.

She could just see the man in the corner now, and the Plague Saint was at the other edge of her vision.

The other man took a step forward. His dark blue suit was one of the nicest Winter had ever seen, and he carried himself with an air of calm confidence. He was undoubtedly an important man, she thought as he moved to examine the bag attached to Mom's IV. Something about that fact terrified her.

"What is this, anyway?" the man asked. "Some kind of poison?"

"Nothing harmful," the Saint told him. "And nothing that would raise suspicion in an autopsy. Simply a blue-dyed saline solution."

"How long do you think she has left?"

"Without real treatment? Not more than a few days. Her immune system is nearly to its breaking point."

Comprehension dawned on Winter slowly. But as it did, she took another step back from the door and pressed a hand over her mouth. Her feet kept moving, despite her making no effort to control them, and carried her ten feet down the hall.

Footsteps approached the room's doorway. She barely processed it through the sensation of her heart pounding in her ears. Through the cold of the wall hitting her back.

The second man stepped out of the room and walked right past Winter. He cast her the briefest glance as he did, but didn't seem concerned by the trembling, disheveled mess backed against the wall. He hadn't realized she was eavesdropping and probably saw people like her all the time. People who'd received what might be the worst news of their life.

Winter's gaze darted to the door as it clicked shut behind him. The Plague Saint was still in there. And it was still visiting hours. If she could avoid acting like a wreck for two minutes, maybe she could learn more about what was happening without letting the Saint know what she'd overheard.

Winter stomped up to the door and threw it open, warning him of her approach. "Oh, you're in here," she said as she entered, hoping the tremor in her voice wasn't too noticeable. The door closed behind her. She pulled her shaking hand off the handle. "Sorry to interrupt, sir. What is that? More Blue-X?"

The Plague Saint turned around slowly. "You're her daughter?"

"I am."

"Yes, this is another dose of Blue-X." The Saint glanced at Winter's sleeping mother. "But I'm afraid she hasn't shown much improvement today. I don't know if the Blue-X will be enough. I'm sorry." Despite the words, the monotone of his voice didn't convey much by way of sympathy.

Winter swallowed. "But that is Blue-X?"

The Plague Saint paused. Then, slowly, he straightened up and took a step forward, and Winter found herself staring into the glassy black eyes of his mask. Her terrified reflection gazed back.

"What else would it be?" the Saint asked, voice low. Dangerous.

Winter's gaze darted nervously to where the Saint's staff leaned against Mom's bed, then back to him. Was there anyone else nearby? Nurses? Other doctors? And even if she could find someone to help her, would they take her side if she accused the Saint of planning to let her mother die?

Probably not.

But Winter couldn't just let this happen.

"I heard you talking to that other man before I came in," Winter said, her growing anger just barely managing to mask her fear. "I'm not stupid, I—"

The Plague Saint cut her off. "Please, come with me. My office is on this floor." He grabbed his staff and bag, then nodded for Winter to accompany him out of the room.

Dumbfounded, all Winter could do was stare after him for a moment. Then, not feeling as if she had any other options, she followed.

When they entered his office, the Saint gestured to the empty chair next to his desk. "Have a seat. I think you may have misunderstood what you heard."

Winter wanted to believe it. Desperately. But what other explanation could there be? While she settled reluctantly into the chair, the Plague Saint closed the door and walked to the counter. After a moment of shuffling and the sound of liquid pouring, he turned around and approached her with a glass in hand. "Care for some water? Most people don't realize how easy it is to become dehydrated when under a lot of stress."

"Sure," Winter murmured. Now that he mentioned it, she was thirsty. She reached out. Her fingers embraced the cold glass. A chill ran down her spine.

Why the hell was she taking this? She'd just told the Saint that she'd overheard him planning to let her mother die. She should have left while she had the chance. She should have told Dad. Or someone. Anyone. Her hand squeezed the glass. Maybe it was poison. Maybe it was—

"I understand how terrible you must be feeling, with your mother so sick," the Saint said, his voice the same cool tone it had always been. He made no move to sit down. "I'm sure you're having a hard time thinking straight."

So, he was going to try convincing her she'd imagined it. Winter cautiously lifted the glass to her lips to avoid answering. Pretended to take a sip. Some of the water touched her tongue. Was it her imagination, or did the water taste strange?

With the mask covering his face, the Saint was unreadable. Winter was an animal in a trap. The only way out was to go along with this and let the Saint kill her mother. She faked another sip. First, she had to convince him she believed he was truly trying to heal Mom. And then find someone she could ask for help…

No. *No, no, no.* No one was going to help her.

"Are you feeling all right, Miss Pierce?" The Saint took a step toward her.

The room spun around her. "What did you—?" The drink slipped from Winter's hand. "You're going to kill me, aren't you?" She was dimly aware of the sound of glass shattering on wood.

The Saint didn't answer. He was waiting for something. Waiting for her to pass out? To drop dead? What *had* he given her?

In desperation, Winter lunged at him.

He sidestepped and dodged her easily. Winter stumbled into a counter, knocking over a couple of bottles. A hand grabbed her arm. The Saint's grip tightened, and Winter blindly reached out with her free hand for something, anything. Her fingers grazed cold metal.

By the time she'd processed that what she grabbed was a scalpel, she'd already jammed it into the Saint's chest.

He staggered back a few steps. Winter didn't stop. She grabbed a jar and smashed it against the side of his head. He dropped to the ground. The jar clattered to the floor with him, the dark brown liquid inside sloshing haphazardly.

Oh. God.

What had she done?

Was he dead?

No. *No.* He couldn't be.

Winter nudged the body with her foot, trembling so violently that she could barely move. The Saint didn't so much as twitch. Blood gushed from around the scalpel wound.

For a long moment, all Winter could do was stare at the body. Minutes passed. She wasn't sure how many. Finally, she acknowledged that she had to do something.

So, who was the man behind the mask?

Winter knelt down and pried off the plague mask with hands that were both shaking and numb. The man beneath was unfamiliar. His dark hair had faint streaks of gray, his light skin had a tan to it, and there was a pale scar running down the right side of his face. He looked to be in his forties. Blood trickled from the wound made by the jar.

Tears blurred Winter's vision. She had the fleeting thought that she should check his pulse or see if his chest was moving, but it was overwhelmed by a dozen other concerns. Should she run? If he somehow survived, she'd be arrested and her life would be over. And Mom would still die.

If he was still alive, she couldn't—she couldn't let him stay that way, could she?

Winter staggered to the office door and fumbled with the handle until the lock clicked. She moved on to poking around the office, throwing frequent glances at the Saint to make sure he hadn't moved.

The tools and vials she found didn't mean much to her. But the notebooks detailed patient logs and treatment records. In the Saint's bag, she found the Plague Bible. Instructions for making medicine. Guides to building treatment plans. And notes explaining which patients had received real treatment, and which ones had received nothing.

The hospital reports were lies, and the truth was here.

There were also more uniforms in one of the cabinets, all identical. Winter held one of the coats up. It would probably fit. Maybe she could...

No, no, that was an unbelievably bad idea. Ridiculous. Completely absurd. *Dangerous.* She should just leave and let someone find the body. After she'd removed any evidence of her presence, that was.

But she was bound to miss something. Something that would tie her to the scene. And if no one found the Saint, no one would know the crime had happened. No death, no murderer. No body, no investigation.

Plus, if the Plague Saint disappeared and no one was around to make his medicines, people who could have been saved would die. And Winter had a chance to do what he wasn't doing: treating everyone who came in. Curing as many as possible. Healing people who deserved help, not just ones the hospital director told the Saint to save.

She didn't know enough about medicine to develop new cures. But she could follow instructions.

You're not thinking straight.

Winter picked up a spare mask from the cabinet and stared at her faint reflection in the eyes. She didn't have all night, and she couldn't think of any better options.

She put on the mask.

Winter had been correct about the uniform fitting. It wasn't perfect, but it worked. She pulled on the gloves last. Now all she had to do was get rid of the—

The—

Winter swallowed and approached the body again. She wasn't strong enough to carry him. Okay, that was fine. The hospital had beds on wheels and carts. But she still had to take him outside.

And then where?

This was an easier question to answer. Devil's Pass was built next to a river. Some of the water was diverted into canals and pipes for the city to use, but the rest continued through the mountains, to lands in the south. Once the Saint left the city, no one would find him. Not any time soon, anyway.

The Saint had said this room was his office. Winter hoped that meant no one else would come in during the time it took her to find something with wheels. Still, she grabbed his arms and dragged him under his desk, hiding him from view of anyone at the door. The act left her exhausted and struggling for air, but she couldn't rest yet.

The hallways were mostly empty. Still, Winter walked fast, hoping if she conveyed enough urgency, people wouldn't bother her. Thankfully, the few staff members she did pass simply gave her polite nods.

She peered through passing windows into rooms until she spotted a row of flatbed carts. Without thinking, she threw open the door and found herself in an office.

"Oh, Plague Saint!" A woman sitting behind the desk looked up. "I wasn't expecting you. Are you looking for someone's bill?"

Winter glanced at the wall of cabinets behind the woman. This was where they kept bill and payment records? Noted.

She opened her mouth to speak but caught herself. She cleared her throat and, in a quiet voice that she hoped was deep enough to resemble the real Saint's, said, "Actually, I need a cart. It's...an emergency." Would that reasoning work? Winter wasn't entirely sure what the carts were typically used for.

The woman hesitated. She looked nervous, Winter realized. "Oh. Are all of your wing's being used?"

Winter nodded. The less she spoke, the better.

"Well, go ahead."

Winter crossed the room and grabbed a cart.

"I'm sure you're very busy," the woman said, her tone bordering on fearful. "But if you could bring it back as soon as you have a chance, that would be great."

"Sure," Winter told her. Was it purely because the woman thought she was the Saint? Was he that intimidating to hospital staff?

The world spun when Winter reentered the hallway and was still spinning when she stumbled back into the Plague Saint's office. When had it gotten so hard to breathe? *Come on. Come on.*

With her shaking hands and stinging eyes and nausea threatening to overtake her, it took nearly ten minutes to get the Saint's body onto the cart. After that ordeal was over with, she staggered to the nearest wall, sank to the floor, pulled her knees to her chest, closed her eyes, counted to ten, counted to ten again, counted to ten again—

Someone knocked on the office door.

Don't throw up in the mask.

The visitor knocked again. Louder.

Winter pushed herself to her feet. "One minute!" she called, her voice straining. If she was going to keep this up, she needed to find a better way to alter her voice.

She opened cabinets in a rush until she found a stack of folded sheets. She grabbed one, threw it over the cart, moved the cart behind the desk, and hurried to the door.

A nurse stood on the other side. "Sorry to bother you, Plague Saint, I know you're leaving soon. But I have the treatment schedule

Dr. Liang made for Miss White." In response to Winter's blank stare, she held up a file. "That was the one you wanted, right?"

"Oh. Yes." Winter took the file. The nurse nodded and hurried off.

Well, at least that was quick. Winter tossed the file onto the desk and assessed the cart. The sheet on top was a bit awkward, but it would have to do. If anyone questioned her, she'd tell them she was getting rid of...biohazard waste? People seemed to be slightly afraid of the Saint, which was going to work to her advantage.

As a matter of fact, no one questioned her during the entire twenty minutes she spent wandering in search of an exit that wasn't out front. She finally found one and emerged in a dark alley between the hospital and the apartment complex next door.

The biting cold was almost an improvement over the suffocating hospital corridors. Almost.

She pushed the cart to the back of the hospital, across a narrow patch of dirt, and to the tree line. The forest terrain was a nightmare to navigate, and snow had begun to fall, but the sound of the river drew Winter forward.

She nearly collapsed when she reached the water's edge. She did trip, and the cart slipped from her grasp. Her hands flew out frantically and barely managed to catch it before it could tumble into the river. She wouldn't have cared about losing the thing otherwise, but she had promised that woman she'd return it.

What a stupid thing to care about at a time like this. Winter shook her head. She wanted nothing more right now than to crawl into her bed. And maybe never come back out.

The wind picked up, and the uniform's overcoat billowed around her. Winter yanked the sheet off of the cart.

Another wave of nausea rolled over her as she was forced to see the body again. She avoided looking too closely, instead focusing on the terrain as she dragged the Saint down the riverbank, searching for a spot that looked deep enough.

Plague Saint. People had been using the title for nearly as long as he'd been in the city. What a stupid name. Who'd thought of it, anyway? Him? Surely he didn't think he deserved to be called a saint.

Winter stumbled to a halt. This spot would do. She pushed the Saint until he rolled into the water.

Everything was a blur after that. She remembered dragging the cart back to the office she'd taken it from, gathering some of the Saint's belongings in a bag, and searching his lab until she found the treatment that would save her mother.

When she returned to her mother's room, a nurse was there scribbling something on a clipboard. She glanced up when Winter walked in.

Winter held out the vial of medicine. "She needs this. All of it."

The nurse didn't question her. She took the vial and nodded. "I'll give it to her once I'm done checking her vitals. Should I note it in her file—?"

"I already did," Winter cut her off quickly. "Don't make any notes. Just give it to her."

Winter wanted to spend more time with Mom, but she couldn't do that as the Saint. It was getting late, anyway. All she could do now was hope the medicine did its work overnight.

She left the room and found her way outside, where she wandered until she found a dark alley she could change out of the uniform in. She shoved it into the bag she'd taken and stumbled to the main road, snow in her hair and wind in her eyes.

The trolley she rode home was nearly empty this time of night, but there were a few other stragglers leaving their late shifts. Winter couldn't shake her paranoia that the people glancing her way could see the blood on her hands. The reflection of a dead man in her eyes. The way she trembled from the effort of throwing his body in the river.

She got off at her stop and hurried up the stairs to the apartment.

Dad and River waited at the dining table. Damn it. Winter had hoped they wouldn't be home yet.

"How's Mom?" River asked.

It took Winter a moment to remember she didn't need to use her imitation of the Saint's voice. She cleared her throat. "Uh, same as she was when we went the other day. But they're giving her a new treatment tonight. If it works, she should be doing better tomorrow." She adjusted the bag slung over her shoulder.

Dad frowned. "Is that a new bag?"

"Oh, um." Winter swallowed. "Yeah, uh, I had to get a new one from the station. The zipper broke on my old one."

"Up for a game of devil's bridge?" River asked, thankfully putting a halt to Dad's line of questioning.

Winter shook her head. "Sorry, not tonight. I'm exhausted."

She wanted to sprint to her room but settled for walking quickly to avoid raising any further suspicion. She shoved the Saint's bag behind her bed before crawling under her blankets. All she could hear was her racing heart. All she could see was the Plague Saint.

What the hell was she supposed to do now?

Chapter Four
Next of Kin

"Red-dyed solution," Winter told Director Adams as the two watched the liquid travel through the IV line. It was difficult to maintain her composure with River in such terrible shape, but she had to keep up the façade. She couldn't let the director know she was giving him real medicine. "Kid's in decent health, though. He might pull through anyway."

"That could be a problem," Adams muttered. "See what you can do. And make sure his bill gets paid."

Winter clenched and unclenched her left fist. "Of course." She'd been working on a plan to sneak into the payment office and destroy her mother's file, and now she'd be adding her brother to the list. But she'd need to wait until he was out of the hospital—and Adams's mind.

"Which reminds me—" Adams began.

"Andersen?" Winter asked before he could remind her again. "I'm going to...speak with his next of kin after I finish this round."

Adams nodded approvingly. "Take your assistant with you. If she proves to be competent, I'll consider putting her in charge of bill collection. As much as I like sending the Plague Saint to collect, you only have so much time to treat patients." His expression darkened.

"And immediately handing the bills over the city guard is...upsetting to some people. Now is not a great time for us to be drawing negative attention."

No way Phoebe was capable of that. Not emotionally. Still, Winter nodded. "Sure."

She finished her rounds, updating her patients' treatment schedules as she went. When she returned to her office, Phoebe was scribbling away in a notebook.

"You're coming on a bill collection trip with me," Winter told her. "Adams's orders."

Phoebe closed the notebook and jumped to her feet. "Oh. Uh, sure. Okay." She grabbed her coat off the rack, and the two set out.

Winter skimmed Andersen's file while they walked. Director Adams had ordered family records from the city guard, revealing that Andersen had a cousin living a few blocks from the hospital.

"It's not really fair, is it?" Phoebe asked. She kicked a stray stone. "Why should they have to pay their dead relative's bills?"

What would the real Plague Saint say? Something profoundly stupid, probably. Winter slid Andersen's file into her bag. "I don't make the rules."

"Why not? You have a lot of sway, don't you?"

Sway that came from being good at killing whoever Adams wanted killed and saving whoever he wanted saved. But that wouldn't last. Winter wouldn't let it last, and Adams wouldn't let her get away with breaking his agenda. She was running out of time. Something had to change, and if she didn't make the first move, Adams would.

"Adams was thinking about promoting you and putting you in charge of collecting payments," Winter said, changing the subject. "That's part of why I brought you."

Phoebe frowned. "I'm not sure I—"

"Want to? I figured as much. But it's your choice. And it might come with higher pay." *And the guilt of harassing grieving people for money.*

"Will he fire me if I say no?"

"I doubt he'd try, but I need you as my assistant. I won't let him."

Phoebe perked up. "You like having me around?"

Winter awkwardly adjusted her grip on the staff. "You make paperwork easier." She wasn't the monster the real Plague Saint was, but she'd never been one to show much affection, either. "Training a new assistant would be a pain in the ass."

Still, Phoebe grinned. "Whatever you say."

The smile faded when Winter stopped in front of a dull apartment complex. "This is the place," Winter told her. Seeing the alarm on Phoebe's face, she added, "Relax. I'll do all the talking."

As Winter knocked on the door, part of her hoped no one would answer. But another part knew if that happened, she'd have no choice but to hand the case over to the city guard.

The door creaked open a few inches. The woman on the other side took in the uniform, the mask, the staff. Her expression darkened, but she did her best to sound polite. "Plague Saint? Can I help you?"

Winter took a deep breath. In the moment before she started speaking, she could hear children yelling somewhere in the house. "Does Erik Andersen live here?"

The woman nodded.

"According to city records, he's Jacob Andersen's closest living relative." Winter drew the bill out of her bag. "I'm afraid Jacob passed away with money still owed."

The exhaustion on the woman's face worsened. "How much?" she asked weakly.

Winter held out the bill. After a moment's hesitation, the woman took it. Her eyes widened.

"We can't afford this," she said. "We didn't even see Jacob that much."

"My apologies, but it's hospital policy." Saying the words made Winter feel sick. But she couldn't blow her stolen identity. Not yet.

"What if we can't pay?"

Winter would have to find some way to make this right. But this poor woman was one of many in the city. One of many that the people in power were eager to squeeze every last dollar they could out of.

For now, Winter tapped a finger against the top of the staff. "You have until the end of the month to make your first payment. You'll receive some payment plan options in the mail in the next few days. If you have any questions, you can call or visit the hospital. And if you can't pay..." She swallowed. "That's not my department."

Contacting next of kin shouldn't have been her department either, but it seemed the real Plague Saint had been happy to perform this task for Adams. He must have liked being present in the lives of the city's people. It added to the persona. Winter had initially found it strange he didn't want to appear completely benevolent, but he had an excuse: if the hospital didn't get its money, he couldn't heal the people.

And the stories the preachers told in church...well, the figures sent by God in those stories weren't always pleasant, either. God's will didn't have to be pleasant.

Winter rejoined Phoebe—who'd waited just close enough to hear the conversation—and they headed back toward the hospital.

"Why is this the Plague Saint's job?" Phoebe asked after a minute, echoing Winter's earlier thoughts. "Wouldn't your time be better spent with patients?"

Winter considered for a long moment, unsure how to convey her true thoughts on the Plague Saint when she was pretending to be him. "Adams has interesting ideas about how things should be done," she finally said.

It felt a bit like deflecting blame, but to be fair, she had no idea how much of this had been the real Plague Saint's idea and how much had been Adams. Maybe the hospital director thought if he sent the people someone they saw as a savior to collect, they'd be more inclined to pay.

"Like harassing innocent people for money?" Phoebe said the words under her breath, but Winter still heard them. She didn't respond.

When Winter had first learned about the next of kin policy, she'd been conflicted. It was certainty unfair, but where was the hospital supposed to get money if so many of its patients died?

It didn't take much time going through the files and letters in the Saint's office to learn the truth: the absurd amount of money on the bills was far more than it cost to actually treat patients, and Adams was taking most of the money that came in for his salary. And even if the hospital weren't profitable, there were plenty of wealthy people in the city who could easily afford to pay more taxes to fund the hospital.

Adams wasn't the entire problem, but as long as he was around, things were going to stay terrible. Winter wondered what the chances were of him catching one of the plagues. Probably slim. He was taking excellent precautions. But if he slipped up...

Back at the hospital, Phoebe returned to paperwork, and Winter returned to sneaking real medicine to patients that needed it. While she was in the middle of taking down the vitals of a red plague victim, Adams entered the room. Winter's jaw clenched under the mask.

"Andersen's bill?" he asked.

"Gave it to his cousin's household. Told them they have until the end of the month to send their first payment." Winter tightened the cap on the blood sample she'd just taken, which she'd figured out how to do from a combination of closely watching nurses and reviewing the Saint's written instructions. "I don't think they'll be able to pay, though."

"Then the city guard will handle it." Adams's tone was as casual as if he were commenting on the weather.

Winter dared to bring up the point that had been on her mind for some time. "That doesn't benefit us, though."

"Not directly. But it helps the city financial advisor, and she's the one signing off on our budget."

City financial advisor. That was someone to look into.

Adams looked Winter's patient up and down. "How's he doing?"

"Not sure. He just came in," Winter answered. "But he's got red plague and he's eighty-three, so I doubt he has much of a chance." That was true, even with Winter giving him the best medicine she had.

"Good."

Adams left Winter to stare at the man, her fists clenched, her jaws tight. The rage burning in her chest was undeniable. Hell, it was the only thing in this city keeping her warm.

Winter opened her hand to study the vial of blood.

If Adams wanted this poor man dead so bad, maybe he could go with him.

Winter returned to her office, walked past Phoebe without a word, and entered the Plague Saint's lab. She pulled out the Plague Bible and read through every entry mentioning the red plague.

Adams was in good health, but he was nearing sixty. If he was infected with red plague, he'd show symptoms within a day. If he received real treatment, Winter estimated he had close to a fifty-fifty chance of pulling through, maybe higher.

But even without treatment, he'd still last a few days. Winter sighed. She couldn't let his death drag out that long. He wouldn't go down without a fight, and if she didn't give him her medicine, God knew what he'd do. She could risk lying and giving him fake treatment, but something told her Adams was too smart for that.

Winter lifted her gaze from the Bible to the freezer on the other side of the lab. Other blood and saliva samples filled the shelves, plenty of specimens from every plague. Her fingers drummed against the counter.

With five plagues running rampant in the city, there were inevitably cases of people catching two at once. Winter had even found records of patients with three in the Saint's files. The only one she'd seen herself was a man who'd died within hours of coming in. While he'd had signs of green plague since the night before, yellow and red symptoms had only showed up the morning of his death.

Winter crossed the room to the freezer.

She told herself she was just looking. Then she told herself if it wasn't Adams, it would be all the dying patients. People like River. *Do it for River.*

Nothing she told herself prevented her hands from trembling, nor her heart from racing, but she didn't let that stop her from taking a sample of each plague.

Chapter Five
Saint, Doctor, Executioner

"How much longer do you want me here?" Phoebe asked as Winter exited the lab.

It took Winter a moment to process the question and glance at the clock. The day had been excruciatingly long. First River, then the trip to Jacobsen's...was it really only six? "Did you finish today's paperwork?"

"Almost. But I was planning on getting dinner soon."

"That's fine, as long as you finish before you go home for the night. Tomorrow's going to be just as busy, and the last thing we need is to fall behind." Winter moved to the door.

"Where are you going?" Phoebe asked.

Winter resisted the urge to touch the vial in her pocket. "I have a few red plague patients that need extra monitoring." It was only half a lie. She did plan on checking on River.

But she had something else to take care of first.

Winter moved slowly through the hospital, pausing to listen for footsteps, ensuring that no one saw her near Adams's office. When she knocked at the door, she was greeted with silence.

She was ready to give up quickly. Her hands still trembled, and if Adams didn't notice that, the panic in her voice was bound to give her away. It was probably for the best that he didn't—

The door swung open. "Plague Saint," Adams greeted her. "I don't believe I asked to see you."

"You didn't. There's something we need to discuss. May I come in?"

Adams's eyes narrowed. "What's this about?"

Say something. Anything. "One of our patients, despite my initial assessment, seems to be making a remarkable recovery. And now he's talking about raising hell over the hospital's billing methods."

"He won't get very far."

"That's what I thought, at first. But he has a lot of interesting friends." *Please let me in.* Winter was in too deep now. If this wasn't enough to pique Adams's interest right now, he was going to want names and details later.

"Well, come in. But I have a meeting with the mayor in an hour, so we may have to deal with this later."

There wasn't going to be a later. Not for Adams. Winter closed the door and twisted the lock. As she crossed the room, her gaze darted to the mug on his desk, sitting in its usual spot. There was just one unfortunate detail: the mug was empty.

You idiot. You've only been in here a couple of times, and that was weeks ago. What made you so sure there would be coffee in the mug? Had she really thought she was going to be able to just empty the vial into the drink while he wasn't looking? Pray the coffee would be strong enough to hide any change in taste?

No, she couldn't panic. If she didn't get a hold of herself, Adams would realize something was wrong. And River would die.

"Long day?" Winter asked, nodding at the empty mug, hoping she sounded casual.

"You could say that." Adams gave the mug a disdainful look. "May need another cup or two."

Winter's gaze moved to the coffee maker on the counter behind his desk chair. "If you are going to make some, would you mind sparing me a cup?" If the suggestion alone wasn't enough to push him to make coffee, maybe she could lure in him with the idea of seeing under the mask.

Sure enough, Adams chuckled. "Are you going to drink it with that mask on? Or have I earned a chance to see the man behind the Plague Saint?" Despite his light tone, there was something darker in his gaze. Winter wasn't sure if he was asking or demanding.

"I suppose it will have to come off." Worst case scenario, she could run away and ditch the costume and pretend this mess had never happened. Find some other way to get River treatment.

"Have a seat, then." Adams moved to the coffee maker. "So, who's this patient you're having trouble with?"

Adams's back was to her. Now was her chance. "His name's—" Winter racked her brain for a fake name while she drew out the vial and silently unscrewed the cap. Her final product was a disgusting shade of brown. Adams's black mug would hide that, though. "—Jim Gomez."

One drop went in. Two. Three.

Adams's head turned to the right. Winter leaned back and tightened her hand around the vial. Adams frowned. Her heart was ready to explode.

"I don't recognize the name," Adams said.

"He came in with that wave the other night." Winter wondered how long it would take for symptoms to appear, if this worked. The

Saint had noted that the plagues had unusually short incubation times compared to most infectious diseases.

After they did appear, Adams would probably have hours. The other doctors could try to save him, but they didn't have the medicine she had. They didn't even know it existed. As long as she kept busy elsewhere and avoided letting him find her, she'd have nothing to worry about.

Other than leaving this meeting without exposing herself, that was.

Adams returned to the desk with the pot of coffee and a second mug. He set the mug in front of Winter and filled it, then moved to his. The sound of the liquid hitting the bottom of the cup was deafening.

Adams sank into his chair and picked up his death sentence, eyes on Winter. His gaze burned through her. "Did this Gomez name any of his friends?"

He took a sip.

Winter forced her gaze to lift from the mug to his face. "Hm?"

"Gomez. You said he had interesting friends." Adams took another sip. "Are you all right, Plague Saint?"

"What makes you ask?"

"You seem distracted."

"My apologies." Winter adjusted her position in her chair and slipped the vial back into her coat pocket. "I am." *Distract him from Gomez. Say something. Anything.* "Someone close to me has caught red plague."

Surprise took over Adams's face, though he tried to hide it quickly. "I didn't think you had anyone of the sort."

"I do."

"And this...loved one of yours? Are they here at the hospital?"

An image of River in his hospital bed flashed in Winter's mind. "No. I'm treating them at home."

Adams opened his mouth, but whatever he wanted to say was interrupted by a fit of coughing.

Winter's stomach flipped. "Are you feeling all right, Director?"

"I'm sure it's nothing." Adams cleared his throat. Hesitated. "Of course, if it were something serious…"

"If it is a plague, early treatment is better." Winter rose to her feet. She'd found a way out. "I have some medicine I take whenever I'm not feeling well. It will have you feeling better in just a couple of hours. And if you aren't infected, it won't do you any harm."

"Well, we still have to discuss Gomez—"

"Your health is of the utmost importance, Director. Besides, it will only take me a few minutes to fetch the medicine and come back." Winter headed for the door to deter further argument. All she had to do once she was out of here was avoid him, maybe feign an emergency elsewhere…

"Well, all right," Adams conceded. "I do have my meeting soon, though."

Winter waved a hand in acknowledgement as she stepped out.

She returned to her own office, mind racing in a dozen different directions. As she flung the door open, she settled on a plan to keep Adams from finding her. "Phoebe," she said.

Phoebe looked up from the file she was reading. "Yes, Plague Saint?"

"I have important lab work to do. I'm not to be disturbed under any circumstances." Winter opened the cabinet behind her desk and dug around until she found a bottle of pale blue liquid. "If Director Adams comes by, tell him to drink a glass of this, and that I'll talk to him before I leave tonight."

Winter set the bottle on the desk. The liquid was used as a base to add other ingredients to and wouldn't do anything to Adams. "If he asks where I am, say that I'm dealing with an emergency with another patient," she continued. "And if he asks you for information on Jim Gomez, tell him I have the file with me."

Phoebe gave her a perplexed look. "Are those—would I be lying to him?"

"You think I'd ask you to lie to the director for me?"

Phoebe hesitated. "I—I don't know—" she stammered.

"Can I trust you or not?"

Phoebe swallowed and nodded. "Of course you can. Don't worry about a thing."

Winter sighed. "Thank you." She glanced at the file in Phoebe's hands. "As soon as you're done with your work, you're free to leave." It would be far better if Phoebe didn't have to deal with Adams at all.

Winter entered the lab, locked the door behind her, and grabbed the notebook she'd taken from the secret laboratory. The key to deciphering the coded text had to be somewhere. Maybe she should search the other lab again. There could be more secret levers or compartments hidden among the cabinets and drawers.

But for now, she studied seemingly nonsensical combinations of letters. Ten minutes passed. Forty. Maybe more. Just as the text was beginning to blur in her vision, Winter turned a page and found something that might actually be useful: drawings.

Winter studied the sketches of the human body. The arrows pointing to various organs were labeled with more coded text, but Winter was less interested in that and more interested in the fact that whatever was written was color-coded. Blue ink, green ink, gold ink, purple ink, red ink...

Winter flipped through more diagrams for a minute before picking one to examine closer. One of the arrows pointed to an arm covered in bruises. At the other end were just three words. The text was in blue, and Winter glared at the letters, willing them to make sense. *Cmvf pwfs hsffo.*

None of them were long enough to be about the bruising. Maybe one of them was a color. That would make sense, given the plagues, but which one? Bruising could be blue or green. Winter tried the next page and found a chart full of numbers.

The categories along the left column looked complicated, but the top row only had five: *hsffo, cmvf, wjpmfu, zfmmpx, sfe.* All in black ink this time, but *hsffo* and *cmvf* had been on the previous page. Maybe they—

Someone pounded on the lab door. Winter jumped. The book slipped from her hands and fell shut on the table. Damn it. Hadn't she told Phoebe not to bother her?

"Plague Saint!" Adams yelled. His voice was hoarse and scratchy. How long had it been since Winter left him? An hour?

Maybe if she were quiet, he would look for her somewhere else.

"I know you're in here! What the hell is going on?"

This was happening faster than she'd expected. Winter pushed her chair back from the table, grabbed her staff, and stood up. She couldn't let Adams die in her office. She had to be as far removed from his death as possible.

Winter flung open the lab door. "Walk with me." She stormed past Adams.

"Wait. Not until you explain—"

"I'll explain while we walk."

"Plague Saint, I—"

Winter spun around. "Do you want to die?" She snarled the words with far more malice than she'd intended. Adams's eyes went wide, and she got a really good look at him for the first time. Faint bruises crept up his neck, the whites of his eyes had gone yellow, and the handkerchief he clutched in his right hand was stained with blood.

"Your office," Winter hissed. "Now."

As they walked the hospital halls, Winter barked questions at him.

"How long ago did you start feeling sick?"

"It really hit me about ten minutes after you left my office," Adams answered. "I came to ask you for that medicine, and your assistant told me to drink from that bottle on your desk and said you were dealing with an emergency."

"Did you?"

"Yes. Half an hour later I only felt worse, so I went looking for you again. I've been searching ever since. Your assistant was gone when I came back to your office, but the light in your lab was on—"

Adams continued to ramble about his symptoms. Winter watched him out of the corner of his eye. His cough interrupted him with persistence, his skin had paled dramatically, and he walked at a slow pace that betrayed his weakness. Thankfully, they made it to his office without him collapsing or otherwise drawing attention. While Adams staggered to his desk and sank into his chair, Winter closed the door. Now she could ask her last remaining questions.

"How many people did you talk to since our meeting?" Winter asked. "Anyone else know you're feeling sick?"

Adams rubbed his forehead. "I called and rescheduled my meeting with the mayor. He said he was busier than expected tonight, anyway, and we didn't talk long. I also told a few nurses I was looking for you, but I didn't say why. I think they noticed something was wrong, though." He frowned. "Why do you ask?"

"I need an idea of whether this is going to spread." Until Winter said that, it hadn't occurred to her that Adams might run around and pass along any of the five plagues he was infected with. Most of the staff wore medical masks, though, and they wouldn't have been keen to get into Adams's personal space. Hopefully, he'd kept at least a few feet between him and anyone he talked to.

"Do you know what I have?" Adams tipped his head back and closed his eyes. "And can you treat it?"

"Did you drink your entire mug of coffee?" Had three drops done this, or had it been even less?

"Yes, I drank all of it. How is that relevant?" Adams burst into another coughing fit. When he was done, he asked, "Do you know what's wrong with me or not?"

Winter walked to his desk and stood over him. "Of course I know what's wrong with you," she said. Her cool, steady tone surprised her, given how fast her heart was racing. "You've been exposed to all five plagues, and most—if not all of them—have already taken hold. The immune system can only take so much. Especially at your age."

For a moment, Winter wanted to pull off the mask. Reveal herself, show Adams that a teenage girl had been the one to kill him. He was dying anyway...

No, that was ridiculous. It didn't matter what Adams did or didn't know about his killer. And she'd acted on enough stupid ideas for one day.

"What?" Adams gasped. "Plague Saint?"

"I'm not your Saint," Winter told him. "I killed him two weeks ago."

"That's why you've been—" More coughing. "Why? Who are you? Who do you work for? Someone after my job?"

"I'm not some political rival, and I don't work for any of your enemies." Winter lifted her chin. "You wouldn't know me. I'm just another poor citizen to you. Someone you wouldn't think worthy of saving."

Adams tried to push himself up. Winter's grip tightened on the staff in her hand, but she had nothing to worry about. Adams collapsed on the floor the moment he was out of the chair.

"You won't get away with this," he hissed. "I have more friends than you know. They'll kill you."

Winter couldn't stand here and watch anymore. Nausea overwhelmed her. Her legs were ready to give out. She backed away from Adams and stumbled to the door.

You wanted this. You did this.

The hallway outside was silent. Winter exited the office, pulled the door shut softly behind her, and walked. She didn't have a destination in mind, only her pounding heart screaming at her to get as far away as possible.

Her free hand slid into her coat. The vial was still there. Her fingers wrapped around it.

Death. She had made liquid death.

Chapter Six
Survival Worship

Eventually, Winter forced herself to walk back to Adams's office and make sure he was dead. It was easy enough to tell from the brief glance at the body—she'd seen more than enough dead patients in the past two weeks to know what death did to people—but she ventured close enough to confirm he wasn't breathing, that there was no pulse, before she allowed herself to leave.

It wasn't until she was walking into the family apartment that she realized she was nearly two hours late for dinner. She'd all but forgotten that Dad was making casserole. As it turned out, he'd forgotten too.

"River has red plague," Mom blurted as soon as Winter entered the living room. She sat on the couch next to Dad, who was studying the evening paper through his reading glasses.

"I know," Winter said numbly. "They called me at the guard office. I stopped by the hospital to see him."

"We must have just missed you, then," Dad said. "Was he conscious?"

Winter shook her head. "They told me there's a good chance he'll wake up sometime tonight." *Hopefully.* She adjusted her grip on her bag. "I'm going to bed."

"Are you sure?" Mom asked. "Don't you want something to eat first? I think there's still some stew in the fridge from the other day."

Winter shook her head. The thought of eating made her want to throw up. "I'm exhausted. Good night."

When she entered her room, she tossed her bag on the floor, too tired to stash it in its usual hiding place. She collapsed onto her bed and waited for relief that never came. When a few minutes of slow breathing did nothing to steady her, she pulled out the locket.

All Winter could do was stare at the photo inside. River laughing, her smiling—a rare sight these days.

She'd had an idea a few days earlier, a way to get out of this mess without dooming countless patients to death: she could reveal everything she'd learned to the public and then disappear.

But would people believe the Plague Saint if the government claimed the better treatments were fake? How easy would it be for people like Adams to cover it all up? As long as people like him were running things, people in the hospitals would continue to die for no reason.

So, she'd mulled over her ideas all week, trying to come up with some sort of foolproof way to stop what Adams and the real Plague Saint had started.

They were both gone now. Winter had to make sure no one took their places.

Sleep took her under eventually, and she came to in the early hours of the morning. It took twenty minutes or so, but she pushed aside her grogginess and started to get ready. Normally, she wouldn't show up to the hospital for a couple more hours, but she wanted to slip into the lab and work on deciphering the new journal.

There was a knock at the door. "Winter?" Dad called.

"I'm up!" Winter yelled back to deter him from entering. "Be out in a minute." Strange. He knew she didn't have to leave yet. Why wake her?

She finished dressing, swung her bag over her shoulder, and left her room. Her parents were both up and dressed, sitting at the kitchen table.

"Are you going to visit River this early?" Winter glanced at the clock. The hospital wouldn't even allow visitors for another hour.

"Not yet," Dad said. He adjusted his tie, and Winter's stomach churned as she realized he was dressed a little too nicely for a trip to the hospital. "We're going to St. Andrew's."

St. Andrew's cathedral. The place sat atop a hill a block from the hospital, at the highest point in Devil's Pass. It was mostly constructed from the salvaged material of another church down south. The original church was one of the few buildings from the old world that survived the floods—enough to be recognizable, anyway—and people thought it would bring the new city good luck.

That hadn't exactly worked out, had it?

"Would you like to come with us?" Dad asked.

It wasn't really a question, but Winter tried to get out of it anyway. "I have to work."

"Your shifts never start this early. You can go straight to the station after."

As far as torture went, sitting on a hard bench listening to a priest or priestess recite passages of old text wasn't the worst thing ever. But all Winter could think about as she walked with her parents to the trolley stop was what she would be greeted with when she returned to the hospital. Had Adams's body been found yet? Would they assume it was simply illness, or would the city guard be called in to investigate?

Hell, if they did decide it was plague-related, they might ask Winter to take a look at the body.

Or they might just arrest her.

After getting off the trolley, Winter and her parents had to trek up a snow-covered hill to the white, black-roofed church—it *had* originally been a rather plain church, after all. The "cathedral" in the name had been slapped on after it was rebuilt. The stone path was supposed to make the hike easier, but it still took all of Winter's concentration to avoid slipping.

She paused at the top and took in the view while she waited for Mom and Dad to catch up. Lights flickered on up and down the pass. The top of the hospital's tower overshadowed nearby buildings, a stark white against the dark sky. A few blocks from there stood the campus of St. Minerva's College.

Then, her parents were passing her, their quiet conversation bringing her back to the present. Winter followed them into the chapel. They chose a seat near the front, to her annoyance.

She surveyed the people around them. Mayor Atherton was here, accompanied by his wife and children. The whole Atherton family was matching, wearing the same shade of deep red. *How cute,* Winter thought sarcastically. That toddler's dress probably cost more than her entire wardrobe.

A woman in the row in front of the mayor had turned so that she could face him. Her mouth moved, but her hushed tone made the words inaudible. Winter studied the woman's sharp features, the lines on her face that put her in her fifties, the blonde hair pulled up in a bun. She wore a purple dress, and her matching heels clacked against the wood floor when she finally moved away from the mayor to take a seat at the end of the row. There was something annoyingly familiar about her.

Other conversations died out as a priest took his place in front of the altar. As he flipped through the pages of a tattered brown book, candles flickered on the table behind him, beneath a portrait of the Storm Saint himself: Saint Andrew. Winter vividly remembered hearing the story of how he'd died while pulling people from floodwaters, as a child no older than six. The priestess who'd told it scared Winter almost as much as the story itself, and she'd had nightmares about drowning inside the church for nearly a week afterward.

Dad nudged Winter, snapping her out of her thoughts. "Do you have a donation?" he asked. "The church maidens are coming up the aisle."

"I don't have any money on me," Winter muttered.

"Put this in for me." He handed her a bill.

Ten pieces? Really? Even with River in the hospital and out of work?

Swallowing her protests, Winter accepted the bill and turned to watch the nearest maiden approach. She restrained a shudder. The white face masks the maidens wore were creepy as hell, especially combined with the black hooded gowns that covered everything else. Winter still couldn't grasp the reasoning for it. Something about separating the maidens from the donation? And why did they all have to be girls, anyway?

Winter dimly remembered something her father had said years earlier about her missing the point by asking all these questions. Maybe he was right. She was never going to understand what people got out of this, was she? She felt a twinge of guilt.

As the maiden approached, her mask slipped from her face. Her hand flew out to catch it. Winter's eyes widened.

Phoebe? Phoebe worked as a church maiden? With two jobs and night classes, how did she have time to sleep?

Phoebe's eyes darted around as she slid the mask back into place and fixed the strap that had come loose. Winter quickly glanced away. When Phoebe held out the basket a moment later, she dropped the ten-piece bill in.

It had been years since Winter had attended one of the formal weekend meetings, but she came with her parents on weekdays every once in a while. From six in the morning to six at night, it was a "come and go as you please" sort of thing. You could come sit while listening to old people tell you all the things you were doing wrong, all while maidens in creepy masks came around with baskets and stared at you until you put money in.

Maybe Winter wouldn't hate it so much if it were actually a place that made her feel "inner peace" or whatever, but that wasn't an emotion she'd felt here. Or anywhere, really. Maybe the problem was her, after all.

She anxiously checked the stopwatch in her pocket until she could finally tell her parents she had to leave for work. Her heart in her stomach and her stomach in her throat, she left the cold church and stepped into the morning sun that failed to make things any warmer outside.

The Plague Saint uniform felt heavier today. Winter stared at herself in bathroom mirror for far too long, the beaked mask staring back, the pit in her stomach outweighing her fear of someone walking in. Finally, she climbed out the window and walked to the hospital.

The atmosphere was tense. Something had definitely changed. Winter didn't make it ten feet past the receptionist desk before someone was talking to her.

"Plague Saint!" The woman was Dr. Liang. "Did you hear about Adams?"

Winter swallowed. "No. Did something happen?"

"He's dead!"

Winter stopped. How much emotion should she show? How would the real Plague Saint react? "Dead? Since when?" She allowed a small amount of surprise into the words.

"A nurse found him a few hours ago," Dr. Liang replied, pausing next to Winter. "But the coroner says he thinks he died last night, though he's still examining the body."

"Any word on cause of death?"

"Not that I've heard. Yet."

Winter nodded. "Well, that's—incredibly unfortunate. Hopefully we'll get answers quickly."

Before going to her office, she stopped by River's room long enough to see that he was still sleeping. She couldn't risk asking about his vitals until she started her rounds. The last thing she needed was for the nurses to suspect she was more interested in him than her other patients.

Once in her office, she sat at her desk and focused on the coded journal entries until Phoebe came running in.

"Sorry I'm later than usual!" Phoebe tossed her bag on her chair, clearly out of breath.

"It's fine. Did something hold you up?" Maybe Winter could get some information about her job at the church.

Phoebe hesitated before answering. "I help out at St. Andrew's early most mornings, and in exchange my tuition at the college is discounted a little."

So, her only compensation was slightly lower bills? Winter turned her attention back to the journal. "Did you hear about Director Adams?"

"How could I not?" Phoebe asked. "With all of those city guards hanging around the receptionist's desk."

Chapter Seven
An Investigation

Winter was painfully aware of the city's police standing around her as she stared at Adams's body. She recognized a few of the guards from her time working at the station, which only added to her anxiety. Fighting to keep her hand steady, she capped the final vial she'd brought for samples. The needle she'd used to draw blood went into the room's biohazard bin.

"I'll test the samples, but based on his appearance, I agree with the coroner's initial findings," Winter said. "He had red plague, yellow plague, and either green or blue. Possibly both. I won't be sure about violet until my tests come back. That one tends to have a longer incubation time."

The guard captain assigned to the investigation, Captain Perry, nodded. "Have your results delivered directly to the north station as soon as you're done."

"Of course." Winter examined the blood sample one more time before sliding it into one of her coat pockets. "Anything else?"

Perry folded his arms. "In your opinion, Plague Saint, what are the chances of someone like Adams catching three or more plagues in such a short span of time?"

"He does work in a hospital," Winter deadpanned.

"But we've never seen anything like this before."

Winter gritted her teeth. "I have, actually. I have several recorded cases of this happening to other people. Adams is just the first one the city actually cares about."

Maybe she should have left that last part out. Perry lifted an eyebrow. "I wasn't aware of that." Was he more surprised by her statement, or the ferocity with which she'd delivered it?

"I'd be happy to send you the case files." Winter picked up her staff form where it leaned against the table holding Adams's body.

"I'll give you a call if I have any other questions," Perry said.

"Great," Winter muttered.

Phoebe looked up from her notebook when Winter returned to the office. Her expectant gaze followed Winter all the way to the lab door.

Winter paused with one hand on the door handle. "Yes?"

"Well?" Phoebe asked.

"Well what?"

"What did the city guard want with you?"

Winter pulled out her sample vials and held them up for Phoebe to see. Blood and saliva. "I have to run tests and let them know exactly which plagues he had."

Winter had half-expected Phoebe to wince at the sight of the samples, but her expression didn't change. "So, did they tell you why they're getting involved with a plague death?"

"It's not my job to worry about that," Winter replied as she returned the vials to her coat. "And if they're looking for something beyond bad luck on Adams's part, they're going to be disappointed." *Hopefully.*

"So, you don't think it was—" Phoebe leaned forward and lowered her voice. "—*murder?*"

Winter froze. There it was. No one else had said the word out loud, yet she couldn't shake the fear that it was what everyone was thinking. She shook her head. "What on earth would make you say that?"

Phoebe shrugged. "The whole thing is just weird. I think we should look into it."

"*We?*" Winter's hands tightened. "The city guard is already investigating. What could we possibly find that they can't?"

"I have a theory," Phoebe replied, her voice low and conspiratorial again. "I think whoever killed Adams killed a few other people as well. Some of the deaths in the hospital that were supposedly from plagues shouldn't have happened. People who were getting better and should have recovered." She reached for a stack of papers on the small table by her chair. "I've been analyzing files since I got here. I've only gone back a few months, but—"

Phoebe was far smarter than Winter had given her credit for, Winter realized as her assistant's rambling continued. And she wasn't entirely wrong. The Plague Saint *was* responsible for those deaths, and if Winter was the Saint now, then the Saint was responsible for Adams's death as well.

"What, you think someone snuck into the hospital and killed them?" Winter asked when Phoebe finally paused for air. She hoped her skeptical tone would deter Phoebe from her theories.

"A lot of those people still owe the hospital money," Phoebe said. "Maybe we could go talk to them under the guise of reminding them about payment and ask a few questions. See if they all had someone in common that might want them dead."

Why did Phoebe care about this? "I thought you didn't want to go into debt collection."

"I don't, but we don't have to let whoever replaces Adams know that." Phoebe's brow furrowed. "Who is replacing him, anyway?"

"No one knows yet. The mayor's supposed to assign someone soon." Another powerful member of the elite to replace Adams. Cut one head off…

"Well? Are you interested?"

The last thing Winter wanted to do was walk around the city for a few hours in this stupid uniform. "I have a lot of work to do here," she said. "But…"

What good would supervising Phoebe do? Adams's murderer wasn't some serial killer sneaking around the hospital. It was her, and she'd killed him to protect herself and her family. And countless other innocent people.

And he was a terrible person with a lot of power, she reminded herself.

Winter pushed aside those thoughts. It would be interesting to see how Phoebe went about her investigation. And maybe Winter could figure out why she was so invested in this. There had to be more to it than simple curiosity.

"I know a girl who works at the north guard station," Winter finally said. "She's not one of them, she's just an administrative assistant—she has a similar job to you, actually. Her name's Winter Pierce."

Phoebe perked up. "How do you know her?"

"I'm familiar with a lot of people at the guard station. For arranging debt collection and whatnot," Winter replied. "If I tell her you're coming, she might be willing to help you out. She'll have access to addresses, too. That should make it easier for you."

The hospital records office had the addresses, too, and they'd be easier to steal from than the guard station. Winter's mind raced. If she met Phoebe on the street outside the station, she could probably get away with the lie.

"Oh, well, I guess I could head over to the guard station after my shift." Phoebe stood up. "I mean, if that's all right. I should be done filing new reports by four."

"I'll have to call the station first and check with her." Winter eyed the telephone sitting on her desk. "While I do that, could you go check my inbox?"

"In the main office?" Phoebe didn't even attempt to hide the hesitation in her tone. It was a long walk. Which was just what Winter needed.

"Yes. Please." Winter started toward the desk. "Like I said, I'm busy. So, it's either that, or I find something else for you to do that might take even longer." *And cut into your time playing detective.*

Phoebe swallowed and nodded. "Right away, sir."

Winter felt a slight pang of guilt as Phoebe hurried out of the office, but she brushed it off. She was helping Phoebe enough as it was.

Things had been quiet all morning, patient-wise. There was the chaos surrounding Adams's death, but that was all the more reason to leave earlier in the evening. There was enough medicine on hand for other doctors to stabilize any new patients that popped up, and Winter had her remote radio to listen for any sudden outbreaks.

Since there was no need to make a real phone call, Winter stepped into the lab and started a mental list of tasks to finish before leaving to help Phoebe with her investigation. First were the sample tests, of course. The violet test would take the longest, but even that would be done in a couple of hours. That would give her time to hunt down some case files she could send along to Captain Perry that would prove Adams's death wasn't unprecedented.

Then, she had to make her afternoon rounds and check on River. If he was conscious, she wanted to visit him out of costume before meeting Phoebe.

And, while her shorter tests ran, Winter had to work on decoding the new journal. She was sure she was close, but she just hadn't been able to catch a minute to take a good look. She also wanted to do another sweep of the secret lab sometime soon. There had been labeled diagrams of the empty cages in some of the journal pages she'd flipped through. Maybe there were clues around them she'd missed.

She set up the sample tests, left a note on Phoebe's chair informing her that Winter would be able to meet her that evening, and headed down to the secret lab armed with the journal.

The five words across the top of the page she'd been focused on were definitely the plague colors, Winter decided. The words all being in black would make deciphering them trickier, but it was doable. With her own pen and a spare piece of paper, Winter scribbled down the colors. *Red. Blue. Green. Yellow. Violet.*

Sfe had to be red, *cmvf* blue, and...if *hsffo* was green, then *f* definitely meant *e*. One letter off...was that all it was? Winter's eyes widened. *S* became *r*, *f* became *e*, *e* became *d*.

At first, she thought it was too simple for a secret code made by someone who was supposedly a genius, but then she realized that despite its simplicity, it was still a pain in the ass to translate. It would presumably get easier as she started to pick up on which letters went with which without having to mentally run through the alphabet, but she didn't make it that far. She only translated one sentence—*plague combinations can be constructed with varying incubation times based on which are used*—when the timer she'd brought down with her went off. Time to check on the tests.

Winter left the notebook, figuring she'd come back to it as soon as she could, and no one else knew about the place, anyway. She threw the empty cages one last glance before making the trip to the upper lab.

The violet plague hadn't taken hold after all, but on top of red and yellow, Adams tested positive for both blue and green. Dread settled over Winter, who'd hoped only one would show up. The more plagues the dead director had, the more suspicious the whole incident was.

She dug out the massive camera stored in the lab and photographed her results. While they took their time developing, she wrote up a report.

Armed with her results, Winter left the lab. "Phoebe?"

Phoebe, back in the office now, looked up from her paperwork. "Yes?"

"Could you spare a moment to round up files on patients who were diagnosed with multiple plagues? Preferably those with three, at least." Winter opened a desk drawer and pulled out a large envelope.

"Sure thing." Phoebe jumped up and walked to the filing cabinet. "So, what's Winter like?"

Winter slid the lab report and photos into the envelope. "Hm?"

"Winter Pierce. What's she like?" Phoebe asked as she eased open a particularly creaky drawer. "I thought it might be nice to know a bit about her before I meet her."

"I don't know her that well. I've only interacted with her briefly." What did Winter even want Phoebe to think of her? "She does seem to be a bit on the quiet side, so I wouldn't be offended if she doesn't warm up to you quickly."

Phoebe laughed. "I put up with you, don't I?"

Winter's hands tightened around the envelope. "Sure," she muttered.

After opening and closing a few more drawers, Phoebe came to the desk with a stack of files. "You want copies of these?"

Winter glanced at the pile. "I'll pick out a few and have you copy those while I make my rounds."

"Sounds good."

Winter selected some prime examples for Captain Perry to study. Four cases of patients with three plagues, all who died within twenty-four hours of showing symptoms. On top of that, she was lucky enough to stumble across a four-plague case. That patient died less than two hours after showing up at the hospital.

While Phoebe made the copies, Winter went on her rounds, updating treatment schedules and adjusting doses. Her final stop was River.

He was awake, sitting up, and apparently feeling well enough to get down spoonfuls of soup while Winter checked his vitals.

"So, what's the word, doc?" he asked as she made notes in his file.

"Word on what?" Winter answered blankly.

"How long until I'm out of here and back to work?"

Winter tapped her pen against her clipboard. "You'll be on bedrest for the rest of the week, at least. I can't recommend you checking out until you go three full days without coughing up blood."

"But I'm feeling much better already."

"You'd collapse as soon as you stood up. Trust me, I've seen dozens just like you." Winter turned to leave.

"Not one for light conversation, are you?" River chuckled. "You remind me of my sister."

Winter froze. "Just...try to get some rest."

Chapter Eight
The Trolley Problem

"I'm leaving early to take these reports to the guard station," Winter told Phoebe as she prepared to leave the office. "Once you're done here, you're free to go meet Winter."

Phoebe nodded. "Good night. And Plague Saint?"

Winter started for the door. "Yes?"

"Thank you."

"Mmhmm." Winter awkwardly fumbled with the door handle and left the office. Instead of changing in the restaurant tonight, she was going to take a risk and change in a hospital bathroom. She had to see River before she left and didn't have much time to spare.

Her pulse quickened when she arrived at River's room and found an unfamiliar man standing outside, peering in through the door's window. He was a stout man only a couple of inches taller than her. Short gray hair was just beginning to recede at the top of his head. His deep green business suit looked expensive, as did the black shirt under his jacket.

Winter glared at him as she approached. "Can I help you?"

The man shot her an annoyed look back. "Doubt it."

For a moment, Winter missed the respect and caution people treated her with when she wore the Plague Saint uniform. Despite her instincts screaming at her to lower her gaze and avoid antagonizing him, she lifted her chin. Sharpened her glare. "Then step aside so I can visit my brother. Please." The bitterness in that last word negated any politeness it might have offered.

The man's eyes narrowed. "You're River Pierce's sister?"

"And you are—?"

"It's none of your concern." The man gave her one last look—the same kind of look he'd likely give a hair in his food—and walked away.

Winter stormed into her brother's room. "Who was that man outside?"

"Well, hello to you too." River leaned over to peer at the open doorway. "There was someone outside? No one's come in since the doctor."

"Fantastic," Winter muttered.

River laughed. "Aw, come on. You can't cheer up just once? For me?"

"You're in a hospital bed." Winter closed the door and walked to his bed. "For once, I have a reason to be grim."

"Oh, please. I'll be out of here in no time."

Winter sank into the chair at his bedside. "And back in the factory, where you'll catch something else?"

"Well, what else am I supposed to do? Not work?" River playfully punched Winter in the arm. It was weak, even for something meant to be teasing. "I know you want me going soft so you can finally beat me at arm wrestling, but—"

Winter rolled her eyes. "I could beat you now!"

"Well, no shit. I'm on the verge of death!"

"Don't let Mom hear you say that." Winter couldn't stop the barest hint of a smirk from finding her lips. "And I thought you were going to be out of here in no time."

"There's a smile. Though less smug would be nice." River coughed. Thankfully, there was no blood. Not this time. "Anyway, the factory would fall apart without me."

"Yeah, I think I heard them crying when I walked by the other day." After a moment's hesitation, Winter leaned forward. "How many other people have gotten sick?"

"Not many before I left, but James mentioned a lot more guys have stopped showing up when he visited me this afternoon." More coughing. "It's all right, though. Heard that Plague Saint's been giving them some new treatment. They should all recover."

Well, that was assuming the treatment worked the way it was supposed to. And assuming no one else got in Winter's way.

River's gaze shifted to the locket hanging around Winter's neck. "Seriously, though. As soon as I'm out of here, I'm kicking your ass at devil's bridge and winning that thing back."

"Can't wait," Winter told him. After a moment's thought, she added, "I could bring the cards sometime this week when I visit."

"Please do," River said. "It's so boring here. And everyone's as gloomy as you."

"It's a hospital." Winter stood up. "I have to drop something off at the guard station, but I'll try to find some books or something to bring you tomorrow."

"Thank you." River leaned back against his pillows. "Try not to let the station suck any more soul out of you, all right?"

Winter rolled her eyes. "Will do." Her hand wrapped around the locket, and she hesitated. "Look, why don't you just take the locket while you're in here—"

"Nope. No way. I have to win it back fair and square," River insisted. "Those are the rules."

"If you say so." Winter rose to her feet. "Good night. Love you." She started toward the door.

"Love you too!" River called after her, his voice hoarse enough to make her wince.

It was already dark outside, though plenty of people were still running errands and finishing up work under the light from streetlamps and windows. Winter wished it was more acceptable to hide away in her room the moment the sun vanished, but the city wasn't ready to sleep at five p.m.

Her apprehension grew as she walked. This would be her first time entering the station since quitting. She'd told them she'd been offered a job at the hospital when she left, and now the lie would actually come in handy. Assuming no one asked too many questions.

And assuming she could keep it together long enough to drop off a simple envelope. The slight tremble in her hands and her racing heart weren't promising.

She also had Phoebe to worry about. Winter had told her to wait outside in her note, but if she decided to come into the station anyway, Winter's entire story would be shattered to pieces.

Winter stepped through the front door and into the familiar chaos of the guard station. Officers hurried about, along with assistants carrying reports and files. The same job Winter had once had. Doors leading to offices lined the walls to the left and right of the foyer, while a hallway beyond led to storage and holding cells.

Winter walked to the reception desk. "I have a delivery from the hospital," she told the woman on the other side. "From the Plague Saint."

Beth looked up at her and smiled. "Winter! How's working at the hospital?"

"Busy," Winter replied curtly. She held out the envelope. "Plague Saint sent this for Captain Perry. It's for the Adams case."

Beth nodded. "I'll get it to him. Good to see you!"

"You too," Winter mumbled before turning around and leaving. The familiarity of the station was oddly uncomfortable, and she wanted out before memories could start clinging to her. Weighing her down.

She found a place in front of the guard station to wait for Phoebe that was out of the way of passersby on the sidewalk. Frigid air filled her lungs with every breath. The occasional flake of snow drifted lazily past her face. Winter wished she could give this terrible weather the plague and make it go away.

Yikes. Calm down. Winter adjusted her coat. All she had to do was put up with Phoebe's investigation for maybe an hour, and then she could go home and sleep.

Phoebe came around the corner about five minutes later. Winter took a deep breath, straightened her coat, and moved to intercept her before she reached the station doors. "Phoebe Blackburn?"

Phoebe spun to face her. "Oh! Winter? Winter Pierce?"

Winter nodded.

"Pleasure to meet you." Phoebe stuck out a hand.

Winter was taken aback by Phoebe's eagerness and strong handshake. "Um, right. The Plague Saint told me you had questions for some families of recently deceased patients. You thought maybe there was something else at play?"

Phoebe nodded and tucked a stray curl behind her ear. "A lot of them should have recovered but took a turn for the worse out of nowhere. At first, I thought it was this new white plague people are spreading rumors about, but now I think it might be a person responsible."

"And what led you to that conclusion?" Winter drew a folded piece of paper from her coat pocket and handed it to Phoebe. "Oh, and here are the addresses. Lead the way. I'll follow."

"Thanks." Phoebe scanned the page for a moment before setting off toward the street corner west of where they stood. "The reason I think there's a killer is because my uncle was one of the victims."

"Oh." Winter shoved her hands into her coat pockets. "I'm sorry for your loss."

Something flickered across Phoebe's face. Not sadness—hesitation? Concern? "Thank you. He was a scientist, working on cures for the plagues. He's the one who first told me about the possible existence of a white plague."

Oh. Great. The rumors would be harder to dismiss if a real scientist believed them. "Who did he work for? The city?"

"Uh, yeah, I think so. He's been on a few projects recently, so I'm not entirely sure." Phoebe looked up from the list of addresses. "Okay, we'll do these first since they're all a short walk from here. Then we can take the trolley a couple of stops to the eastern blocks and visit some people there."

"Sounds good."

Phoebe took the lead with surprising ease, pressing everyone who answered the door with questions. She asked whether anything strange had happened before the deceased passed, or if they'd interacted with anyone out of the ordinary. And through it all, she managed to maintain a tone of sympathy that kept the people she interrogated comfortable.

Winter stood behind her at every stop and watched, unable to help but be a little impressed. And unable to help feeling guilty—she had all the answers Phoebe was looking for. Her uncle was, more likely than not, just another victim of a doctor who didn't care to save his poorer patients.

It took about forty-five minutes for them to finish with the addresses in the northwestern apartments and head to the trolley stop. As they climbed aboard, Phoebe shook her head. "They were all just—people. People with nothing. They won't even be able to afford to pay the hospital." Her hand tightened around one of the trolley's poles. "It doesn't make sense. Adams was the first wealthy person to be killed."

Winter hesitated. "What about your uncle?"

"What about him?"

Was he rich? Poor? Winter shrugged instead of elaborating. It was probably the latter. "I don't know. Never mind."

Phoebe seemed to realize what she meant, anyway. "My uncle lives with me and my parents. He's my dad's brother. His research was valuable, but he hadn't seen any money for it. Yet." Her gaze dropped to the floor as the trolley jerked forward. "We were really hoping he'd find a real cure and finally get a good payout."

Lives? Present tense? Winter's chest tightened. Poor Phoebe. It sounded like she hadn't completely processed her uncle's death.

"Do you think his death could have to do with his research?" Winter asked.

"I did think about that," Phoebe replied. "But it doesn't really make sense to kill him because of it. Who *wouldn't* want a cure?"

"Maybe it's not about stopping a cure. Maybe it's about stopping people from knowing a cure exists."

Phoebe stared at her. "You think someone's keeping plague medicine a secret?"

Think? More like know. Winter didn't know of any true cures yet, but there was better treatment than the hospital claimed to have. "Maybe," she answered Phoebe with a shrug. "I mean, people in the government might want to keep themselves safe without wasting resources helping people who—" She swallowed. "People who won't be able to pay for it."

"Huh." Phoebe's brow furrowed. After a long moment, the concentrated expression fell away, and she straightened up. "Thank you for your help. Do you have a phone?"

Winter's mind went to the ancient thing hanging on the wall in her family's kitchen. "Yes. Why?"

"Why?" Phoebe laughed. "Because you just gave me a new direction to take this case!"

"Case?" What the hell had Winter gotten herself into?

"If you're not busy this weekend, we could go to my uncle's lab," Phoebe continued. "It's locked up, but I have one of his keys."

Say no. It's a bad idea. A waste of time.

But what if Phoebe's uncle had new research on the plagues? Cures or treatments that the Saint hadn't discovered?

"Sure. I'm free." Winter usually left weekend mornings to the other doctors, anyway. She searched her coat pockets until she found a stray pen. Phoebe gave her the crumpled piece of paper that held the addresses, and Winter scribbled down her number.

"What did you say your uncle's name was?" Winter asked as she handed the paper back. She wanted to search the Saint's personal reports and see if she could confirm whether his death really was on purpose.

"Oh. Um. I didn't." There was clear hesitation on Phoebe's face as she accepted the paper. It took another moment before she answered, "Uh, Marcus Blackburn." She glanced at the list of addresses, then flipped the paper over to study Winter's number.

"I think we should call it a night," Phoebe continued. "Whatever the reason for these people's deaths, I don't think they know anything that will be helpful."

Winter held back a sigh of relief. She was eager to get out of the cold and away from the shadows lurking just beyond the streetlamps. "Sure thing. Where's your stop?"

"Next one, actually."

"Oh. You're not far from the hospital, then."

Phoebe leaned against the trolley's railing. "Yup."

"Careful," Winter found herself muttering as the wind whipped Phoebe's hair around.

Phoebe laughed and straightened up again. "Right. Wouldn't want to end up in someone's philosophy experiment."

"Hm?" The hell was that supposed to mean?

"Oh, sorry. I don't know why I thought you'd get that. We learned about it in one of my elective classes." Phoebe traced a finger across the railing. "The trolley problem. Let's say you're standing by a switch in the tracks and the trolley's coming. If it continues, it'll run over five people."

Winter stared at her blankly. "What? Why?"

"I don't know. It doesn't really matter, but the point is there's five people tied to the tracks and the trolley can't stop. But you can pull the switch."

"Well, do that then."

"There's more." Phoebe held up a finger. "There's a sixth person on the other track. To save the five people, you have to kill one."

"Is this what they teach at the college?" Winter asked incredulously. "I thought you were studying nursing."

Phoebe chuckled. "Technically, yes. But I'm also taking an old world history and philosophy class. The whole point is to study what people thought and believed hundreds of years ago, and why that might have led to things falling apart around the world the way they did."

"Okay, well, what did people think back then? Would they kill the five to save the one?"

"This isn't the kind of class with simple answers." Phoebe smiled, but it didn't reach her eyes. "And even if you think killing the one is the right thing to do, could you actually do it? Could you pull the switch? Lots of people say they'd do one thing, when in reality they might do the opposite."

Winter rubbed her forehead. "I'm still not sure I understand the point."

"It's just a thought experiment. And it's only a small part of what we're covering." Phoebe shrugged as the trolley rolled to a stop. "Anyway, this is my stop. Good night, Winter! I'll call you sometime tomorrow."

"Good night," Winter mumbled in response as Phoebe hurried past her.

That girl had too much energy, Winter thought as she watched her hop off the trolley. Before walking off, Phoebe turned and waved. Winter offered a half-hearted wave in return, still not entirely sure what she'd gotten herself into.

Chapter Nine
Doubled-Edged Sword

Marcus Blackburn did not exist in the hospital records. Not the official ones, not in the debt reports, and not in the Plague Saint's notebooks. Either there had been some sort of mistake, Winter had missed something, or Phoebe was lying.

That last option was hard to believe. Phoebe had never struck Winter as anything more than a hardworking—and sometimes naïve—assistant. So, Winter set aside the thought for now. She could reassess after the visit to Blackburn's lab. Phoebe had called earlier that morning, and they were going to visit the lab the next day—Saturday.

At least, that was the plan. Winter had been at the hospital for nearly an hour, and there was no sign of Phoebe.

She ventured down to the secret lab and decoded a few more sentences from the journal. *I've been able to isolate strands of DNA from samples. I believe I've identified bacteria responsible for blue and yellow plagues. I will test the colonies I'm replicating to be sure.*

Isolating DNA? That required technology Winter hadn't seen at the hospital. She only had the vaguest idea of how that sort of stuff worked, and that knowledge was based on brief notes the Saint had made elsewhere. Where were the machines he'd used for this?

Winter glanced around at the emptied shelves. They must have been in this lab at some point. Had someone been sneaking in here while she wasn't around? And if the Plague Saint had been able to get his hands on advanced enough technology to work with DNA, would it have killed him to install some security cameras, too?

She sighed. It was time to do her rounds. Deciphering the text was a frustratingly slow process, and as much as she wanted to keep going, a break to clear her head would be good. She set the notebook in its usual place on the counter and left the lab.

Phoebe was in the office when Winter returned, digging through a drawer in the filing cabinet.

"Where have you been?" Winter asked.

"I'm so sorry!" Phoebe spun around. "I had a—a family emergency. But it's all sorted out now. Sort of."

"Oh." Winter awkwardly picked up her bag and staff from her desk. "Okay. I'm off to do rounds."

She started in the tower, checking in on two new patients in critical condition before moving on to her brother. River was recovering as fast as could be expected. It would still be a few days before he'd be able to walk around at all, but he was doing as well as Winter had dared to hope.

She'd just left the tower and was headed for a batch of green plagues when a man called to her from behind. "Plague Saint!"

Winter paused in the middle of the hallway, trying to place the familiar voice before she turned around. Her eyes went wide under the mask. "Mayor Atherton?" She could barely keep the surprise from her voice. "What brings you here?"

"You, of course," Atherton said as he approached.

He wore a similar dark red suit to the one he'd worn at the church yesterday. The pale red shirt underneath wasn't far off in shade from his flushed skin. And Winter swore that under the hospital lights, there was a hint of red in his neatly gelled dark brown hair, too. Maybe he wore the suit to bring it out.

"It's been some time since I last saw you," Atherton continued. "We've never really had a chance to talk one-on-one, have we?"

"No, we haven't." Thankfully, it sounded like Winter wouldn't have to figure out what kind of conversations the mayor and Saint had been having before his death. "I am rather busy, after all. In fact—"

"Oh, I assure you, this won't take much of your time. I'm only here to extend an invitation. We can have a real discussion later." Atherton lowered his voice. "I'm holding a general assembly meeting Sunday night at St. Andrew's."

General assembly meeting? The hell was that? Some sort of city council thing?

"With the unfortunate passing of Director Adams, we thought it would be wise to ask you to join us," Atherton went on, oblivious to Winter's confusion. "We have some very important decisions to make regarding the hospital, of course, and Adams spoke highly of you."

The mayor—and possibly his council of politicians who ran the city—thought Winter was the man who saved their friends and killed their enemies.

"Of course," Winter said as smoothly as she could manage. "What time?"

"Seven o'clock. It'll be a pleasure to have you." Atherton extended his hand.

Winter shook it. "I look forward to it."

She finished her rounds, returned to her office, and ventured back down to the secret lab.

The notebook she'd left sitting on the table was gone.

Shit.

Winter raced back up to her office. Once she'd regained her breath, she forced a casual tone. "Phoebe, have you been in here all morning?"

"Uh, yes?" Phoebe didn't look up from the drawer she was organizing.

"And no one else has come through here? Gone into the lab?"

"Nope." Phoebe slid a folder into place. "Why? Something wrong?"

Two options. Phoebe was lying, or there was another entrance. Phoebe wasn't a liar. Then again, this was the second thing she'd said that was a little suspect.

Still, Winter searched for other possibilities. If there was another way into the basement lab, who else could possibly know about it?

"Plague Saint?" Phoebe was looking up now, nervous gaze on Winter.

"Nothing. Everything's fine. Just checking." Winter grabbed her staff. "I have to run some time-sensitive tests, so I'll be in the lab for a while. I'd prefer not to be disturbed."

"Understood." After one last concerned glance, Phoebe returned to her work.

Back down to the lab. Winter moved to the center of the room and turned in a slow circle, scanning for anything out of place, anything strange, anything that might be a way in.

A metallic clang came from her right. Winter's gaze snapped to the wall in time with her heart's skipped beat. She lifted the staff and fought to keep her hand steady. Another clang, this time farther up.

Was there something in the wall?

Someone?

A thud came from the ceiling. Winter grabbed the closest chair and dragged it in the direction of the sound. She stopped underneath a vent, hopped onto the seat, and pointed the staff toward the opening.

"Someone up there?" Winter hoped she sounded intimidating. The voice modifier could only do so much when fear was making every inch of her tremble.

Another thud, right over the vent. Winter jabbed up with the staff. The vent opening was loose, to her surprise, and the grate lifted and banged against the inside of the vent shaft. There was a squeak, and then a blur of white flying at Winter's face.

She yelped and swung with the staff. It collided with something solid before she could build up much speed and sent whatever it was crashing to the floor.

Winter whirled toward the spot where the white *thing* had landed. A clattering sound distracted her; the collision seemed to have loosened something inside the staff. Frowning, she held it up and pushed her thumb against the very tip.

It clicked. A new section of staff sprang up above the wings—a handle. The rest of the staff's outer shell slid off entirely and clattered to the floor.

Underneath was a blade. A narrow sword.

Movement on the floor made Winter jump. She hopped off the chair and pointed the blade at the—rat?

A white rat sat on the floor, dazed by the fall but seemingly unharmed otherwise. Winter took a step toward it and knelt down. She slowly extended a gloved hand. The rat cautiously approached and sniffed her fingers before stepping into her palm.

Winter rose to her feet. "Sorry about hitting you, little guy," she muttered. "You scared me." She turned around, and her eyes fell on the empty cages. Was this what had been in them? Rats? And if so, where were the rest of them?

After deciding the rat was fine, Winter put it back in the vent shaft. She had no idea what else to do with it, no way of feeding it or taking care of it, and a dozen far more pressing matters to deal with.

Chapter Ten
So Below

Winter had warned Phoebe in advance that she would not be leaving her home until the sun was out. Phoebe had laughed but agreed they could meet after sunrise. Winter told her parents she'd picked up an extra shift at the station.

When Winter hopped off the trolley at the stop they'd arranged to meet at, Phoebe was already waiting.

"Good morning!" she said brightly.

Winter rubbed one of her eyes, still fending off the last clutches of sleep. "You haven't been waiting long, have you?" She wasn't late, but she would still feel bad if Phoebe had been standing around in the cold for more than a couple of minutes.

"Not long at all," Phoebe replied as they started walking. "The lab's pretty close to my house."

"Have you been there before?"

"Uh, sort of. I've been outside of the building to meet my uncle when he was done working, after my classes. He never took me inside, though." Phoebe paused. "Oh, shoot! I forgot I need to drop off an assignment before my professor marks it late."

"Oh." Winter paused. "Right now?"

Phoebe nodded. "I'm so sorry. I swear it won't take long. I just have to drop it in a box outside the classroom."

"Sure, no worries. I'll just...follow you." Walking to the college and back would only delay them, what, twenty minutes? Twenty-five? Winter forced herself to take a deep breath. No need to rush. There was nothing to get worked up over.

They made the walk to the college in just under ten minutes. Phoebe led the way to one of the many brick buildings, and Winter anxiously followed her inside. She had to remind herself that it didn't matter that it wasn't a student, and that she was with Phoebe, and that no one cared about some random girl walking the halls. But she couldn't shake the feeling that everyone they passed knew she didn't belong.

The corridors they walked through smelled like old books. Posters and diagrams Winter didn't understand covered the walls, along with portraits of people who looked a lot smarter than her.

"Here we are." Phoebe stopped in front of a door and drew a bundle of papers from her bag. "I spent all night on this essay. I'd hate to get docked for being late." As she slid it into the metal box hanging next to the door, she chuckled. "Maybe if I'd gotten some more sleep, I would have remembered to drop it off before coming to meet you."

"What's the essay on?" Winter asked.

"Oh, it's for a history class," Phoebe explained as they began walking again. "Stuff about politics when Devil's Pass was founded. Here, let's go down this hall, it'll put us out closer to the lab."

Winter followed her until they were almost out the doors. A massive painting, much larger than any of the other portraits they had passed, made her stop. She stepped back to take in the woman's cold face, the sword in her hands, the blood dripping from the blade.

"Who's that?" Winter asked.

"Huh?" Phoebe was almost to the door. She turned around and glanced at the painting. "Oh. Saint Minerva." Winter swore there was a hint of disdain in her voice.

"*That's* Saint Minerva? She looks like she just killed someone!"

"Because she did." Phoebe closed the distance between herself and Winter. "I don't know why they made the War Saint the school's patron—well, I do know, I just think it's a bad choice."

Winter shot her a sideways glance. "Why did they, then?"

"Something about knowledge being our best weapon against our enemies." Phoebe gave a half-hearted shrug.

"Devil's Pass has enemies?"

"We did when the school was founded, in the early days of the city. Different communities were fighting over resources in these mountains. Still, you'd think they'd have taken this down at some point." Phoebe turned away from the painting. "I just think it's a bit much. You ready to go check out the lab?"

Winter nodded. "Let's go." As they reached the exit door, she asked, "How did the War Saint die again? It was in battle, right?"

"Yeah. The last battle Devil's Pass fought, over a century ago. Saint Minerva led her army to victory, but the last enemy soldier killed her before dying from their wounds."

They left the campus behind and walked the city streets for nearly fifteen minutes before Phoebe stopped. "This is the place." She gestured to the plain stone building in front of them. "It also houses some offices. My uncle's lab is in the basement." She held up a key. "And this is for an entrance in that alley over there."

Winter followed her to the side of the building. "We're pretty close to the hospital," she noted.

"Yup. He worked with them a little. Requested samples and whatnot." Phoebe walked up to the only door in the alley, inserted and turned the key, and attempted to push it open with a grunt. It didn't budge. "Stupid thing," she muttered.

"Here, let me try." Winter took a step forward and a deep breath. With one swift movement, she shoved the side of her body against the door, shoulder first. It gave way and opened with a groan.

"Wow." Phoebe folded her arms. "Uh, thanks."

Winter gestured to the open doorway, hiding the pain shooting through her upper body. "After you."

Phoebe stepped into the darkness. "There must be a switch around here somewhere—aha!" There was a click, followed by a dim light flickering on up ahead.

Phoebe led Winter through a narrow hall and down a flight of stairs. Winter pressed a gloved hand to the wall at her right. She wasn't ordinarily one to get nervous in places like this, but the tight space was making her claustrophobic. The flickering, exposed light bulbs weren't helping.

The hallway led them directly to the lab. And disappointment. Any equipment or supplies the space once held were gone.

Winter examined a dust-covered table near the entrance. "This place looks pretty empty."

"There has to be something." Phoebe strolled in and began trying cupboards. "Keep looking."

Winter wasn't optimistic. Still, she dropped to the floor, tried not to focus on how dirty it was, and peered under the counter wrapping around the lab. Her eyes caught a clear path through the dust. She reached out, and her hand found something. A gold-banded black pen. Not terribly notable.

"This is all I've got." Winter rose to her feet and held up the pen for Phoebe to see.

Phoebe threw a drawer shut with surprising force. "Why would he clean it out?" she muttered.

"Well, he had to have taken it all somewhere, right?" Winter tried. "Do you know of any other places he might have kept his things?"

Phoebe closed her eyes and took a deep breath. "I'll just have to ask him again."

It was a whisper, barely audible, but Winter heard it all the same. She took a hesitant step toward Phoebe. "What was that?"

Phoebe's eyes flew open. "Okay, I lied. I'm really sorry. I didn't want to, but—" She brushed a piece of hair out of her face. "I just—didn't want you thinking I was crazy for thinking he was still alive. But I knew he was."

"Your uncle?" Winter asked, brow furrowing.

Phoebe nodded. "He didn't die in the hospital. He went missing. I thought maybe it had to do with his research, but I was sure he wasn't dead. And then the other night he showed up at our apartment."

"Where was he, then?"

Uneasiness settled over Winter.

"He hasn't told us much. All he said was that someone was after his research, and he'd been in hiding." Phoebe was pacing now. "And he won't answer my questions. It was this killer. It has to be. There's some sort of conspiracy with the plague cures, or—"

This didn't make any sense. Winter could account for every death. They were all either her, or the real Saint. Was someone else after the cures? Maybe the incident with Marcus Blackburn was completely unrelated to what was happening at the hospital, even if he'd gone missing from there.

Wait. Maybe the Plague Saint *had* gone after Blackburn. If Blackburn's research was leading him to promising cures, the Saint might have decided he needed to be eliminated. It was just...odd that he'd never mentioned the man in his journals. But not impossible.

"My uncle doesn't know I came here," Phoebe continued as Winter tuned back in to her rambling. "I found the lab key last in his bedroom last week, but I put off coming here because I was scared. But I need answers. He could still be in danger, and people are dying." Her eyes found Winter's. "I need your help."

"Me?" Winter sputtered. "I don't know how I could be of any help—"

"I think you're right about people trying to hide the plague cures."

Winter's desire to remove herself from this mess entirely was at war with her burning curiosity about Blackburn's research. She sighed and shook her head. "What can we even do about it, though?"

"We have to persuade my uncle to tell us what he knows," Phoebe said. "And I think you can help with that. Since you work at the guard station, you can get information about the investigation into Adams's death, right?"

"It doesn't really work like that," Winter said. "I just organize—"

"There has to be something you can do," Phoebe interrupted, pleading. Desperate. "Anything."

There was something. But that would be a job for the Plague Saint, not Winter Pierce. "I'll see what I can do. I have a shift tomorrow night."

Phoebe's face lit up. "Thank you. I'm going to talk to my uncle. Maybe you could come over for dinner Monday night and tell him what you find out about the investigation. And I can bring files from the hospital—"

"That would be illegal," Winter told her.

"Fine. I'll *look* at some files and bring the information I learn in my brain. That work?"

That was still a violation of hospital conduct, but Winter wasn't exactly one to lecture Phoebe on following the rules. "Sure. Sounds great." She looked around the dusty lab as the lights overhead flickered. "Can we get out of here? This place is creeping me out."

"I was thinking the same thing," Phoebe said. "Let's go."

A minute later, they were stepping out into the alley. Winter breathed in deeply, taking in cold air that held the scent of cooking meat from a nearby restaurant. Chatter from the streets nearby washed over her.

"What are you up to after this?" Phoebe asked.

"Hm?" Winter held up a hand to shield her face from the blinding sun. She supposed she should have been happy to see it so bright out, but it felt like a lie with the biting cold, like the weather was mocking her—

She shook off her thoughts and processed Phoebe's question. "I'm going to visit my brother in the hospital," she answered as they made their way toward a trolley stop at the end of the block.

Phoebe shot her a wide-eyed glance. "Your brother's in the hospital? Is he—?"

"He's got red plague," Winter replied. "But he's recovering. As long as he rests, he should be fine. Eventually."

"Well, that's good!" And just like that, Phoebe's overly cheerful demeanor was back.

"You two would get along great," Winter muttered.

"I'm headed to the hospital, too, actually," Phoebe said. She slowed, then halted next to the sign marking where the trolley would arrive. "Plague Saint won't be dropping by until later today, but I don't like letting new patient reports pile up. The workload always gets crazy on weekends."

Winter stopped next to her. She had forgotten that she'd told Phoebe she'd be coming in for a little bit today. Part of her regretted not taking the day off, as she usually did on weekends, but she was eager to decode more of the Saint's notebook.

Assuming she could find it, Winter reminded herself. The book's disappearance from the secret lab was deeply unsettling.

An idea crossed Winter's mind as the trolley approached the stop. "Say, do you by chance have any work to do that doesn't involve sensitive information on patients?"

"Ugh, where do I begin?" Phoebe began counting off on her fingers. "Orders for chemicals and tools need to be filled out and sent to factories, stock records need to be organized, finance reports need to be added up and checked for accuracy..."

"Could any of that be done while, say, sitting in bed?"

"Oh, absolutely!" Phoebe's brow furrowed. "Why do you ask?"

A small smile found its way onto Winter's face. "I think I know someone who would be more than happy to help you with your workload, if you want it."

They stepped onto the trolley as Winter explained her idea. Phoebe nodded eagerly. "That would be a huge help. I'd have more time for my schoolwork." She hesitated. "Are you sure he'll be okay with it?"

"Of course," Winter told her. "River's bored out of his mind. And if he knows he's helping someone out, he'll be all the more eager to do it."

The trolley jerked forward. Winter grabbed onto a pole, and Phoebe's hand found a hold below hers.

"You know, I was thinking about that trolley problem thing," Winter began. "Does the problem say anything about the people involved?"

Phoebe frowned. "What do you mean?"

"Like, are they good people? Bad people?"

"Well, that would affect your decision, wouldn't it?"

"Exactly. Like, if the five are all ordinary people, and the lone one is, I don't know, a serial killer…it's an easy choice, right? You flip the switch." Winter's hand tightened around the pole. "Hypothetically, of course."

Phoebe hesitated. "I mean, sure. There are versions where you swap in criminals or even people you know, but the basic version is just…people. If you just stumble across the tracks and see this situation, not knowing anyone involved, what would you do?"

Winter turned her head to stare at the city passing by outside the trolley, the people on the sidewalk, the brief glimpses of her reflection in dark windows. "Hm."

"But hey, let's consider your situation," Phoebe said. "The one is a bad person, the five are good." Under her breath, she added, "Subjective as that may be."

Winter glanced at her. "Would you flip the switch?"

"Do you think that's the right thing to do?" Phoebe asked.

Winter shifted, growing uncomfortable in the tight space of the trolley. "Well, if you're keeping good in the world and getting rid of some bad…" She let the implication hang in the air, not sure how to finish the sentence.

"It's a fair thought." Phoebe tipped her head back to stare at the trolley ceiling. "You know, I work as a church maiden, and I hear those passages they read every morning. There's a lot of talk about how killing is bad, no matter what."

"So, the right thing to do is let the five die, because choosing to kill the one is a bad thing for you to do? Even if they go on to kill other people?" Winter asked. "Do you really believe that?"

"Not saying I believe it. That's just what the books say." Phoebe shrugged. "I guess killing—even bad people—is interfering with things you shouldn't."

Interfering with what? Some divine plan? Winter stared at Phoebe, watching the way her dark eyes swept the trolley ceiling. "Maybe the right thing is to do the wrong thing."

"Huh?" Phoebe lowered her head to look at Winter again.

"Like, maybe killing is bad, but you do it anyway because you care enough to save more people, even if you get some sort of cosmic weight put against your soul." At the blank look in Phoebe's expression, Winter shrugged. "But what do I know? I'm not in college."

Phoebe nodded, but there was apprehension in her gaze that made Winter feel like she'd said the wrong thing.

Chapter Eleven
Council

As Winter expected, Phoebe and River got along great, and River was grateful to have something to keep him occupied. Now she had to hope he wouldn't let it stop him from resting. His cough was still too strong for Winter's liking, though it was blood-free.

After leaving the two to their work, Winter spent as much time as she could spare on Saturday searching for the notebook that had vanished from the secret lab. By noon on Sunday, she had to face the fact that despite her desperate hopes, she hadn't misplaced it. Someone had come into the lab and stolen it. Not only was there another way in, but there was someone else out there who knew about it.

The question was whether they were a friend of the Plague Saint, or an enemy.

Winter's search for another hidden passage yielded nothing. Wherever it was, it was far better hidden than the entrance from the first lab.

Finally, she was forced to quit for the night. She had the general assembly meeting at the church and still had no idea what that was going to entail. And before she left, she had one last thing to do.

Instead of combining every plague in her new serum, she left out yellow and green. She didn't plan to use it, but knowing she had the option made her feel more secure.

She made the trek to St. Andrew's alone, for the first time in her life. She'd never expected she'd visit the church without her parents dragging her along. But she'd also never expected to become a killer.

The lights were on in the chapel, casting a warm glow across the snow. *You are the Plague Saint*, Winter reminded herself as she reached the double doors at the entrance. She had nothing to fear. These people needed her. They thought she was on their side.

The chapel was full of people dressed in the nicest suits one could find in Devil's Pass, with the occasional dress here or there. Winter stood out, but she'd expected that.

"Plague Saint!" Mayor Atherton noticed her as soon as she entered—most people did—and hurried to meet her. "Follow me. There's a spot for you at my table."

Winter scanned the clusters of people as they walked and was surprised to glimpse a familiar face near a drink table: the man who'd been standing outside River's hospital room. Did she dare ask?

"Mayor," she said, hating the way the word slid off her tongue. She nodded to the man in the green suit. "Who's that? I noticed him at the hospital the other day."

Atherton followed her gaze. "Oh, George Gordon. Smart man. He runs the city's largest food packaging factory."

River's boss. That explained it.

"He'll be joining us soon, actually." Atherton stopped in front of a table and gestured to an empty chair. "Once he's finished discussing trade with those diplomats from south of the pass."

The mention of visitors from other communities surprised Winter, but she didn't have time to dwell on it. There was another familiar face at the table. As Winter settled into her chair, she studied the woman in the lavender pantsuit across from her, trying to place her.

Atherton introduced her. "This is the city's financial advisor, Ellen Bates."

Winter had seen her speaking to the mayor at church, she realized. She nodded. "Pleasure to meet you."

Sitting to the right of Bates right was a man Atherton introduced as Jonathan Forrest. Winter knew the name. He was responsible for designing the trolley system that had been installed in the pass a decade earlier, a welcome upgrade from the old vehicles that had been used to bus people around. Rumor had it the money the city had paid him in exchange was exorbitant.

Forrest also had a reputation for being a charming and funny guy, and he had plenty of admirers among the people of Devil's Pass. If they hadn't met him, they'd read interviews with him in the paper, where his strong persona came across even in print.

He was younger than most of the others in the room—late thirties, probably—and had a messier look than the city officials. His clothes were just as expensive, though, even if he'd abandoned his suit jacket and failed to button his bright yellow shirt up all the way. His auburn hair wasn't slicked with gel or neatly combed, either, but his confident air made it look playfully ruffled rather than unkempt.

Though his obvious wealth undoubtedly helped, Winter thought bitterly.

For the next few minutes, Atherton and Forrest did most of the chatting. Then, they were joined by George Gordon. Winter seethed quietly under her mask as he took the last empty seat at the table.

"The supplies?" Atherton asked.

Gordon nodded. "They have the resources to double our orders, if we can afford it."

"Shouldn't be a problem." Atherton chuckled. "Especially with the new laws going into effect."

A commotion at the edge of the chapel made Winter turn. A wave of church maidens entered the room one by one, carrying platters of food and drink. One approached their table quickly.

The others at the table eagerly took small plates of meat and salad. As Atherton took a glass of wine, he glanced at Winter. "You're not going to eat, Plague Saint? I'm sure everyone here would be delighted."

"I think the city knows me well enough by now to know the mask stays on," Winter replied coolly. After a moment's hesitation, the church maiden hurried off to the next group.

Across the table, Bates raised an eyebrow. "And why is that?" she asked. "What reason do you have to hide your identity?"

Winter's fists clenched in her lap. "The last thing I need is people banging on my door all hours of the day, begging for a cure I can't give them."

It was convincing enough, apparently. "Fair enough, Saint," Atherton said with a smile. "Though I hope you'll come to trust us."

"I'm sure, with time." Winter needed to change the subject. "Mayor Atherton, what's this new law you mentioned? I'm afraid the hospital's been keeping me too busy to follow politics as closely as I'd like."

"Oh, you wouldn't have heard about this in any of the papers," Atherton told her. "My council hasn't announced it yet." He leaned toward her and spoke in a low voice. "I'm going to do what no one before me was able to do: I'm going to end the plagues."

Sure. Because that worked out so well for all the previous politicians who thought they could do it.

"And I'm going to need your help, Plague Saint." Atherton gave her a cold smile as he continued. "You've done so much for us already, under Adams's direction. And it's all been building toward this."

It should have been a good thing to hear that the mayor had a plan for the plagues, but Winter couldn't believe it. What the hell was Atherton going to do that no one else had thought of? The plagues were too damn persistent, and even the real Plague Saint hadn't found a permanent cure. Only treatments that kept the patient alive long enough for them to hopefully recover on their own.

"And how exactly do you plan to do that?" Winter asked.

Atherton straightened up in his seat. "Well, we're in a bit of a lull right now, but before long we'll have another serious wave of cases. You know how it goes."

Winter nodded. It might be strange to think of the city as being in a lull with the number of patients she saw every day, but she could recall times in years past when things had been much worse. Times when it had been better, too. Another spike would come along sooner or later.

Atherton went on. "People get less careful, the hospital loosens restrictions on quarantined patients, medicine production goes down, and then there's another big outbreak."

"We've tried to prevent that in the past," Winter said. "No matter what precautions the hospital takes, people relax. Become less careful. Especially younger ones who haven't seen a lot of outbreaks."

"Exactly!" Atherton exclaimed, his abrupt increase in volume nearly making Winter flinch. "They get sick and spread it around. How many stories have you heard of sick people still going to work?"

"Well, most of my patients tell me they have to get back to work as soon as possible, or they won't be able to afford to pay rent or feed their families—"

It was as if Atherton hadn't heard her. "They have no regard for others. They put themselves above the rest of the population."

The irony of Atherton's words would have been funny, if they didn't make Winter want to kill him then and there. River wasn't selfish. He'd been ready to die to earn enough for another meal for his family. And the man who owned the factory, the man who was really at fault for letting River stay at work while sick, was sitting mere feet away from Winter.

Atherton's rant wasn't over. Completely oblivious to the fact that Winter was fuming, he added, "And then, when they finally do go into the hospital, they waste valuable supplies that could have gone to someone actually contributing something to this city."

"Like the people in this room?" Winter deadpanned.

"Exactly." Atherton took another sip of his drink. "So, I was saying this at the last meeting, and I said—Jonathan, what was it I said exactly?"

Forrest laughed. "You said, 'it ought to be illegal.'"

The words turned Winter's blood to ice. "Illegal, to—?"

"To put us decent people in danger like that," Atherton said. "And Gordon told me..."

"'You are the mayor, after all,'" Gordon chimed in. "I see kids get carried out of my factory every damn day. If I could do something to stop them from showing up sick in the first place, I would."

How about not punishing them when they call out, moron. Winter swallowed her rage, but she couldn't stop it from simmering in her chest. *Give them sick pay so they can keep themselves fed until they can come back in.* That had to be cheaper than burning through employees and constantly training new ones, right? It had taken River months to learn the full scope of his job and work at the same speed as the employees who'd trained him.

Even if not, Winter was sure that punishing them with threat of termination was stupid. Especially if Gordon was going to turn around and act like they wanted to come in sick.

"I thought we could throw them in prison, but I don't think there'd be enough room," Atherton continued. "And why lock 'em up, anyway? If they want to work so badly, let them work. We'll just put them all somewhere where they won't infect anyone else. The new law will get them assigned somewhere, and our first new location will be run by Mr. Gordon here."

Gordon nodded. "I have a few workers in the hospital right now," he said.

River. Panic joined Winter's fury. Her pulse quickened. *What are they going to do to River?*

"Once they're released, they're not going back to their old jobs." Atherton took a sip of his wine. "They'll get a community service sentence to work in the new factory we're building at the edge of the city. The supplies I've got coming in are to finish up the construction."

A prison. Atherton might say otherwise, but that's what it was. Hell, it was death row. And...it didn't make any *sense.* Despite what the mayor said, this wasn't going to stop the plagues. This was just going to get people killed. A bunch of workers whose immune systems were already compromised from being sick, thrown together with people recovering from different plagues? People who might still be contagious, if they weren't properly tested before being discharged from the hospital?

"They'll all die," Winter realized. She didn't mean to say the words aloud, but they came out all the same. Quiet. Cold.

The sentiment didn't bother Atherton. "And they'll do us some good before they do."

Not just the people working in the new factory, but the families they went home to...

"What are you making in the new factory?" Winter asked. Her mind was screaming at her, her body throwing out alarm signals like a racing heart and nervous sweat. She needed something to focus on. And gathering information was her best move right now.

"It's a bottled drink factory," Gordon told her. "Nothing terribly interesting. Obviously, we'll take precautions on the production lines, but it's not the kind of stuff anyone in here would be drinking, anyway."

He meant people in this room, Winter realized.

As long as they were safe, they didn't care that they'd be putting more lives at risk. What a terrible way to stop the plagues. Making it illegal to be sick. And they'd even found a way to profit from it.

"And when will this new law be put into place?" Winter asked. She couldn't bring herself to sound thrilled about it, but she could manage the usual deadpan tone of the Saint's persona.

"I'm announcing it at the city council meeting at the end of this month." The wine glass went back to Atherton's mouth. "Of course, a majority of the council will have to approve it, but that won't be an issue."

"There's more to stopping the plagues than just punishing the people who are spreading them," Bates said. "Plague Saint, would it be possible for you to treat people in advance? Give us something that will make us immune?"

There wasn't a way to guarantee complete immunity, as far as Winter knew. Maybe giving them the treatment while they were healthy would help prevent infection, but she wasn't the scientist the real Saint was. Not that it mattered to her. "I have been working on something along those lines," she said. "It will be expensive to make, though."

"Not a problem." Bates gave her a thin smile. "I assure you, there's room in the budget."

But not room to pay Phoebe?

"We'll get you the money and the supplies you need to make your treatments," Atherton said. "We can discuss numbers later this week."

"Hopefully, we can avoid another tragedy like Adams's death," Bates added.

Everyone else at the table nodded solemnly. Winter tapped her fingers against her lap. Her next question had to be navigated carefully. For all she knew, she could be a suspect, after all. Voice low, she asked, "Has the city guard revealed anything new about the investigation into his death?"

Atherton sighed. "I spoke to the captain on the case this morning. He can't find any evidence that it was anything other than serious illness, but I'm not entirely convinced. Adams was a powerful man. He had enemies like the rest of us."

"Of course," Winter said. "Have you decided who you're going to assign to replace him, yet?"

"I've narrowed it down to a few candidates."

The conversation moved away from the Saint and the hospital, leaving Winter to silently battle the anger threatening to boil over within. The others at the table discussed people's lives like they were nothing more than gears in a machine. As if all that mattered was whether they were making the city money or losing it. The night dragged on.

Maybe rage was overwhelming any other emotion Winter might have felt—guilt, fear, hesitation—but the decision to poison George Gordon was an easy one to make.

Slipping the new serum into his drink was trickier.

Winter kept an eye on him as she endured over an hour of conversation, hand on the vial in her pocket, waiting for the perfect opportunity to strike. Her chance finally came when Bates and Atherton left to discuss budgetary matters with an education director. Gordon and Forrest remained at the table, deep in conversation about something related to trolley maintenance. And another round of church maidens arrived to circle the chapel with trays of drinks.

Winter pushed her chair away from the table and rose to her feet. "Would you two care for another drink while I'm up?" she asked. "I'm afraid it's about time I left."

"Yes, thank you Plague Saint," Forrest said. Gordon nodded, and Winter took that as yes.

She walked toward a maiden lingering at the edge of the table arrangement, drawing the vial from her pocket and unscrewing the cap with one hand as she moved. With the other hand, she reached for the maiden's tray. "I'll take two, please."

The maiden nodded silently. Winter took the first glass and passed it to her other hand, the one with the vial. As her hand wrapped around the glass, she tipped the vial and let a few drops spill into the drink. She grabbed the second drink quickly and hurried back to the table.

She set Forrest's glass in front of him first, then used her now freed hand to grab Gordon's while leaving the vial hidden— hopefully—in the other. Her hand closed around the vial the moment the glass was free, and she could only hope the movement of the drink was enough to distract anyone looking from glimpsing the poison.

Winter's eyes darted to Forrest as he picked up his own, untainted drink. She didn't have much of a read on him yet, and although she doubted he was any better than the other people here, she wasn't ready to kill him about it.

Yet.

That thought made her freeze. Gordon was taking his own drink now, and oh god she was really doing this again, wasn't she?

She left the table quickly after that but paused on her way out to say goodbye to Atherton. "I'm afraid I have other matters to attend to tonight, but I hope I'll be able to help you fix the problems plaguing Devil's Pass," she told him. "Thank you for inviting me."

Outside the church, Winter stumbled down the snow-covered hill and into an alleyway, where she leaned against the cold brick wall of a building and pulled off the hat and hood and suffocating mask. Cold air flooded her lungs. For the first time in her life, it felt good. With a shaking hand, she pulled out the locket. Opened it. Stared at the old photo.

She'd killed the Plague Saint for her mother, and Adams for her brother. And now Gordon would die for her family too.

Not just for River, she reminded herself. *For all the people they're going to kill.*

This was the most anger she'd felt in a long time. The most *anything* she'd felt in a long time. For once, she wasn't just going to work day after day, wondering if things would ever change.

Now, she had a mission.

Chapter Twelve
Thin Ice

That night, Winter's dreams were shaped by long-forgotten memories. Snowy forests. Frozen ponds. River's laughter. She awoke with a start at the realization that she'd met George Gordon once before.

Three years earlier, River was eighteen and had already spent a year working at the factory. Fourteen-year-old Winter spent several months bemoaning how bored she was without him around in the afternoons to play card games or read her stories. His help with her schoolwork was missed, too, as their father was considerably less patient when Winter was confused. Her complaints about River's absence only stopped when she got sick of her parents' lectures about bills and adulthood and supporting the family.

She gradually got used to her brother not being home when she returned from school, got used to him only being around in the late evening, got used to him already being gone when she woke up in the morning. The two tried to make the most of the weekends, but he spent most of those resting up from his days of hard labor.

It was an unusually sunny Thursday in the middle of December when River shook Winter awake. She blinked at him in confusion as her dreams faded from her mind. She had the days leading up to the end of the year off from school, but he was supposed to be at work.

"River?" Winter rubbed her eyes. "Why are you still here? Are you sick?"

"Nope. I've got the day off."

He quickly explained that, as an incentive to encourage employees to work harder and faster, the employee with the highest productivity at the end of each month would receive one paid day off. And River was the latest winner.

That news was enough to chase off Winter's grogginess. She sat up. "So, you'll be here all day?"

"Well, not exactly." One of River's arms had been behind his back, and he moved it forward to reveal the two pairs of ice skates he held by the laces. "I thought we could enjoy the nice weather, while it lasts."

"You got us both ice skates?" Winter asked incredulously. She'd been begging her parents for a pair for nearly a year now, to no avail.

"We're only renting them," River explained. "It was that or buy one pair, but they've yet to invent shoes that can change size, so..." He lifted the ice skates higher. "You in?"

Winter grinned, already envisioning herself twirling on a frozen pond, like the skaters she'd seen in the town square once. The fountain at the square's center had broken and flooded the area, causing it to freeze over and draw in the skaters who ordinarily had to venture to ponds outside the city proper. Winter had been helping Mom carry home groceries when they saw the skaters.

Mom had been too busy to let Winter stand around watching the performance for long, but the sight had stuck with her.

"Obviously, I'm in," she told River. "But where are we gonna go?"

"One of my friends at the factory gave me directions to a pond that's not too far from Oak Street. It's supposed to be great for skating."

River left to wait in the kitchen while Winter changed out of her pajamas into clothes more suited to the temperatures outside. She knew better than to let the blindingly bright sun deceive her.

She finished zipping up her coat as she walked out to the living room. River was by the door, putting the ice skates into a bag for easier transport. Mom was apparently already off to work. Dad sat on the couch reading the newspaper.

He didn't so much as glance up from the paper as Winter crossed the room to join River. But he did speak. "Take the dog with you."

"Planning on it." River turned toward the corner of the room where a mass of white and red-brown fur was dozing contently. "Daisy! Wanna go out?"

The Saint Bernard was on her feet in an instant. She lumbered over to where River and Winter stood by the door, tail wagging behind her. Winter dropped to one knee in front of her and scratched her behind her ears. "Lucky you, already nice and warm in that fur coat of yours."

No leash was needed to keep Daisy at Winter's side as she and River left the family's apartment and took the stairs down to the street.

"I wish we could have the snow without the cold," Winter said as they began the trek to the edge of the city. "I bet ice skating would be more fun if I weren't wearing fifty layers to keep myself from dying."

River laughed. "You'll forget all about the cold once we're out there."

They walked ten minutes to the city's edge, then another fifteen along the trail to the pond. Between the snow-dusted pine trees, an expanse of ice took up most of the small clearing that waited for them at the end of their journey.

"This is the pond you were so excited about?" Winter asked as they entered the clearing. "I thought it'd be bigger. Isn't the one south of the city supposed to be huge?"

"That one's more dangerous. It doesn't freeze as deep. People have fallen in trying to skate on it." River moved to a log at the clearing's edge and sat down. As he slid off one of his shoes, he added, "Of all people, I'd think you'd be the most concerned about freezing to death in a pond."

"I guess," Winter grumbled. She settled onto the log next to him and began pulling on her skates. Despite the pond's small size, she was still excited to get on the ice.

Daisy interrupted by resting her head on Winter's lap. Winter laughed and pushed her back. "I'm trying to put my shoes on, girl. Hold on a moment."

River grinned. "Too bad they don't sell dog ice skates."

Winter snorted. "Yeah, that would go over well. Are you trying to break her ankles?"

"I think she'd be very graceful."

"Daisy? Graceful? Where have you been the past ten years?"

While River laughed, Winter briefly found herself dwelling on how long they'd had Daisy. Ten years was probably near the end of her lifespan, wasn't it? She didn't seem to have as much energy as she'd had even just a couple years earlier...

River rose to his feet. "Come on, enough staring off into space. The pond is waiting."

"The pond's been there for centuries, I'm sure. It can wait a few more minutes." Winter went back to tying her laces.

Finally, she was ready to go. She rose to her feet and took a shaky step toward the edge of the pond. Then another. So far, so good.

Her first step onto the ice was far less dignified than she'd imagined it would be. Her foot slipped out from under her, and she landed hard on the pond's surface with a yelp of surprise.

River stepped onto the ice next to her and kept his balance just fine. "Are you okay?" he asked.

"Ow. Yeah, I'm okay." Winter climbed back to her feet with a slight groan. Her blades slipped across the ice a little, nearly making her fall again. "How do people do this?"

"Practice." River held out his arm. "Here, hold onto me while you figure out how to move."

"I'm just going to bring you down with me."

River laughed. "No, you won't. Come on."

Winter grabbed her brother's arm and inched forward. He kept pace with her as she figured out how to move her feet in a way that would carry her forward without sending her crashing onto her back.

Daisy settled down at the edge of the pond, content to watch the two struggle across the ice.

"See?" River said once they'd finished a loop around the pond's edge. "Not so bad, once you get used to it."

"Yeah. I still don't understand how those skaters in town square did all those tricks, though." After a moment's hesitation, Winter let go of River and tried moving forward on her own. When she didn't immediately fall, a smile crept onto her face, and she pushed herself to go a little faster.

Gradually, Winter got the hang of gliding over the ice. She wouldn't exactly call herself graceful, but she was doing loops around the pond at a speed that she thought was pretty decent. River was definitely better, but even he slipped a couple of times trying to push his limits. Winter laughed at him both times. The second time, he responded by grabbing a handful of snow from the grass, shaping it into a snowball, and chucking it at her. She laughed even harder when he missed.

They got to enjoy the pond for half an hour before they were interrupted.

"There you are, River!"

River and Winter turned their heads as the man emerged from the trees. The dark green coat he wore was thrown on over a business suit that looked out of place in the wild forest. As he approached, Winter found herself inching closer to River, overcome with an apprehension she couldn't explain.

"Mr. Gordon?" River's brow furrowed. "What's so important that you'd come all the way out here looking for me?"

"I would have sent one of the supervisors, but they've got their hands full keeping things from falling apart at the factory." The man—Gordon—stopped at the edge of the pond.

Daisy rose to her feet and let out a low growl.

River glanced at her and lifted a hand. "Daisy, it's okay." Daisy stared back at him for a long moment before sinking into the snow and resting her chin on her paws. Her eyes stayed fixed on Gordon.

River glanced at the man that Winter figured must have been his boss. "What's happening at the factory?"

Before Gordon could answer, Winter jumped into the conversation, eyes narrowing. "And how did you know we were out here?"

"Winter—" River started, a warning in his voice.

"I went to your apartment to find you, and your father told me you'd come out here," Gordon replied.

Winter didn't like that this guy knew where they lived.

Gordon returned his gaze to River and continued. "Eight people called in sick today. We could really use your help."

River hesitated. "Are you asking, or…?"

"We need dependable employees at the factory, River. Are you someone I can count on?"

"Of course, sir."

"River!" Winter hissed. "You're supposed to have the day off!"

River responded in a low voice. "Sorry, Winter, but I have to go help them."

"No you don't!"

"I could lose my job."

"Can't you just get another job somewhere else?" Somewhere that wouldn't snatch his days off away from him when they'd barely begun?

"You know Mom and Dad would be upset," River replied, and Winter couldn't argue with that. "And it's better to stay at one job for a long time than to jump around. Especially after all the time I spent training."

"Whatever." Winter stormed to the edge of the pond as dramatically as she could manage without falling.

"I'll make it up to you, all right?" River promised as he followed.

"You'd better," Winter muttered. She dropped back onto the log with a heavy sigh.

While Winter started taking off her skates, River waved to Gordon. "I'll be right over, sir."

"Thank you, River." With one last look at Winter that made her stomach turn, Gordon left.

River joined Winter on the log. "Would you let Dad know where I went?" he asked.

Winter nodded.

River changed back into his boots quickly, and Winter was still pulling hers on by the time he stood up and put the skates back in his bag.

"I have to go. Are you okay to walk back home?" he asked. "I wouldn't let you go alone if you didn't have Daisy."

"Yeah, we'll be fine," Winter told him.

"Okay. See you tonight." River walked backwards and waved. "Love you!"

"Love you, too." Winter had to fight to keep her annoyance out of the words. It wasn't really River's fault. He was doing his best.

River had disappeared from view by the time Winter was ready to go. She stood up. Nearby, Daisy mirrored the motion and moved to her side. Winter gave her head a quick pet and sighed. "Come on, Daisy. Guess it's just you and me, now."

Together, they returned home.

Chapter Thirteen
The Patron Saint of Killing You Slowly

The morning after the assembly meeting, George Gordon came into the hospital complaining of a cough.

"I know you said you'd get us preventative treatment as soon as possible, but I need whatever this is gone now," he said. The handkerchief he'd been coughing into didn't show any signs of blood, but that could always change.

"Of course," Winter told him.

She gave him a useless serum and told him to drink half at noon and half at three.

"I wouldn't do this for any ordinary patient," Winter said after handing him the bottle. "I don't have the time for them. But I can come by your office at the factory this evening with a new batch of medicine I'm making this afternoon. If you're still not feeling better, it'll be the most effective thing for you."

Gordon believed her, took the bottle, and left.

Winter left around five, early enough to stop by the factory before meeting Phoebe for dinner at her family's apartment. Per Gordon's instructions, she made her way to a door at the back and knocked.

Gordon opened the door. He looked terrible. Bags under his eyes, bruising on his neck, deathly pale skin. "Come in," he said, his voice hoarse. "And please tell me you brought something better."

"Of course I did." Winter followed him into his office. The door clicked shut behind her, leaving the two of them alone in a quiet building. All of the workers had gone home for the night. "How are you feeling?"

"Awful!" Gordon sank into the chair behind his desk. "Just getting up to answer the door felt like enough to kill me."

"I'm sure it did." Winter took a deep breath. No going back, now. "You make a lot of money running your factory, don't you?"

"Well, yes." Gordon coughed. "What—?"

She cut him off. "But none of that would have been possible without your workers."

"Technically, but—"

"They seem to be disposable to you, though."

More coughing. Then, "It's not exactly a high skill job. As long as there are people who need work, I do fine." Gordon's eyes narrowed. "Are you going to help me or not?"

"I'm not saying you don't do work. But is your labor really worth ten times what theirs is?" Winter held up the staff and pressed the button on the top. The handle popped up, and she pulled the blade free.

"What the hell?" Gordon moved to stand but didn't make it more than an inch off the seat of his chair.

Winter pointed the blade at him. "So eager to sentence innocent lives to death. For what, a little more profit? The city will be better off with you gone."

Finally, he realized what was happening. His eyes went wide. "You—you're supposed to be a saint!"

"Then consider me the patron saint of killing you slowly." Winter laughed, a cold laugh that took her by surprise. "Besides, a saint? Really? Adams had the Plague Saint killing anyone he considered a political rival, and letting those who wouldn't be able to afford real treatment die with fake medicine in their blood." Her grip on the weapon tightened. "And I know he worked with the mayor. A wolf parading around in saint's clothing."

"You're—someone else?" That tremble in Gordon's voice was satisfying to hear.

Winter lifted her chin. "I'm the saint that's really going to save Devil's Pass."

"So, you're just going to wait here with your blade pointed at me until I die?" Gordon spat. "I'm not gone yet."

Winter should have known she wouldn't be that lucky with timing. Her gaze darted around the office. A phone hung on the wall, and she certainly couldn't let him get to that. She carefully circled around the desk. Gordon's eyes followed the blade.

Winter kicked the chair he sat on, sending it and him toppling to the ground.

Gordon hit the floor with a thud and went into another coughing fit. Blood sprayed from his mouth.

"I don't get it," he hissed, glaring up at her. "You could be rich. You're in Atherton's good graces. Why give that all up to kill me?"

"This didn't start with you, and it won't end with you. You're just a name on a list." Winter took a step toward him. His words were nothing more than fuel added to the anger burning bright in her chest. "And you tried to kill my brother."

"Please," Gordon wheezed. "I'll do whatever you ask. Cure me. I won't tell anyone what you did. I'll help you. I'll—"

Winter felt a new emotion swell in her chest, almost enough to drown out that hot anger. Gordon had acted so high and mighty, so sure he was an untouchable elite. And now he was pleading for his life at her feet. It made Winter feel...

Good.

Satisfaction. She had the power now. Winter dropped to one knee and brought her face as close to Gordon's as she dared. Even with the mask protecting her, she didn't want to put herself in the path of his exhaled air. "There is one thing you can do," she told him, voice low.

"Anything, Plague Saint."

Winter slid the blade back into its scabbard and pushed the handle in. "Shut the hell up."

She straightened up and swung the staff against the side of his head.

Maybe the coroner would believe the head injury, if he discovered it, came from the desk as Gordon slipped from the chair. Winter wasn't too concerned with that matter right now, though. She was too distracted by the buzzing in her skull. She clutched at her chest. Her heart was going to explode.

But despite her body's physical reaction, this didn't feel as awful as the first two kills. There was a steady resolve growing, swallowing her dull nausea. She was succeeding. River would live.

On her way out, Winter checked that the door into Gordon's office from the factory floor was locked. She also loosened the phone cord enough that it wouldn't work, but not so much that it would be noticed anytime soon. She'd come back later tonight—or early in the morning—to make sure he died before anyone else found him.

Would she kill him with the blade, if it came to it? She didn't want to make it obvious that he was murdered. It might make the mayor and the city guard rethink Adams's death. It might make them take a closer look at her.

The snow came down hard outside. Winter crossed the street to a bar and snuck into the bathroom. After changing and shoving the uniform into her bag, she remained hidden in the stall, checking her pocket watch every few minutes until she had to leave to meet Phoebe on time.

"Stupid snow," Winter muttered as she climbed out the bathroom window and back into the cold's embrace. "Stupid frozen city."

Phoebe was already at the trolley stop when Winter stepped off. "Sorry," Winter said, rubbing her gloved hands together as she joined her. "You weren't waiting long, were you?"

Phoebe shook her head. "It's all right!" She was oddly upbeat, considering the many snowflakes clinging to her dark curls and the red tinge the cold had brought to her cheeks and nose. As they walked, she asked, "Did you learn anything new about the Adams investigation?"

There wasn't much happening on that front, but exaggerating the truth to convince Phoebe's uncle to give them information wouldn't hurt anyone. "They're having a hard time finding evidence," Winter said. "But there are more than a few people at the station who find the whole thing suspicious."

"I know the city guard asked the Plague Saint for information, but he didn't give me any details about what was going on." Phoebe sighed. "I just hope we can convince my uncle to give us something. Maybe even tell us how his research was going. If he was close to a breakthrough with the plagues..." She sucked in a slow, steadying breath. "I just can't shake the feeling it's all connected."

"You might be right," Winter said, choosing her words carefully. "But if you are, that's all the more reason to be cautious. We don't want to become targets ourselves." If she had to scare Phoebe to keep her from getting too close to the truth, so be it.

They turned a corner, and Phoebe pointed to an apartment complex a few buildings down. "That one's mine," she said.

They reached the old brick building and approached a door at a ground level. When Phoebe opened the door, a shred of the peeling white paint drifted to the ground. Unlike Winter's apartment building, this one had interior hallways. An exterior window at the end of the hall ahead offered a glimpse of the dark city outside. The two walked the corridor and took a corner before arriving at the entrance to Phoebe's home.

Anxiety welled up in Winter's stomach as Phoebe led the way in. When was the last time she'd been to someone else's home? What if she did something wrong and offended them? What if—?

"Right through here," Phoebe said. "You can put your shoes there."

"Phoebe?" A woman called from another room. "That you? Are you with Winter?"

Oh, God. These people knew about Winter. What all had Phoebe told them?

Before Winter could completely wrap her mind around the concept of other people perceiving her existence, the woman poked her head in from the next room. "Hello! You're just in time. Dinner's ready."

"Is Uncle Mark home?" Phoebe asked.

The woman—Phoebe's mother, Winter assumed—nodded. She gave Winter a warm smile. "He's looking forward to meeting you."

Winter offered a smile in return and prayed she didn't look as much like a frightened prey animal as she felt. Looking forward to meeting her? Why? It was probably politeness, but alarm bells were going off in Winter's head.

Phoebe led her around the corner into the dining room. Winter's gaze moved from her mother, setting a pot of soup in the center of the table, to her father, reading a book, to—

"How are you feeling?" Phoebe asked the man sitting at the other end of the table.

"Better." Marcus Blackburn smiled at his niece and ran a hand through his dark hair. Light from the fireplace illuminated the faintest streaks of gray mixed into it. And the scar running down the right side of his face.

Winter was staring at the man whose body she'd thrown in the river.

Chapter Fourteen
Two of Saints

Impossible.

Impossible.

Impossible.

There was a fresher scar on his left jaw, and a fair number of scrapes and bruises, all matching the wear and tear from Winter dragging him out of the hospital. *Do something. Say something.*

Marcus Blackburn didn't miss a beat. "You must be Winter Pierce." His expression was still warm, still friendly. "Nice to meet you."

Why not tell them? Why not tell his family that Winter had tried to kill him?

"Nice to meet you, too." Winter held out her hand to shake the one he offered. Of course he wouldn't tell them. He had kept his identity as the Plague Saint a secret from them. Was that only so he could keep all of the money for himself, rather than share it with his brother's struggling family?

How had he *survived*? In her panic, Winter hadn't really made sure he was dead, she reminded herself. He hadn't been breathing after his collapse, she'd thought, but...maybe he'd started again, and she hadn't noticed. But she'd thrown him in the river!

And then you walked away.

"You can sit down," Phoebe said.

"Huh?" Winter's gaze darted to her right, where Phoebe was pulling out a chair.

"You okay?"

"I'm fine. Sorry." Winter sank into the chair next to Phoebe. "I just...remembered something I need to do when I get back to the guard station. It doesn't matter."

While she made conversation with Phoebe and answered her parents' questions, Winter tried to figure out Blackburn's side of the story. After pulling himself out of the river, why not go back to the hospital? How long had it taken him to find out she'd taken his place—if he even suspected it was her who now wore the persona? Why not go to Director Adams? And why hide from his family for over two weeks?

Winter tried to avoid looking at him, but then she wondered if that was weird. Did he notice? Did anyone else notice?

"What do you do at the guard station, Winter?" Phoebe's mother asked.

"Oh, I uh, I organize case files, pretty much," Winter answered. "Sometimes they have me deliver messages or fill out reports, too." She risked a glance at Marcus, who was nodding along to her answer.

The conversation shifted to Phoebe's work and school after that, to Winter's relief. She focused on downing the rest of her soup.

After dinner, Phoebe insisted on making cookies, so the family and conversation moved to the kitchen while she worked. As she was putting them in the oven, her parents announced they were going to bed.

Winter could have choked on her own anxiety as she watched them leave. Just her and Phoebe and Marcus now.

"Let's wait in the dining room while they bake." Phoebe led the way back into the room where they'd had dinner. Marcus sat down first, and Winter took a seat on the other side of the table. Phoebe sat down next to her, close enough to make her already racing heart feel like it was going to burst. She hid her shaking hands in her lap.

"Uncle Mark," Phoebe said. "Winter's been hearing some interesting things about the hospital director's death." She gave Winter a pointed look.

"Right." Winter cleared her throat. "There are rumors going around the station that Director Adams's death wasn't an accident."

Marcus's expression was almost unreadable. Almost. He lifted an eyebrow and the barest hint of amusement danced in his eyes. "I heard the tests for some of the plagues came back positive, though."

Winter had expected she would need to convince Phoebe's uncle of foul play to get him to divulge information about his research. But giving him information now would be a mistake. Surely he'd figure out that she'd been the one to kill Adams, right? Maybe even assume that she was responsible for Gordon's death, too, once that became public? He knew she was capable of it, after what she'd done to him.

Phoebe was waiting expectantly. She couldn't clam up now. Winter forced herself to continue. "I guess there are some theories about how someone could have made him sick deliberately, but I don't know the details. But I did hear someone say they think it's connected to plague research." She swallowed. "As in, someone had new information on how to cure them, but someone else wanted to keep it secret. I don't know exactly what that has to do with Adams though."

Winter hoped she looked as ignorant as she sounded. "But—" Her eyes darted to her right, to Phoebe, who was nodding encouragingly. "Phoebe mentioned you were involved with that kind of research."

Marcus really was unreadable now. He pressed his lips into a thin line and nodded slowly. "I was afraid some people were after my work. And when I was attacked in my lab a couple of weeks ago, I took that as confirmation. Truthfully, I always expected something like that might happen." Blackburn's gaze darkened as his eyes locked with Winter's. "If you control the plagues, you control the people."

The ding of a timer came from the kitchen. "Oh, the cookies!" Phoebe jumped to her feet. "I'll be back in a minute."

Winter's heart skipped a beat. "Do you want help?"

"No, I've got it. Be right back!" With that, Phoebe darted out of the room, leaving Winter alone with the man she'd tried to kill. After he'd tried to kill her mother.

"So, Winter." Blackburn leaned back in his chair. "Do you enjoy working at the guard station? It must be an exciting job."

"It's actually pretty boring for me," Winter told him, a bit surprised by the seemingly casual question. "Like I mentioned earlier, I mainly do paperwork."

He responded with a slow nod. "Ah. Not much work on your part, then. Just working with what other people accomplished."

Winter's eyes narrowed. "Well, not entirely. People make mistakes. I have to correct them."

"How do you know what's a mistake and what's simply something you...don't see eye to eye on?"

"To begin with, I don't see helping people as a mistake."

A cold smile crossed Blackburn's face. Mistake. What Winter had just said was a mistake. He knew she was the one who'd taken his place.

"Help some, hurt others...that's how it goes, isn't it?" Marcus asked.

"It doesn't have to be." *Shut up. Shut up. Shut up.*

"So, you help everyone you possibly can? No matter what they can offer in return?"

Winter had nearly killed him, taken his job, and was undoing his work at the hospital. Why did he seem so damn amused?

Winter didn't have to come up with a response. Phoebe returned with the tray of cookies, oblivious to the tension between them. "So," she said as she set the tray down. "I know we asked you this already, but you've been pretty vague. Where did you go after you were attacked? Why were you gone for two weeks?"

Marcus sighed. "I was trying to keep you all safe," he told Phoebe, completely falling back into the persona of a concerned uncle. "I was afraid my attackers would follow me if I came back here. I had to stay away long enough that I could be sure they didn't know where I was. Even now, we have to be alert. That's why I've been so on edge."

Phoebe swallowed and nodded. "I'm so sorry, Mark. I—"

"You have nothing to be sorry for," Marcus interrupted. "I knew my research would put me at risk, and I did it anyway, because I knew it was important. I won't give up until I find a cure for every last plague."

The way he pretended to be noble, and the way Phoebe watched her uncle with admiration in her eyes...it made Winter sick.

"Do you know who's after you?" Phoebe asked. "Names? Or faces? Because they could be responsible for Adams's death too, and maybe other people who died in the hospital—"

"Phoebe, if I knew that information, I wouldn't give it to you," Marcus said. "I don't want you getting involved in this any more than you already are. It's too dangerous. I've given the city guard everything I know, and they'll handle the situation better than anyone else could."

Winter's jaw clenched. She'd learned everything she was going to from Marcus. He'd learned from her, too, far more than she should have let him, but nothing could be done about that now. She needed to figure out how she was going to move forward.

Marcus hadn't given any indication that he planned to reveal what she'd done. But surely he intended to do something, and soon. If Winter gave up the Plague Saint persona and backed away from this whole mess, would he let her go?

Even if that were an option, she couldn't just let things go back to the way they were before. She'd killed two people already, and until about an hour ago, she'd thought that number was three. Mayor Atherton would proceed with his plans and new law, even with Gordon dead, and there were people in the hospital who needed the treatment that only Winter could give them.

Plus, River still needed medicine.

Now that Winter knew Blackburn and the Plague Saint were one and the same, she wanted another look at his lab. Did Phoebe still have the key? Could Winter persuade her to take another look? Probably not, now that she seemed to have sorted things out with Marcus.

Winter cleared her throat. "Phoebe, may I use your bathroom?"

"Of course!" Phoebe rose to her feet. "Follow me, I'll show you where it is."

They entered a dim hallway, and Phoebe lowered her voice. "Thank you for your help," she said. "I'm sorry we couldn't get much information about whoever's behind all this, but that conversation made me feel a lot better."

"I'm glad it worked out," Winter told her, quickly running through a few ideas before settling on one. "Would you want to go back and look at his lab again, now that we know a little more?"

"You'd do that?" Phoebe asked.

"Of course!" Winter feigned enthusiasm, though she kept her voice hushed. "This entire thing is crazy."

Phoebe considered the idea for a moment before shaking her head. "I appreciate it, but I think Mark's right. There's no point in putting ourselves in danger when the city guard is already investigating."

Seriously? What had happened to the girl who was so eager to play detective? It wasn't about the killer, really, Winter realized. Phoebe had been trying to find her uncle, and now that she had him back, she didn't need to solve the rest of the mystery. His vague answers about people wanting his research were enough.

Phoebe took a few more steps down the hall and paused in front of a door. Her hand slid into her pocket, and she pulled something out.

The lab key.

"I'm just going to put this back where I found it," she said. "Hopefully he hasn't noticed it's gone. But I doubt he's going back any time soon, anyway, since the place was empty."

Winter pulled her eyes from the key in Phoebe's hand. "Where did you find it?" Did that sound suspicious? "I mean, I would think he'd have kept it well hidden."

"It was just sitting in the top drawer of his nightstand. I was surprised, too." Phoebe shrugged. "But hey, we got in, didn't we?" A grin flashed across her face.

"Fair enough, I guess." Winter jutted a thumb at the door behind her, just a few feet down from the one Phoebe stood in front of. "Bathroom, right?"

"Oh, right, yes!" Still clutching the key, Phoebe inched open the door to Marcus's room. "I'll just put this away and head back to the kitchen."

Winter entered the bathroom and pulled the door shut behind her, trembling violently. The girl in the mirror stared back, wide-eyed and struggling for air.

She needed that key.

Forcing her breathing to quiet, she kept her back to the door, listening. Faint creaks followed Phoebe into the next room. There was the sliding of a drawer, and then the soft click of the door closing. Phoebe returned to the kitchen, and a moment later her voice drifted down the hall, followed by a reply from Marcus.

While their conversation continued, Winter slipped out of the bathroom and crept to Marcus's door. She pushed it open. Swept her gaze across the room.

There. She moved to the nightstand as fast as she dared and opened the drawer. The key rested on top of a stack of notebooks inside. Had Phoebe bothered to give these a look? Winter resisted the urge to dig through them; there wasn't time now. She grabbed the key and shoved it in her pocket.

She paused. Over the sound of her thudding heart, she could just make out Phoebe's voice. She closed the drawer and left the room.

As Winter was easing the door shut, another door opened at the far end of the hallway. *Damn it.* She frantically pushed the door the rest of the way closed with an alarming thud and stepped away from it.

Phoebe's mother emerged from the darkness of her bedroom. "Hi, Winter."

"Sorry," Winter stammered. "I hope I didn't make too much noise. I was just using the bathroom."

"You're fine. I wanted a glass of water."

Winter breathed a small sigh of relief and hurried back to the dining room ahead of Phoebe's mother. "Thank you for having me over, Phoebe," she said. "But my parents are expecting me home soon."

"Of course!" Phoebe sprang to her feet. "I'll show you to the door."

Winter pulled on her coat as she stepped out of the apartment, eager to get home as soon as possible.

"So," Phoebe said slowly as they approached the exit door. "I guess I'll...see you around?"

There was something in Phoebe's tone that made Winter think there was more she wanted to say, but Winter didn't have the mental capacity to try and decode it right now. "Sure."

Phoebe waited in the doorway while Winter hurried out into the cold night. "Good night!" she called as Winter reached the sidewalk. Winter glanced back, and Phoebe waved.

Winter waved back. "Good night."

She had new plans for tomorrow. Instead of having lunch in her office, she'd visit Marcus's lab and try to find something— *anything*—that could help her. She also needed to somehow stop the mayor's law from passing, figure out the most effective way to get word out about the better plague treatments, and get River all the way healed.

And she had one new item to add to her to-do list.

Winter had to make Phoebe see who her uncle really was.

Chapter Fifteen
As White as Snow

River took a turn for the worse.

Winter stared at him Tuesday morning, his patient file in hand, half-listening to the nurse explain that he was coughing up blood again and his skin had gone deathly pale and sometimes he seemed to be hallucinating—

"We followed the treatment schedule perfectly?" Winter finally cut her off, unable to listen any longer.

"Of course!" the nurse exclaimed. She frowned. "You know this happens sometimes. We saw this just last week with that woman—"

"You're right. My apologies." Winter sucked in a deep breath. River was going down the same path as those other unusual red plague patients.

No. He was going to recover. He had to. "Keep his Red-X dose the same, but double that new medicine I added." Winter handed the file to the nurse. "I'm going to check on my other patients."

She tried to stay focused as she finished her rounds, but it was difficult to care about anyone besides River. Information on other red plague patients rolled through her mind, patients who had seemed to be getting better before abruptly dying. She'd assumed before that the Plague Saint had killed them, but maybe there was more to it.

Rounds finally finished, Winter entered her office. Phoebe had mentioned rumors of a new plague, and Winter had dismissed the idea. But Phoebe had said her uncle had told her about it and—

Oh. God.

That meant the Plague Saint believed there was a white plague.

Winter threw the staff down on her desk with more force than she'd intended. Out of the corner of her eyes, she saw Phoebe jump.

"Plague Saint?" Phoebe asked cautiously. "Is something—wrong?"

Winter rested a gloved hand on the edge of the desk and leaned against it. "What all have you heard about white plague?"

"Uh, just rumors," Phoebe said. "I would think you'd know more than me."

"Didn't you say your uncle thought it might exist?"

Phoebe frowned. "When did I tell you that?"

Damn it. She hadn't told the Plague Saint, she'd told Winter. "I...don't remember, exactly. Last week, maybe?" Oh god, had Phoebe even said anything about her uncle to the Plague Saint? "Maybe Winter mentioned him to me. She was concerned about her brother and asked me if I thought the white plague was real."

There. That was reasonable, right?

Phoebe's expression didn't reveal whether or not she believed Winter. Still, she nodded. "Uh, well, he didn't tell me much about it. Just that he thinks it's basically a worse version of red plague. Much worse."

Well, that might explain why white plague hadn't been identified at first, but surely the other doctors would have realized it was separate from red by now, right? Had it only developed recently? A strain evolved from red plague?

That wasn't important right now. And, as anxious as she had been about it all day, neither was the fact that Winter hadn't heard anything about Gordon's death yet. What she really needed to know was whether the Plague Saint had developed any form of treatment for white plague. She'd been through the entire Plague Bible, all of the notes he'd left in his office and lab, every last scrap of paper. There was no mention of it. And if it was in the coded journal, well, she was screwed.

Or maybe not. There was one upside to the Plague Saint being Marcus, and Marcus being alive. Now that Winter knew his identity, she had new places to look for information. Those journals in his nightstand, for a start, although that would involve breaking into Phoebe's apartment. Phoebe was here now, and Winter had learned at dinner that both parents worked. But what did Marcus do all day?

Winter could consider a breaking-and-entering plan later. Her first stop would still be the lab Marcus had worked in.

Phoebe was still looking at her with an expression somewhere between confused and worried. Winter straightened up. "I'm leaving to get lunch. I'll be back in about an hour."

"Oh. Okay." Phoebe's gaze lingered a moment longer before she returned to her work.

Winter changed in a hospital bathroom so that she could stop by River's room before she left. She also brought along the staff. It barely fit into her bag, squeezed awkwardly between the two sides and stretching it oddly. But it fit, and the black material prevented it from being too noticeable.

River was fast asleep and running a high fever. Winter didn't stay long. With grim determination, she left the hospital and retraced the path she and Phoebe had taken to the lab.

It looked just as they'd left it. At first, anyway. It didn't take long for Winter's eyes to trace new paths in the dust that hadn't been there when she and Phoebe left. She circled the room, wondering if Marcus had come by. Had he been the one to clear it out, or was there a third party after his research, after all?

Winter knelt by the counter she'd found the pen under. That little detail was still bothering her. The pen had looked familiar, and—

Something shiny on the dark floor caught her eye and stopped her train of thought. Winter picked up the scalpel and nearly dropped it again when she saw the drops of blood on the metal. It was dry, but it still took her a moment to steady her hand enough to pick it up again.

This definitely hadn't been here before. But there had been scalpels in both of the Saint's labs at the hospital, which had struck Winter as odd. She'd never needed one to treat plague patients.

If this was one of the Saint's scalpels, why was it here? And how had it been taken from the hospital without her notice in the few days since she and Phoebe had been here? And why had the pen—?

Wait, she'd seen a pen like the one she'd found here earlier that morning. At the hospital. There were a variety of pens scattered around the Saint's quarters, including gold-banded black ones. In fact, Winter was fairly sure she'd left one with the coded notebook that had disappeared.

She stood up slowly, suddenly unsettled. Deeply unsettled. The notebook had been stolen while she was just upstairs. Marcus was the most likely suspect now, and that meant he must have been watching her before he stole it. And probably after. How many times had she been wrong when she thought she was alone? She shuddered.

Winter moved to the center of the room and turned in a slow circle, orienting herself. If the hospital was north of here, that put the wall opposite the door closest to it.

She looked over the counter spanning the wall. After nearly ten minutes of running her hands over every surface and finding nothing, she was almost ready to give up. Then she remembered River lying unconscious in his hospital bed. She took a step back and stared at the wall. Her vision blurred. *Something. There has to be something.*

Maybe she was wrong. Maybe it would take her a hundred years to find what she was looking for. Maybe she wasn't even looking in the right place.

Winter wiped away the tears stinging her eyes with her arm. Anger took control, making her fists tighten and her jaw clench. She let out a cry of frustration and kicked the counter.

Something inside the cupboard—the cupboard that was supposed to be empty—made a *clink*. Distracted from the pain shooting through her foot, Winter dropped to her knees and opened the cupboard. The light caught something shiny. A loose screw. She frowned. The screw didn't appear to be doing anything useful. Then again, she wasn't an engineer.

She grabbed it. It twisted in her fingers, and the back of the cupboard clicked and slid back an inch. Winter gave it a push, and it swung open.

The opening was definitely large enough for Marcus to squeeze through, and it opened into a taller passage. Winter backed out of the cupboard and grabbed her bag off the floor. The smart thing to do would be to wait and come back when she knew Marcus was at home, to ensure she didn't run into him. But River might not have that long.

Winter entered the passage.

The flickering light bulbs in the ceiling were few and far between. Winter stumbled through one stretch of darkness so long she began to fear she'd never see day again. Then, finally, there was a new source of light, a bright white pouring out from the bottom of a door. Winter hurried forward, grabbed the handle, threw the door open—

—and was greeted by the sight of Marcus Blackburn standing in the middle of the secret lab.

Winter spun around as the door slammed shut behind her. From this side, it was simply a section of wall that blended seamlessly into the rest.

"It's much harder open from in here," Marcus said. "You'd never figure it out on your own."

Winter frantically unzipped her bag and pulled out the staff.

Marcus chuckled. "There's no need for that, I just want to talk."

Winter yanked the blade free. She pointed it at him. "Talk, then. How did you know I'd come this way?"

He held up his hands, but the cold smile on his face didn't fade. "Really, I don't want to hurt you. I'm impressed with what you've accomplished, actually," he said. When Winter jabbed the sword at him again, he continued. "I knew Phoebe stole the key. I let her go because I'd already cleared the lab out. After your visit, it was a pretty reasonable guess that you'd take the key for yourself.

"I couldn't be entirely sure you'd go back," he added with a slight shrug. "Or that you'd find the passage. But if you didn't show up through that door, I knew you'd come back the other way eventually." Marcus's gaze drifted around the lab. "You figured things out pretty quickly. But you don't know nearly as much as you think."

Winter's eyes narrowed. "What about the white plague?"

"How long did that take you to figure out?" Marcus asked, his eyes snapping back to her. Amusement danced in his expression, provoking her rage, tipping the balance between her anger and her fear.

"I didn't want to believe it, at first," she said, jaw clenching. "But I'll do whatever it takes to save my brother."

"Oh, yes, Phoebe mentioned him when she was telling me about you. River, right?"

Winter's grip on the sword's handle tightened. "If you lay even a finger on him, I'll kill you. And you know I can do it."

"Really?" Marcus raised an eyebrow. "Because you failed the first time."

"This time, I'll make sure you're not breathing," Winter hissed.

Marcus chuckled. "Don't worry, I haven't done anything to your brother. But I'm afraid his chances aren't good. White plague is the worst of them all."

"Well, do you have a cure?" Winter hated the way her voice cracked, hated the way her desperation crept in. "You knew about it before everyone else. And you made better treatments for the others."

"I said I was impressed by you, not that I liked what you were doing," Marcus replied. "Why would I help you when you've made my friends your enemies?"

"Your friends?" Winter asked. "Like Adams? And Mayor Atherton? The people who want to let us all die?"

"They don't want everyone to die. Obviously, they need people to work." Marcus folded his arms. "But making medicine costs money. They run the city, they put themselves first. Why should they just hand treatment out to people who won't provide anything in return?"

"You could have saved so many people. Do you have any idea how many lives I saved in just a few weeks?" Winter's arm ached, but she didn't dare lower her weapon. "And we have no reason to go after our patients for money they don't have! The taxes coming in and payments from those who can afford it are more than enough. I've seen the financial records."

"I didn't have anything personal against most of those people I let die," Marcus said. "I was just doing what the man signing my paychecks asked. He hired me to do a job."

"So, this was all about money to you?"

"No." Marcus shook his head. "The money's nice. But I'm working toward something bigger. And if you think I'm going to let a teenage girl stop me, I have some bad news for you." His hand moved behind his back. A heartbeat later, he had a revolver pointed at Winter.

Her blood froze, her heart stopped, her eyes were glued to the end of the gun. Marcus said something, and she didn't hear it.

"Wh—what?" Winter stammered. Her hands were numb. She was barely aware of the blade in her hand, useless now.

"I don't need the Plague Saint persona anymore," Marcus said. "I created it to get into the hospital so that I could use their machines and experiment with patients. But now I have all the information I need."

"Need for what?"

"You think I would just tell you my plans? Maybe you're not as smart as I thought." Marcus took a step forward. Light glinted off the gun's barrel. "Now, if you don't want me to shoot you, you're going to do exactly what I say. You can keep playing doctor, but I want every last notebook of mine back. Plague Bible included."

Winter lowered her blade, arm unable to take the strain anymore. It wasn't doing her any good, anyway. "You think I don't have copies of your treatment recipes?" She didn't. Why hadn't she thought of making copies?

She'd never thought she was in danger of having her notes stolen.

"Even if you do, you couldn't possibly have saved enough information to treat your patients as well as you are now," Marcus said. "Let's see how you handle yourself without my years of research and experience." He gestured to Winter's bag with the gun. "Put on the costume. Bring back my notes, or I'll tell Phoebe who you really are."

Two could play at that game. "Do that, and I'll tell her the truth about you."

"And if I denied it, do you think she'd take your word over mine?" Marcus asked.

"Do you really want to find out?" Winter retorted.

"Only one way to be sure."

Either way, Winter couldn't say no to the gun. She told herself she didn't care what Phoebe thought either, but that was harder to believe.

She picked up her bag and walked to the door. Maybe she was being overly optimistic, but Marcus didn't seem too serious about shooting her, or he wouldn't be letting her leave alone. The real threat was having her identity exposed.

Winter paused at the door to the upper lab. "Before I grab those," She began, glancing back. "I'll admit it was stupid of me to not make sure you were dead. But even if you were breathing, I thought there was no way you'd survive the river."

"I regained consciousness while you were moving me," Marcus told her. He lowered the gun as he spoke, putting her further at ease regarding his desire to shoot her. "But I was weak from the blow, so I decided feigning my death and crawling out of the river downstream was my best option. But it was cold. And painful. You can't blame me for harboring some resentment."

"Right. Sure. And you didn't do anything wrong," Winter muttered. It did make her feel a little better to know he'd decided going into the water was a better option than fighting her. "Were—were you going to poison me? Or was that really plain water you gave me?"

"It was tainted with a combination of plague samples and something that would knock you out quickly," Marcus admitted. "But I just wanted time to come up with a plan. You wouldn't have died, necessarily."

"But I could have." Despite his claim he only wanted more time, she doubted he would have put much effort into treating her.

Marcus's eyes narrowed. "Just go already. Before I change my mind about letting you live. You have five minutes, or I come out behind you."

Chapter Sixteen
Smoke and Fires

Winter scribbled away on spare sheets of paper. She wrote down what procedures and measurements and chemical names she could remember, frantically trying to save them before they were gone from her memory. She still had the ingredients. She still had nearly three weeks of experience. She still had—

"They found him dead in his office!" Phoebe exclaimed. She was reading from a newspaper she'd picked up on her lunch break, the front page of which advertised the sudden death of a certain factory owner. "There really is a killer on the loose."

"It was plagues." Winter tapped her pen against the desk. What the hell was the stuff in that dark red bottle called? Whatever it was, it was ten ounces of that per...half liter of base? Or full?

"There has to be more to it than that." Phoebe folded up the paper. "Maybe I should call Winter and ask her what she knows about the guard investigation."

Was she waiting for permission? "She'll be on a shift right now."

"Well, no, I wasn't going to call now," Phoebe mumbled.

This wasn't going to be enough. Maybe it was the panic blanking Winter's mind, but she couldn't remember any of the full recipes the Saint had written down, despite how many times she'd made them.

She had to steal back the Plague Bible. And get her hands on his white plague cure, which was hopefully somewhere in Marcus's coded notes.

She turned to study Phoebe, who'd returned to sifting through an open drawer of files. "Do you have any plans tonight, Phoebe?"

"Uh, besides school?" Phoebe asked. "I've got evening classes until nine."

"What about your family?"

Phoebe shot Winter a confused look. "I think they're all just going to be at home."

Winter would have to lure them out. Still tapping her pen against the desk, she sighed.

"What are you writing?" Phoebe asked. "You seem...stressed."

"Nothing you need to worry about." Winter rose to her feet, overwhelmed by the sensation to move. To do something. Anything. Now was a good time to start afternoon rounds, anyway. She gathered up the scraps of paper, folded them up, and shoved them in her bag.

She managed her rounds as best she could without the Bible. The lab had enough medicine stocked to handle most of the patients for a few more days. But if River didn't get whatever the hell treated white plague soon...

Back in the office, time dragged by until Winter could finally justify leaving. She said a quick goodbye to Phoebe, who was finishing up her last report before heading out herself.

Before Winter could make it out of the building, a nurse caught her attention.

"Plague Saint!" he waved his hand as he caught up to her. "My apologies, I know you're on your way out, but we're having some issues with a red plague patient."

Winter's heart skipped a beat. "In the tower? What floor?"

"Second."

Not River, then. Thank God. Winter nodded. "Lead the way. What kind of issues?"

"The medicine schedule we started a few days ago was working really well. Then a few hours ago, the patient's symptoms suddenly got worse, and the dose we just added to the IV line isn't doing anything."

Just like River. All the more reason to find the cure for white plague.

Winter and the nurse entered the patient's room. A man laid unconscious in the hospital bed, and a woman sat at his side. On the table next to her was a newspaper, a few lit candles, and an untouched sandwich that smelled like it had been sitting there for hours.

"His wife," the nurse explained quietly, nodding to the woman.

Winter walked to the man and looked him over, studied his vitals, read his chart. As if there were anything she could do. Some bit of good news she could give his wife.

"Well, this isn't the first case of this happening," Winter finally said. "I suspect that there's—" She couldn't be honest. Announcing the existence of a new plague would cause panic. "There's a new strain of red plague that's more resistant to the medicine. For now, I'm increasing doses." *Great thing to do with supplies running out, genius.* "But I'm also working on a more effective treatment."

Winter handed the file over to the nurse. "In the meantime, we'll do our best to keep him comfortable." Before moving toward the door, she glanced at the bedside table. At the candles.

She had an idea. A terrible idea, probably, but it was the best she had.

"You use a lighter, or matches?" Winter asked.

The woman's brow furrowed. "What?"

Winter gestured to the candles.

"Oh, uh, matches," the woman stammered. "Is that all right?"

"Perfectly fine. Do you have a few you could spare?"

The woman reached into her bag, pulled out the matchbox, and held it out. Winter selected a few and slid them into her pocket. "Thank you." Before leaving, she paused and added, "I'm going to do everything I can for your husband."

By the time she left the hospital, changed into black clothes, hid her hair under a knit cap, and made her way to Phoebe's apartment building, it was nearly seven. Her parents would start to wonder where she was soon, but she could come up with some excuse when she got home. Besides, this wouldn't take long.

Hopefully.

Winter crept around the side of the building, back pressed against the wall to keep herself out of view of the windows above. Phoebe had been on the first floor, west side...

Winter recognized the curtains in the dining room window. She scanned the wall next to it, estimating the length of the hallway within, how much space the bathroom took up, and recalling what she could of the layout from her brief time in Marcus's room.

There. That window had to be his. His curtains were drawn. Winter continued moving toward the dining room and inched away from the wall until she could just make out movement inside. One, two, three figures. If Phoebe was at school, then both her parents and Marcus were home.

The windows weren't out of reach, but the incline of the alley did put them higher than Winter had expected. Climbing up to Marcus's room would be doable with a running start, but it would be difficult to avoid being seen.

First, she had to get the Blackburns out of the apartment.

The hallway outside their home would be a good place to start, Winter decided. She circled to the back of the building, found the fire escape, and climbed up from the back alley level to the first floor of apartments.

Like she'd seen during her visit with Phoebe, there was a window at the end of the main interior hallway, and it led out onto the fire escape platform. Winter, after some struggling, was able to shimmy the window open. As she'd suspected from the building's shabby appearance, the windows weren't exactly secure.

She fished around in her bag until she found a washcloth she'd taken from the lab. It didn't appear dirty, but God knew what traces of chemicals lingered on it. The bottle she'd shoved the cloth in was also from the lab. Winter pulled off the cap.

Still leaning in through the window, clutching the bottle and cloth in one hand, Winter pulled out a match. *Just a small fire.* Something that could be put out quickly once it was discovered.

She swiped the match across the brick wall. The flame that came to life danced in front of her. For a moment, all she could focus on was the tiny beacon of warmth in the otherwise freezing alley. She could barely feel it, and she couldn't help but think how nice it would be to be in front of a roaring fireplace right now.

Winter lowered the flame into the bottle, touching it to the towel. Her eyes scanned the hallway and found the Blackburns' door. Faint voices drifted from other doorways, and a chorus of laughter told her someone was about to come around the corner at the other end of the hall.

She chucked the burning bottle and screamed, "Fire! Evacuate!"

The laughter stopped, replaced by confused chatter and racing footsteps. Winter ducked out of sight. There were shouts of alarm, and then doors opening and closing and slamming up and down the hall. Perfect. She scrambled down the fire escape and ran back around to the side of the building.

Winter sprinted at the wall beneath Marcus's room and jumped. Her hands found his windowsill. She pulled herself up enough to peer inside. Empty. A door slammed somewhere beyond the room. The front door, maybe?

Grunting with the effort, Winter quickly moved a hand from the ledge to the side of the window and pulled. It jerked open a centimeter. She lost her grip, slipped, and crashed to the ground.

Ignoring the various aches she'd acquired from the fall, Winter ran and jumped up to the window again. This time, she pulled it open enough to get a hand inside, barely saving herself from falling again. She inched the window open farther, until it was just wide enough for her to squeeze through. She collapsed face first onto the floor with a thud. Fear froze her in place, and she listened for voices. Or footsteps.

Nothing but distant shouts from the hallway outside the apartment.

Winter jumped to her feet and moved to the nightstand. When she pulled the drawer open, she was greeted with empty space. Damn it. She spun around, searching for somewhere else the notebooks could be hiding. They had to still be here. *Please. Please they have to be somewhere—*

There. The edge of a black bag poked out from under the bed, just like the one Winter had taken from the Saint's office after she'd thought she killed him. She grabbed the bag, slid it out, and yanked it open.

God, there was a lot. She couldn't take all of this. Piles of notebooks—some she recognized and some she didn't—were mixed in with empty vials and folded papers and envelopes.

She dug through the bag until she found the notebook she'd started to decode. With her free hand, she kept searching, but there was no sign of the Plague Bible. She grabbed a red journal she recognized instead. It didn't have most of the information in the Bible, but it did have medicine recipes. As she shoved it into her own bag, her gaze swept across the rest of the contents. If she took only a few things, maybe Marcus wouldn't notice the theft right away.

She picked up one of the envelopes. It was addressed to Marcus Blackburn, from Mayor Atherton. It had already been opened. She added it to her bag.

A shout rang out nearby, and while Winter couldn't make out what was said—nor did she recognize the voice—it sounded alarmingly close. She closed the bag and shoved it back under the bed, into as close to its original position as she could manage.

She was halfway out the window when the sound of footsteps coming down the hallway reached her. She grabbed the window and yanked it shut, wincing at the sound. Without a spare second to prepare for the fall, she slid off the windowsill.

It wasn't a far drop, but the landing was awkward and sent pain shooting through her right leg. It was enough to make her limp to the back of the alleyway.

Winter followed the rear alley past two more buildings before she reached a dead end and was forced to return to the main street. A new chorus of voices reached her ears as she approached. Familiar voices. City guard voices, deepened and magnified by the modifiers in their helmets.

She had the good sense to set the bag down while she investigated, leaving it hidden underneath a dumpster, along with her hat.

But stupidly, she kept going, moving to check out the commotion instead of hiding. And before she could process what was happening, she was surrounded.

Chapter Seventeen
Dig Yourself in Deeper

Winter had seen the guard station interrogation rooms before. From the outside. Being locked up in one was new.

She hadn't said a word the entire journey to the guard station, too in shock to even ask what she was being arrested for, and more than a little worried that speaking might get her in more trouble, anyway. She sat in silence in the back of the armored guard vehicle, the only kind of machine ever seen on the streets besides the trolleys. Well, and the rare car owned by those wealthy enough to have them imported.

One of the guards up front, an officer Winter was somewhat familiar with from her time working at the station, spoke into a radio as they neared their destination. "We picked up a girl who matched the description of the suspicious figure the resident reported. When we arrived, everyone was freaking out about a fire, but we don't know if it's connected yet. We'll have to question her."

Thank God she'd ditched the bag with everything tying her to the fire, but it was a small comfort. Someone had seen her sneaking around.

"Get this, it's Winter Pierce," the officer added. "The girl who quit a couple weeks ago."

Upon arrival, the guards escorted her inside the station to an interrogation room and left her handcuffed to the table. A captain—Captain Perry, of all people—came in after an excruciating ten minutes.

"Why were you sneaking around the apartment building on Rose Street?" he asked, not bothering to take the chair opposite her at the table.

The upside of the grueling wait was that Winter had plenty of time to come up with a story. "I'm friends with someone living there, and I think I lost my key when I was visiting her a few days ago," she told him. "I was trying to see if I'd dropped it along the sidewalk while we were walking over. But I wasn't sneaking around!"

"Really?" Perry asked. "Someone called in and said they saw a kid trying to look into windows and climbing up a fire escape."

Bristling at being called "kid," Winter's eyes narrowed. "I don't know. Maybe there was someone else there too."

"There was also a fire started inside the building."

"I was just looking for my damn key, okay? And I didn't find it, which means its God-knows-where and I need to figure out what happened to it before someone else takes it!"

Perry sighed. "Fine. Did you see anyone else around while you were there? Someone who might be responsible for the fire?" He still didn't sound convinced she wasn't the one responsible.

Winter needed someone else to point a finger at. She frowned. "Well, I thought I was being paranoid, but there were a few minutes where I felt like someone was watching me."

Perry studied her in silence for a few long moments before nodding slowly. He left without another word.

When he returned a few minutes later, he was holding a clipboard. Processing paperwork. Winter swallowed. "Am I being detained?"

"Not for long, just until your parents arrive to check you out."

No. No, no, nonono— "But I didn't do anything!"

"We aren't keeping you in the arson case, but we did pick you up for questioning and since you're underage, we can't let you leave without an adult." He didn't even glance at her, his eyes still on the paperwork. "We also need to inform them that we may have further questions for you. We didn't find anyone else in the area, and even if it was bad timing on your part, you are still tied to this case."

"Look, you know me!" Winter protested. "I worked here for a year!"

"Doing paperwork for a year doesn't mean you can't be a criminal, Winter. I'm sorry. The receptionist said your parents are already on their way."

He walked out, leaving Winter to sit with the fear snaking its way through her chest, squeezing her heart until she thought it would explode, tightening around her lungs until she couldn't breathe. Maybe her parents wouldn't find out that she didn't work here anymore. Maybe the station wouldn't contact her again about the case. The apartment building was a poor one, so the whole thing might be dropped, anyway. That happened all the time.

When Perry returned for the final time, it was to escort her to the front desk, where her parents were waiting. Talking to Beth. The world's chattiest receptionist.

Their heads turned at the same time at the sound of approaching footsteps. Mom looked upset. Not angry, necessarily, but distressed. Dad was unreadable.

"Good night!" Beth called as the Pierce family walked to the front doors. No one responded to her.

Winter had barely processed the shock of the cold, dark night when Dad was talking.

"What the hell, Winter?"

"I didn't do anything!" she protested. "I was in the wrong place at the wrong time. Why would I set a fire in—"

"They told us you quit three weeks ago! Why did you lie to us?"

Shit. They knew.

"I—" Winter stammered. "I got a similar job at the hospital. I guess I forgot to mention it."

"Forgot? Forgot to mention it? For three whole weeks?"

"I'm sorry! I was really busy!" Winter knew her protests sounded stupid. But what else could she say?

"Isaac," Mom murmured to her husband. "Is now really the time? We could at least wait to discuss this until we get off the trolley."

Dad sighed. "Fine. Let's go."

They walked to the trolley stop in heavy silence. Winter wiped snowflakes off her face, wishing she had her hat.

Damn it. Her hat. And bag. The whole reason for this mess. She needed to get back as soon as possible and pray that city guards weren't searching too hard for evidence. Or sticking around to watch for suspects. The thought of what might be waiting in the journals took over her train of thought.

"Winter," Mom said softly.

"Hmm?" Winter looked up from the sidewalk she'd found herself staring at.

"Trolley's here."

They climbed on. Silence. "Did either of you see River today?" Winter finally asked.

"We went by this morning," Dad replied plainly.

More silence. The trolley arrived at their stop. They were barely off when Dad was speaking again.

"What were you doing by that building, if not setting the fire?" he asked.

Did he seriously believe she'd done it? Sure, it was true, but she'd thought her parents would have a little more trust in her. Even if it was undeserved.

"A coworker from the hospital works there, and I went to say hi," Winter lied. "I was walking down the street after I left, and the next thing I knew, I was being arrested."

"I overheard one of the guards talking to the receptionist. He said they had a call about someone sneaking around and acting suspicious before the fire was started."

"I swear to God, it wasn't me."

Dad stopped at the bottom of the staircase leading up to their apartment, blocking her path. "That's a serious thing to say, Winter."

Mom, who'd been leading the way, paused a few steps up.

"Why would I set the fire?" Winter asked again, slowly, her jaw clenched.

"I don't know," Dad replied. "Why would you lie about your job? Or get home hours later than your shift was supposed to end the day River got sick?"

They'd never asked about that, with everything that happened with River. And Winter couldn't tell them she'd been busy killing Director Adams.

"Sometimes we get behind. It happened at the guard station too," Winter reminded him.

"But you didn't call like you usually do!"

Winter tore her gaze from her father's cold blue eyes to her mother, whose expression held concern.

"Isaac, we're all worried about River, and that's put us all on edge. I think we should get some rest and discuss this in the morning."

Dad didn't even glance Mom's way. "They told us they might have more questions for Winter. As far as I'm aware, she's their only suspect!"

"Isaac!" Mom's voice was more stern now.

After a long moment, to Winter's relief, Dad relented. His shoulders sagged. "All right."

And Winter thought that would be the end of it, until they reached the door. Dad paused again before stepping inside. "But I'm going to call the hospital tomorrow to make sure she's not still lying to us."

Chapter Eighteen
Our Saint is a Liar

Winter lay on the floor in the dark, her ear pressed to the gap beneath her bedroom door. Her parents talked quietly in the dining room for nearly an hour before going to bed. After that, Winter waited another hour to ensure they were asleep before dressing in all black, bundling up as well as she could, and creeping out of her room.

The snow had picked up outside, but it wasn't enough to deter Winter. She waited nearly half an hour for the trolley—late night service was sporadic—and rode it to the stop near Phoebe's apartment. Her hand remained on the knife in her pocket the whole way.

The bag was right where she'd left it. It was covered in an unidentifiable liquid that smelled awful, but it was there. Winter slung it over her shoulder and walked the streets until she found a bench under a streetlight. Her hand occasionally drifted back to the pocketknife at her side, but she didn't see another soul.

She started with the letter from the mayor. The date at the top indicated it had been written yesterday.

Mr. Blackburn,

Apologies for the letter, but I have meetings all day with the council to finalize the new laws.

We are delighted to have you helping out the city council. The city meeting at the end of January will be very important, so we're hosting an "emergency" general assembly meeting Thursday night to address the more immediate aspects of our plans. Dinner and drinks will be served, which will serve our purposes nicely.

Gordon's death is unfortunate, but also serves as a reminder of what we have to do. Forrest said he would be happy to buy out Gordon's factories.

Let me know if you need more supplies by Tuesday.
Mayor Atherton

Well, most of the useful information that could have been gleaned from that was clearly based on private conversations. But the bit about the assembly meeting in a couple of days could come in handy. Though, that sounded more like a celebration of sorts than an actual meeting.

The note about Forrest buying out the factories was interesting, too, but not exactly surprising. Winter had expected someone else would take control of Gordon's assets. She needed a better plan to stop the mayor from filling a building with sick people and working them to death.

She moved on to the journal and started by decoding sentences here and there, trying to get a sense of what information each page held. The chart with the five plagues listed turned out to be a description of combinations of the plagues, not unlike the combinations she'd made herself to kill Adams and Gordon. Average time to show symptoms, average time to death...how many people had he experimented on?

The rats, Winter remembered. He had to have been using them too. In addition to patients, undoubtedly.

Disgusted, she flipped a few pages. The next section mostly turned out to be failed recipes, as far as she could tell. She moved to the back of the book, to pages she hadn't examined at all yet. More graphs, lists, ingredients—

Whoa. A boat?

Winter squinted at the drawing, a sketch of a boat on a river. There were a few notes scribbled next to it. *Equipment fits. Not all cages can go, euthanize the rest. Dissect notable subjects.*

Maybe this was where Marcus had moved his stuff after clearing out his other lab. Winter frantically translated the entire page, but there was nothing even hinting at the boat's location.

Well, it had to be on the river somewhere. Winter stood up. Fatigue tugged at her eyelids and her limbs, begging her to go home, to sleep. But she thought of River in his hospital bed. All the people she'd seen die in the past few weeks, leaving grieving loved ones. The city council's plans that would bring more suffering to Devil's Pass.

She set off toward the edge of the city.

Marcus would have had to strike a balance between putting this boat within reasonable walking distance and keeping it far enough from the city streets that no one would stumble across it accidentally. The closest point of the river was where it wrapped around the northeast edge of the city. The area around where Winter had thrown Marcus's unconscious body.

Winter hit the northeast edge of Devil's Pass. Buildings and sidewalks faded from view, replaced with trees and dirt. Streetlights disappeared. The faint glow from the hospital windows had guided Winter the night she thought she'd killed the Plague Saint, but she didn't have that now.

Thankfully, she did still have a few matches. And a spare piece of cloth. She searched the ground for a large stick, wrapped the cloth around the end, and lit it. Doing her best to shield her small flame from the wind with her body, she followed the sound of rushing water to the river's edge.

Farther north, or farther south? To the north was a barely used bridge, and just upstream from that was where water was diverted into city canals. Downstream, the river ran parallel to the city for a few blocks—too far into the trees to get many visitors—before diverging and flowing out of the mountains.

South, Winter decided. She began to pick her way over rocks and branches along the riverbank. It didn't take long for her mind to get lost in the sound of roaring water. The cold night air slowed her body, but she occasionally snapped out of her mental fog long enough to berate herself and pick up the pace.

One moment she was walking, the next she was stumbling. Her heavy eyes shot open. She met the rocky ground with a painful thud and a splash. Shallow, frigid water swallowed her hands, turning them to ice through her gloves. Her makeshift torch landed in the water with her. The flame went out in the blink of an eye.

Damn it. Winter struggled to her feet and picked up the bag that had slid off her shoulder. She blindly dug around in the bag, praying for another match. As she searched, she cautiously crept forward.

It didn't take long for a dark shape to rise out of the water up ahead.

The appearance of the boat made Winter give up her search for the match. The faint moonlight would do for now. Besides, there was probably some source of light inside. She just had to find her way in.

She walked to the point on the shore closest to the boat and squinted into the darkness. A few planks of wood fastened together acted as a makeshift dock, stretching from the rocks out to the boat. A rope ladder seemed to be the only way onto the deck.

Winter cautiously made her way out to the middle of the river, aware of how fast it was racing by. The cold would kill her in minutes. God, Marcus really was lucky to be alive. He must have crawled out of the water pretty quickly after Winter threw him in.

The rope ladder swung around freely in the breeze. Winter grabbed it and nearly lost her balance. Jaw clenched, heart pounding, she pulled herself up and collapsed onto the boat's deck.

The deck wrapped around a cabin. Winter stood up and grabbed the handle of the door leading inside. It flew open and slammed against the wall. The resounding thud made her wince, but there was no one around to hear it.

She closed the door behind her and tried to make out what she was looking at. Her hands blindly moved across the counter at her side, and she walked until she found a lantern. A search of the drawers eventually led her to a matchbox. Winter ignited a flame inside the lantern, peeled off her soaked gloves, and held her hands as close to the hot glass as she dared.

Now that she wasn't blindly stumbling around and making a racket, she could hear a new sound, barely audible over the river. Scratching. Squeaking.

Winter stood frozen for a minute before mustering the strength to pick up the lantern and turn around.

The entire back wall was covered in cages, and each cage held a rat. Winter moved closer. A few moved to the bars, drawn to her presence, but others were sleeping or apparently didn't care. Winter frowned. Actually, several of them looked rather sick. She knelt to examine the bottom row and noticed drops of blood on some of the rats' bedding. Others clearly had eye infections.

"I'm sorry," she whispered, wondering if they could be cured. The thought of these animals dying in cages for Marcus's research made her angry. It would be one thing if he was using them to test medicine intended to save as many as possible, but his plans for treatment were aligned with the council's. It was only for the rich.

Besides, these rats might have been kept for a different purpose than medicine development entirely. Marcus's notes indicated he'd been testing combinations of plagues to make something even deadlier than the diseases already choking the city.

Winter stepped away from the cages and examined the rest of the cabin. There was a table in the middle of the room, and counters lining the other walls. One corner of the room had a seat in front of a steering wheel and other controls for the boat.

In true Marcus Blackburn fashion, there was no shortage of notes and equipment on every surface. Winter moved toward a stack of notebooks. How many of them had Marcus filled, in all? There were three here on the counter, next to petri dishes and microscopes and scattered pens. She opened one.

These ones were coded too. Groaning, Winter pulled out a stool from under the counter and sank onto it. Shadows danced across the pages in time with the flickering flame as she worked.

It only took three pages to discover the horrifying truth.

Marcus made white plague.

And it wasn't the result of one of the combinations he'd thrown together, something that could be treated with a concoction. It was so much more than that. He'd taken red plague and altered it into a worse disease, one with more severe symptoms, one that even caused hallucinations in some patients.

It seemed to be the result of developing the worst of the red plague strains, forcing them to evolve into something new. The notes on how he'd developed it were unclear in many places. He used terms Winter didn't understand. But the how didn't interest her as much as the why.

Winter stared at what she'd deciphered, hardly able to believe it. He hadn't just made white plague; he'd been infecting people with it. Deliberately. *Testing* it. For nearly a year, and that was just based on the first date in this notebook.

Despite everything she'd seen and read already, Winter pressed a hand to her mouth. The pen she'd been using slipped from her fingers, rolled across the counter, and fell to the floor. He'd been poisoning food and drinks. And not just at the hospital. There were notes made about going to restaurants, stores…

She forced herself to read through more entries. He'd wanted to figure out the incubation time. Survival time. Incubation was unpredictable, ranging anywhere from eight to twenty hours from infection to symptoms. But it was typically only another few hours until death after that, without any treatment whatsoever. Some patients had received medicine, though. They were guinea pigs in Marcus's search for a cure.

The first dozen or so recipes failed. And when the medicine did finally start working, Marcus had what he needed from the people who had no idea their Saint was poisoning them.

Winter decoded the recipe that was circled in red. The final cure recipe. He'd noted that, like the others, it could be administered orally. But putting it directly into the blood was far more efficient. She recognized a few chemical names from the hospital labs, but others were new to her. Where the hell was she supposed to get this stuff?

Maybe she could trick someone like Atherton into helping her. But River needed this medicine now. Winter stood up and started searching cupboards. Marcus had to have some extra cure he hadn't used yet. Or maybe some of the ingredients she needed. She sifted through empty bottles, blood samples, and vials. Some were unlabeled, but others had names. *Red plague. Red plague treatment. Blue + green. Yellow treatment, version 3.*

Plague cure.

Frowning, Winter held up the small bottle. It was two-thirds full with a clear liquid. She put it in her coat and searched every inch of the rest of the cupboards, but that was all there was.

No color. Was this meant to cure everything? Winter went back to the notebooks. There was a tiny number on the cap of each vial that corresponded with entries one of them, she'd noticed. It took ten minutes to find the matching number, which was written above a recipe. This one had a few more ingredients and slightly different instructions than the white plague cure recipe, but it was definitely similar.

Winter copied down the recipe into the journal she'd stolen from Marcus's room, returned the lantern to the spot on the counter she'd found it, and left the boat.

Her first priority was getting what she had of the plague cure to River. Then she'd figure out where to get what she needed to make more. She walked with her back to the river, hoping that as long as she moved in a straight line, she'd reach the city eventually.

It took longer than expected, but streetlights finally cut through the trees ahead. Winter staggered onto an empty street. She spotted a bench and hurried to sit down. *Just a few minutes to rest before going to the hospital*, she told herself.

She laid down on her back and stared up at the black sky. The nothingness weighed down on her. Miles and miles of nothingness. What time was it, anyway? Would the other doctors be suspicious if the Plague Saint showed up to the hospital early? Whatever, she could make up an excuse. They'd believe her. They always did, just like they'd believed Marcus's lies. *Idiots.*

Winter blinked, and the sky was a pale gray. Sunlight crept over the horizon. She jolted upright. A few people walked by and shot her dirty looks. Judging by how they were dressed, they were probably far more well off than her family. Business owners, maybe. Or, hell, they could have been city council members.

Winter hopped off the bench and stumbled a few steps. Her stomach growled. Where was she? How far was the hospital from here? She walked to the nearest intersection and studied the street signs. She didn't recognize Ash Street, but Stone Ave ran up the east side of the city.

She walked into the street and paused halfway across when a glimpse of the church between buildings caught her eye. That was farther than she expected. She must have veered south walking back. Well, if the church was that far, the hospital was going to be a thirty-minute walk. She didn't know where the trolley stops were in this area, and they'd be full of people trying to get to work anyway.

Speaking of trolleys, the ringing of a bell made Winter's head snap to the right. A trolley was rolling straight toward her, and the conductor was shouting at her to get out of the street. She darted to the sidewalk.

Her stomach growled again. "Ugh, fine!" she snapped, louder than she meant to. People were giving her weird looks. Ignoring them, she kept walking and scanned buildings until she spotted a cafe.

She dug out the cash she kept in her coat as she walked in. The only people inside were a man reading the paper in the corner, a woman encouraging her son to eat a pastry, and the girl working behind the counter. All eyes moved to her as she entered.

"Uh." Winter's gaze flickered to the woman, who looked away when Winter met her gaze. She turned back to the menu. "I guess I'll have a croissant and the biggest, strongest coffee you can give me. To go."

The girl lifted an eyebrow. "Sure thing."

Winter paid her and sat down as far from the other patrons as she could while she waited. She turned to look out the window and finally understood why everyone was looking at her. Her faint reflection was ragged, with unruly hair and bags under her eyes. Winter glared at the girl staring back at her for a moment before pulling out the journal and flipping through it.

Minutes later, the employee brought Winter her order. Winter eagerly took her breakfast and left the building. She ate the croissant in a few large bites before moving on to chugging the coffee, relishing the way it burned her tongue.

Chapter Nineteen
Undercurrent

The hospital receptionist was the first person to not blink at Winter's ragged appearance. She had seen far worse. Winter nodded at her as she passed, walking quickly, coat billowing behind her. She headed straight for River's room.

Winter threw open the door with enough force to make Phoebe yelp in surprise. Phoebe spun around. "Winter?"

"Phoebe?" Winter crossed the room. "What are you doing here?"

"I'm sorry, I was just going to be in and out real quick. I didn't want to disturb River, but there were some files left in here that I needed." Phoebe held up the folder in her right hand. "Say, you didn't see the Plague Saint on your way here, did you? He's usually here by now."

Oh. Right. Winter looked down. She was Winter Pierce, not the Plague Saint. "Uh, I—" Her hand slid into her pocket. Her fingers wrapped around the vial of plague cure. "I did see him, actually, but he was on his way to meet the mayor. He gave me this." She held up the cure. "Said he made it last night and I had to get it to River right away. It's an emergency."

Phoebe stared at her blankly. "He gave it to...you? Not a nurse or doctor?"

Winter shrugged. "I must have been the first person he saw, and it's for River anyway. I don't see why it matters."

"Well, hospital protocol, for starters."

"Since when have you cared about following protocol?" Winter asked. "My brother's going to die if I don't get him this damn medicine!"

She immediately regretted raising her voice. Phoebe didn't even look angry, she just looked...worried.

"I'm sorry," Winter said, forcing some calm into her voice. "But he's on the verge of death." She walked to the IV stand and fiddled with the bag. Nothing she hadn't done before. Just open the bottle, and—

"What are you doing?" Phoebe rushed to Winter's side. "At least let me get a nurse—"

"Relax, I know what I'm doing." Winter moved quickly, leaving Phoebe to watch with a stunned expression.

"How did you know how to do that?" Phoebe asked. She looked Winter up and down. "And are you okay? You look awful."

"I didn't get much sleep."

"Have you eaten?"

"I had a croissant. And coffee." Winter swung her bag around to her front to put the empty bottle back in.

Phoebe's eyes widened. "Where did you get that bag?"

"Uh, it's mine?"

"It looks exactly like the Plague Saint's." Phoebe folded her arms. "Seriously, what's going on? Everyone I know is acting super weird. And by everyone, I mean you and my uncle and the Plague Saint. And apparently someone set a fire in our apartment building last night, on top of all that."

"A fire? That's crazy." Winter zipped the bag up before Phoebe could see its contents. "I have to show you something."

"What?"

"What part of that was unclear?" Winter headed for the door. *Take Phoebe to the boat. Come back to check on River. Find the rest of the ingredients.*

Phoebe jogged to catch up. "What do you have to show me?"

"You'll see. I promise, you're going to want to see this," Winter told her. "It's going to explain everything that's been happening."

"Can you at least tell me where we're going?"

"Not really."

They were nearly to the lobby. Phoebe looked around. "I can't just leave! I'm in the middle of my shift—"

"You get a lunch break, don't you?"

"It's nine a.m.!"

It was already nine? "Breakfast break, then. Like I said, the Plague Saint's going to be gone a while, anyway."

Winter led Phoebe back the way she'd come. Phoebe's worried demeanor worsened dramatically when they left the city and crossed the tree line.

"Winter..." she started when they reached the river.

"You said your uncle's been acting weird, and I have answers."

"Maybe weird wasn't the right word," Phoebe said. "He went to the city with his research and now he's working with the mayor, which is great!"

No, it's not. Winter stopped herself before she could say the words. She might be able to get more information first. "Did he tell you anything about what the mayor's planning, specifically?"

"No, he hasn't been home much the past few days. He gets back later than he used to. And he leaves early."

They reached the boat faster than Winter expected. What a difference daylight made. For a moment she worried that Marcus might be at the boat, and she held up a hand to stop Phoebe from taking another step. She scanned the cabin windows for movement. Listened for sound. Nothing.

"Why is there a boat out here?" Phoebe asked.

"It's your uncle's." Winter walked to the makeshift dock. "Come on."

"What?"

"I said come on."

Phoebe hesitated before following. "How did you even find this?"

Winter climbed the ladder. "Long story." She grunted with the effort of pulling herself onto the deck. When Phoebe reached the top of the ladder, Winter held out a hand to help her up.

"I know you said you didn't want to investigate anymore, but I couldn't stop thinking about the weird deaths and the plague research," Winter said. "I found a lot of stuff. I can't explain it all right now, but I can show you this."

They entered the cabin. Winter stood and watched with folded arms while Phoebe took it all in: the rats, the labeled vials of medicine and plague combinations, the petri dishes and microscopes and blood samples.

Once she was done looking around, Winter picked up one of the notebooks she'd left on the counter. "He used a really simple code. Just moved all the letters back one in the alphabet. It is pretty jarring at first glance, and a pain to translate, but I decoded all of these entries. See for yourself, its consistent."

Phoebe's brow furrowed as she took the notebook. Winter pulled the scrap pieces of paper she'd written the translations on from her bag and let Phoebe compare them. Minutes dragged by.

"How—" Phoebe looked up, eyes wide, confusion twisting her features. "How do you know he wrote this? That this is all his?"

Winter searched for an answer. She couldn't explain to Phoebe that Marcus had been the Plague Saint, because that would force her to explain that he wasn't anymore, and that she only knew that because she was the Saint now, and that was because she'd tried to kill him—

"I followed him," Winter said. "I wasn't planning on it, but I was at City Hall trying to get information on a new law I heard a rumor about, and he was there talking to the mayor. I overhead them saying something about white plague."

Her explanation came off as frantic, but that was fine. She continued. "I was scared that might be what River has, so I followed him here and found the truth." She nodded to the notebook. "White plague is real, and it's because Marcus invented it."

Phoebe closed the notebook and gingerly set it on the counter with shaking hands. Her eyes closed. "That—that doesn't make any sense."

"Well, it's all in writing." Winter gestured around the lab to the other notebooks scattered about, her proof undeniable. But her triumph faded when she saw the pain twisting Phoebe's expression. Her shoulders sagged. "I—I'm sorry, Phoebe. I know he says he's trying to help people, but—"

"I don't get why he would do this." Phoebe turned around. Her shoulders lifted as she sucked in a sharp breath. "Why would he want more people to die?"

Winter grimaced. She opened her mouth to offer up something, anything to make Phoebe feel better, but that was impossible.

Phoebe walked toward the rat cages and stopped in front of them, still not facing Winter, not even throwing a glance back. "There must be some sort of misunderstanding."

"Phoebe, his journal entries were pretty clear." Winter's fists clenched at her sides. "I'm sorry, but he was poisoning people to test the plague."

"Ow!" Phoebe yelped and yanked her hand back.

"What happened?" Winter asked.

Phoebe shook out her hand and turned around. "It's nothing. I have to get out of here. I have to talk to him."

"He's just going to keep lying to you!" Winter exclaimed.

Phoebe shook her head and stormed past her. Winter reached out and grabbed her arm. "Phoebe, please, I'm trying to help you!"

"Winter, this is a lot, okay?" As Phoebe pulled her arm away, Winter noticed a drop of blood on her finger. Before she could press the matter further, Phoebe was out on the deck, grabbing the ladder.

Winter followed her to the shore. Phoebe finally stopped at the tree line, letting Winter catch up.

"Some of those vials were labeled as cures or medicine for the other plagues," Phoebe said.

Winter nodded. "I think he's had those for a while now." She hadn't even known there were true cures until she'd found the boat. How many more secrets was Marcus hiding?

"He told me he hadn't been able to make anything stronger than the hospital drugs. Red-X and Blue-X and—" Phoebe cut off and squeezed her eyes shut.

"The notebook disagrees."

Phoebe shook her head. "I—there has to be a reasonable explanation." It sounded like she was trying to convince herself more than Winter.

Winter wanted to refute the statement, but a distant sound stopped her. Branches snapped. A voice rang out. Phoebe opened her mouth, and Winter held up a hand to silence her. "Stay here," Winter whispered.

Winter walked to a tree that had branches hanging low enough for her to reach. She awkwardly pulled herself up and rose to as close to a standing position as she could manage. She peered around the trunk and surveyed the direction the sound had come from.

There was movement. People. City guards. What the hell were they doing out here? Winter didn't want to wait for them to get close enough to find out. She slid out of the tree.

"We're going to run," she hissed to Phoebe. "I'm not getting arrested again."

"Again?"

Oops. Whatever. Winter sprinted down the shoreline away from the approaching guards, watching the ground in front of her for tripping hazards. She glanced back occasionally to make sure Phoebe was following.

Once Winter felt it was safe, she took a sharp left and raced through the trees toward the city. Phoebe was lagging, so Winter slowed her pace, despite every part of her itching to move at full speed. As soon as she stopped, though, a wave of dizziness hit her. Oh, God. She stumbled to a nearby tree and leaned against it.

"Are you okay?" Phoebe asked.

"I'm fine." Winter glanced to her right. They were almost back to the streets, and she couldn't hear the guards anymore. She took a few more seconds to catch her breath before gesturing for Phoebe to follow. They walked the rest of the way.

Winter relaxed when the streets around them filled with people going about their day. She undoubtedly still looked as ragged as she had after waking up—maybe even more—but there were too many people around now for her to stick out as badly.

"Winter, I—I have to get back to work," Phoebe stammered.

Winter stopped. "What about everything I just showed you?"

"I'll stay up to talk to my uncle tonight. Get some rest, okay?" Phoebe started toward the hospital.

"Phoebe, wait!" Winter reached for her, but she was too slow. "He's just going to lie to you more!" She jogged after Phoebe, but quickly fell behind.

Winter doubled over and pressed her hands against her legs, struggling for air. The world spun around her.

Phoebe was right. She needed rest. But she also needed to keep Marcus from lying to Phoebe, and check on River, and go to work as the Plague Saint, and...

Winter wandered to a nearby bench and sat down. Just a quick break. Then she could go after Phoebe. *Phoebe*. Was she really going to ignore all of the evidence Winter had shown her? It was as plain as could be.

If someone told Winter that a person she loved and trusted— River, maybe—was doing something horrible like this, would she be able to believe them? Even with proof?

Her fists clenched in her lap. She wanted to believe she would never deny hard evidence. Even if it hurt. But maybe she was wrong.

Or, maybe, she and Phoebe were just too different.

Chapter Twenty
The Deal

Winter downed two more cups of coffee before changing into the Plague Saint uniform and returning to the hospital. She didn't bother stopping by her office, instead going straight to River's room. To her relief, he was awake and talking to a nurse.

"Plague Saint!" the nurse exclaimed as she entered. "I've never seen anything like it. He's doing so much better."

"See, doc?" River grinned. "I knew I'd pull through."

"I gave him new medicine this morning," Winter said.

The nurse frowned. "New medicine? Should we be giving that to other patients?"

"Yes, but unfortunately, we're in short supply. I'm off to find the ingredients I need."

"Right now? Nobody's seen you all day, we were starting to get concerned. Three new red plague patients came in this morning, and—"

"I'm sorry, you'll all have to handle yourselves for a few hours." Winter winced at her own bluntness. It was something that the nurse should have been used to, but she couldn't help but add, "I promise this is a better use of my time. Those patients will have a much better chance with the new medicine." Shooting River a glance, she added, "He'll probably need some more, too, to ensure he remains stable."

Winter left the hospital and headed for City Hall. If the mayor wasn't there, there had to at least be someone who could tell her where he was.

She'd only walked the streets in daylight on a few occasions to deliver bills to next of kin. Marcus had done it plenty when he was still the Saint, and when Winter did it, people tended to steer clear of her. Today, for some reason, they dared to move closer and whisper to each other while they stared.

The staff. Winter usually carried the staff, but right now it was shoved awkwardly into the bag. Had Marcus actually threatened people with it? She slipped into an alley to dig it out. She wouldn't use it, but if it kept people away, she'd carry it.

Sure enough, that made all the difference. Winter didn't have the energy to let her rage boil over even more, so she pushed the thought of Marcus's cruelty down and continued her journey to City Hall.

The shining white building and its bronze dome overlooked the town square, surrounded by shops and other businesses. At the center of the square was a fountain that sat empty. It was only usable in the summer months, when the nights in Devil's Pass remained consistently above freezing.

Winter stormed into City Hall and walked up to the front desk. Alarm flashed across the face of the young man sitting on the other side. "Plague Saint? I—"

"Is the mayor here?" Winter asked.

"He's in a meeting, but—"

"Any idea how long he's going to be?"

"No idea, but he said he was going to St. Andrew's after, so he'll be coming through here." The receptionist swallowed. "I can tell him you asked to see him…"

"I can wait." Winter looked around the lobby until her gaze rested on a bench.

"Uh, sure. Go ahead."

Winter waited on the bench for ten minutes, according to the clock hanging over the receptionist's desk. She passed time by decoding more sentences here and there in the journal, but she didn't find anything terribly shocking or interesting.

As she was translating a line scribbled off to the side, apparently related to the sketches of petri dishes on the page—*further evidence for gene editing, but lack of close relation to other species indicates possibility of creation from*—a voice reached her from the nearby stairwell. No, two voices. Mayor Atherton, and—

"Two of those jugs should be enough for the assembly meeting, based on my calculations," Marcus said.

Winter shoved his notebook into her bag and stood up. As soon as the two men emerged from the stairwell, their conversation came to a halt. Two pairs of eyes rested on her. Atherton's expression was curious, while Marcus kept his blank.

"Mayor Atherton," Winter said. "I needed to speak to you."

Damn it. She couldn't ask for ingredients in front of Marcus without him realizing she'd his plague cure, and his boat. Did she care if he knew? Phoebe was going to tell him tonight, anyway. But Marcus wasn't going to let her make the cure to hand out freely.

"Plague Saint! This is perfect timing. I have matters to discuss with you as well. Marcus Blackburn here has been researching the plagues, and he's come up with some rather groundbreaking stuff."

"Wonderful," Winter said. Maybe her best chance was to pretend to be on their side. Marcus wouldn't buy it, but would he expose her in front of the mayor? She glanced at him. He was eyeing the staff in her hand. "I need some new ingredients for an improved version of the medicine I'm making for you."

"Perhaps we should compare notes," Marcus said. "I had some formulas I was going to send you, Plague Saint."

Was he lying? Or was he going to really send her the cure?

"The ingredients involved are expensive," Marcus continued. "We need to monitor the handling of them very closely, to ensure they don't end up in the wrong hands."

To ensure they don't end up helping anyone who actually needs them.

"I agree," Atherton said. "And since I'm appointing you as the new hospital director—"

"What?" Winter couldn't keep the surprise out of her voice.

"Mr. Blackburn is brilliant, Plague Saint. You have nothing to worry about. He's going to be an excellent director."

"Thank you, mayor." Marcus smiled. "Plague Saint, you don't need to worry about acquiring ingredients. I'll handle that. You're needed at the hospital. All you have to do is make the medicine for us with your equipment, and we'll make sure it goes where it needs to."

"You're a symbol to the people," Atherton added. "And that's going to be very useful in the coming weeks."

A tool. The Saint was a tool for the mayor to use. Did Marcus seriously expect her to play along?

"Blackburn has proof of the effectiveness of his formula," Atherton continued. "And Forrest has contacts to get all the ingredients. He's arranging for that as we speak. We'll have them sent to the hospital tomorrow morning, so that you can make what we need for the assembly meeting."

Marcus lowered his voice. "Perhaps we should be more careful with that information. It's a bit sensitive." The hint of annoyance in his voice told Winter he really hadn't wanted her to hear that. Was it the bit about the assembly meeting that bothered him? The mention of Forrest? Or both?

Regardless, she had somewhere to look, now. And a new bit of information to work through. A new clue about Marcus's true plan.

"Of course. Thank you, Marcus." Atherton glanced at the clock, oblivious to the severity of his mistake. "My apologies, you two. I have another appointment I have to get to."

As soon as Atherton was gone, Winter voiced her confusion. "Why not tell him the truth? Why are you keeping me around?"

"Do what I ask, and you can go back to your old life," Marcus replied, ignoring her questions. "I'll even let you cure your brother, as long as you don't cause any more trouble."

Winter gritted her teeth. "Why do you need me?" She shot the receptionist a nervous glance, but he was too far to hear their hushed conversation.

"What makes you think I need you?"

"I'm not stupid. You could reveal my identity and have me locked up for murder. Continue with your plan without any chance of me getting in the way."

"Fine," Marcus conceded. "Making the plague cure takes time that I don't have. I'm juggling a lot right now, and you're the only person who knows my recipes and procedures well enough to make it for me on such short notice. As I said, it's impressive how well you took on my role. Even if it's only because I made such detailed notes."

"So, I make the plague cure, you give it only to your rich friends, and I go back to scraping by?" Winter hissed.

Marcus chuckled. "I know you have good intentions, Winter, but you're misguided."

"What, because I killed people? You have no right—"

"The killing isn't the issue. I actually find that to be the most impressive thing you've done, even if it's been an inconvenience," Marcus said. "You just chose the wrong targets. You're right: Devil's Pass is dying and change needs to happen if we're going to survive as a whole."

"If you only save the rich, you'll all starve to death without the rest of us to do your work."

"I know that. I'm not stupid. I'm not just going to save the rich, I'm going to save the people we need, too."

"Everyone deserves medicine, not just the people who are valuable to you!" Winter's voice was rising to a dangerous volume. She had to make an effort to curb her anger.

Marcus shook his head. "They can't all live, Winter. Not if I'm going to wipe out the plagues once and for all. Only so many people can be cured, and the rest have to go entirely. One swift wave of death to take out the last of the sickness. The cure will prevent it from taking hold in everyone else."

"But you can cure everyone! You know how!"

"The costs would be through the roof. We'd have to convince every business in the city to sacrifice months of profits to pay for the supplies." He sighed. "It will be a tragedy, but everything after will be better. We'll have more resources, more—"

"What the hell is wrong with you?" Winter hissed.

Marcus's expression darkened. "Don't act like your idea is any better. Killing only the people at the top? People like Adams and

Gordon keep the city running. Go ahead, kill all of us. Devil's Pass will descend into chaos."

He did have a point. Winter couldn't just wipe out the city's leadership. Who would replace them?

Better people. There were better people in the city. People who would do what it took to get a cure to every last person. People who would give up a few months of profits to wipe out the cures in a way that didn't mean letting innocents die. Or, if it came to it, people who would *force* the businesses to sacrifice money instead of lives.

Maybe that was what had to be done.

"Trust me Winter," Marcus said, pulling her from her train of thought. "This has to be done in one fell swoop. I've had to update my treatment formulas as the plagues evolve, and white will be no different."

"But you made white cure!" Winter protested.

"It's still a living thing," Marcus said. "Just like the other plagues. And like them, it's been genetically engineered to be resilient. To adapt."

Genetically engineered? "Someone...made the other plagues?"

Marcus's smug expression made her want to drive her blade into his chest. Winter flinched at the violent thought.

"You believed the story that they escaped from melting ice caps?" Marcus asked. "Plenty of diseases did, sure. But these five plagues were weapons, used in wars for resources when societies were crumbling. But unlike their creators, I've waited to unleash white plague until I had a cure. And I've found a cure for the others, too.

"I'm not stupid enough to hand out something so valuable for free," Marcus continued with a glance at the clock on the wall. "I'm going to do what it takes to save this city, and people will thank me for it. The smart ones will, anyway."

He was too proud of himself. He genuinely thought he was smarter than everyone who'd come before him, and everyone around him.

"But you'll save my brother." Winter let her voice sound broken, let her own fear crack it into pieces.

Marcus's gaze returned to her. "If you make the cure for me, and agree not to give it to anyone else," he said. "And don't think you can trick me. If you try to back out or make any move to distribute the cure, the guards I've bought into my employment will stop you."

"Guards?"

"Given Adams's and Gordon's deaths, I was able to convince Mayor Atherton you should have guards in your lab while you're working. You're welcome."

"What else do you have guards doing for you?" *Keeping an eye on your boat?*

"That's none of your business. You'll begin tomorrow morning, when the rest of the ingredients you need get delivered. I'll arrange for the other doctors to handle your patients."

"They're already struggling with their workloads—"

"They'll have to deal with it," Marcus said coolly. "Now, go make yourself useful until your lab is ready."

Marcus left Winter standing alone in the lobby, processing and planning. To serve his own purposes, he was letting the elite believe she was on their side. That was going to be a mistake.

Now, where could she find Forrest?

Shoes clicking against tile made her head turn. Ellen Bates walked up to the young man at the front desk and handed him a folder. Winter waited for their conversation to end before approaching.

"Oh, Plague Saint." Bates frowned. "What are you doing here?"

"I'm actually looking for Forrest," Winter told her. "He's handling the transport of supplies I need for my new medicine."

"Forrest? Last I heard from him, he was planning a party at his house tonight," Bates replied. "But if I had to guess where he is now, I'd say look at the Diamond Club. Just down the street. It's his favorite, of the ones he owns."

"Thank you."

"Best of luck with your transport," Bates said. "I've been trying to get Forrest to approve a new tax law for weeks now. I know as well as anyone the economic benefit he's brought to the city, but he tends to get...distracted."

"Right." Winter paused. "Sorry, I'm not as familiar with the council's lawmaking process as I should be. Why do you need Forrest to sign off? He's a businessman, not a politician."

Bates responded with cold laughter. "Sometimes, there's not much of a difference," she said. "Because of donations he's made to certain city funds, we have to go to him when we want to make adjustments to tax laws."

The casual tone with which she said the words made Winter bristle. How was that legal? "Right. Of course," she forced herself to say. "I'm going to go find him. Thank you."

Chapter Twenty-One
King of Clubs

Ten minutes later, the Plague Saint stood in the middle of the flashing neon lights and blaring electronic music of the Diamond Club, completely out of place and clutching her staff like it was her only lifeline. Lights reflected off the beak of her mask, and Winter might have laughed at the image under different circumstances. Right now, she was in shock. She had no idea anything like this existed in Devil's Pass.

"Excuse me, I'm looking for Forrest!" she yelled over the music, hoping one of the people pointing at her and whispering to their friends could help. Either they couldn't hear her, or they didn't care.

Thankfully, word of the Plague Saint wandering the club spread quickly. Forrest emerged from the crowd before long and waved. "Plague Saint! What brings you here?"

Winter could barely hear him. "I have to talk to you about the transport of—"

"What?"

"I have to—!"

"Come with me!" Forrest gestured for her to follow him through the crowd. They passed through a door labeled "Employees Only" and entered a cool, quiet hallway. Another door brought them into an office.

"Atherton said he arranged for you to get me some medicine ingredients by tomorrow morning, correct?" Winter asked.

Forrest collapsed into the chair behind his desk and spun in a slow circle. "Uh, yes. Well, a couple of my employees."

"Well, there's been a new outbreak in this part of the city. With City Hall and other important businesses so close, he's asked me to get a head start on making medicine. I'm going to need some of those supplies right away."

"Right now?" Forrest groaned and rubbed his forehead. "I have a lot going on at the moment."

In the light of the office, Winter could really study him. His hair was a mess, his yellow shirt was half unbuttoned, and his eyes were bloodshot. "Do you know what time it is?" she asked.

"Uh, six?"

Winter didn't bother asking if he meant a.m. or p.m. Apparently, this place was open all day. "It's noon. First case was reported an hour ago, and there have been four more since." She slammed her hands down on his desk, making him jump. "This is more serious than red plague. They'll all be dead by the end of the night if they aren't cured."

"So? Who are they, anyway?" Forrest's brow furrowed. "Anyone I know?"

Winter took a deep breath. "Doesn't matter. They were in this part of town. There is a very high chance of someone coming into this club with it and infecting everyone else. It may have even already happened. And it'll spread like wildfire in there. Do you understand?"

Forrest's frown deepened.

"If I start making batches of cure right away, we'll have enough to treat your customers. But if we don't, they'll all die." Winter leaned forward. "Which means you lose a good portion of your income. And it's only going to get worse from there."

That got through to him. Forrest straightened up. "Well, shit. And all you need is to grab the stuff I bought for the hospital?"

"Yes. Where is it?"

"My house." Forrest stood up and stumbled a few steps before regaining his balance. "It's on the south side."

Go figure. That's where all the nice houses were. The only houses in Devil's Pass, really. Everyone else was crammed into tiny apartments.

"Short walk from here," Forrest continued. "I'll lead the way."

Winter assumed they would take a back exit, but Forrest returned to the club floor. He shouted at the top of his lungs, "Party at my house starts now!"

People gradually joined the pack trailing behind him, which made it difficult for Winter to keep track of him. Irritated, she lifted her staff. "Excuse me, coming through!"

"Damn, Forrest got the Plague Saint?"

"Forrest's friends with the Plague Saint!"

Heavens above. *Just get the stuff and get out.* Winter found herself trailing behind a crowd of people as they moved south. She hadn't been in this part of the city, and despite her concerns about a crowd of drunk people walking around at noon, they were surprisingly not out of place. Not on this side of Devil's Pass. She couldn't believe there were this many people that could afford to sit around doing nothing all day.

Forrest's home was more extravagant than Winter had expected, too. She'd known it would be big, but the house he led the crowd to was ridiculous. What did he need all that space for?

The home's interior held expensive furniture and the nicest appliances money could buy, but it was also a mess. Empty bottles and trash littered the tables and floor. While guests helped themselves to food and made themselves comfortable, Forrest fiddled with a big black box. A speaker that would play music. Winter had noticed some of the odd machines back in the club, too.

"If you could just show me where you're keeping the supplies, I'll be out of your hair in a few minutes," Winter told him.

"You can stay as long as you like!" Forrest exclaimed. "It's no trouble."

"As nice as that sounds, I'm rather busy."

"I think you oughta learn how to balance work and play, Plague Saint. Like me."

Balance? "Right. Sure."

"See, I have nothing going on today. Why waste time sitting around?" Forrest pressed a button, and music similar to what had been playing in the club blasted from the speakers. Winter wondered how much the machine cost. And why anyone bothered making them.

"Look, maybe I can take you up on your offer some other day. But right now, I'm trying to save your life and your money."

"Right, right, right," Forrest muttered. He opened a cupboard over the speaker and grabbed a bottle. "Follow me."

He led the way down a staircase, through a hallway, and into a large, empty room. Empty, that was, except for the boxes stacked up against the far wall. Winter examined the labels. Some of the chemical names were unfamiliar, but others she recognized from the cure formula. She breathed a sigh of relief.

"Thank you, Forrest," she said as she straightened up. "I'll take what I need, and you can have the rest sent to the hospital tomorrow morning as planned."

"Sure thing. Help yourself." Forrest took a sip from the bottle in his hand and walked off.

Winter dug through the boxes, grabbing vials and bottles and packing them into her bag. Strangely, rather than medical ingredients, some of the boxes were filled with plain water bottles. As she worked, she wondered how the hell she was going to make the cure and get it to people like River with guards in the lab.

Wait. There was one lab Marcus had all but forgotten about. And she still had the key somewhere in her bag. Winter picked up the pace now that she had a plan, grabbing the last few things she'd need. She also hunted down some empty bottles, since she couldn't risk going back to the hospital to get anything. Based on the formula she'd skimmed, she had everything else she needed.

Her bag much heavier now, she trekked back up the stairs. More people had arrived, filling the rooms around the entry way. Winter scanned the crowd and spotted Forrest arguing with someone. Curious, she moved closer.

"—and I don't remember inviting you in the first place!" Forrest's words slurred together, barely audible. It was almost impressive how much drunker he'd gotten in the time Winter had been downstairs.

"You invited every damn person in earshot," the man in front of him snapped back. "And I'm not here for the party. I'm here to ask you where my payment is."

"Payment for what?"

"My company spent weeks installing equipment in your new factory. You agreed to the price when you signed our contract. Send me my check, or I'll take this to court!"

"Whatever." Forrest sipped his drink. "My lawyer's cheaper, anyway."

"This isn't the end of this, Forrest." The man stormed off, shoving his way through the crowd of oblivious partiers.

Winter wanted to kill Forrest. Not to save her brother. Not to save the city. She wanted to watch the light leave his eyes.

She needed to get out of here before she did something rash.

Plus, it was uncomfortably hot under the uniform. Almost enough to make her miss the cold.

The walk to Marcus's lab changed her mind on that pretty quickly. It wasn't snowing at the moment, but gray clouds loomed over the horizon in every direction, warning that precipitation was on the way. And while it was warmer inside the lab, there was still a definite chill.

Winter took off the mask and set it on the counter. The lab was still empty, and unlike her last visit, there were no signs of recent activity. No new footprints in the dust or random tools under the counters. Still, she worked quickly and jumped at every sound.

The instructions involved a painful amount of waiting. While she waited for the final chemical reactions to run their course, Winter paced back and forth for a while, then laid on her back on the floor and tried not to think about all the terrible things clawing at her chest.

The ringing of the timer she'd set made her jerk awake. The cure was ready, it was near seven p.m., and Winter was starving. She'd never had anything to eat after the croissant, had she? She climbed to her feet. She had to get the medicine to River first. Then she'd worry about food.

Winter didn't make it ten feet into the hospital before she was swarmed. A couple of visitors asking about their loved ones, nurses inquiring about treatment schedules, and Dr. Liang wanting to know when the new batch of Red-X would be available.

"One at a time, please." The words came out snappier than Winter had intended. "I'm sorry for my absence, but I've been dealing with something important. Now, has anyone seen my assistant?"

The receptionist chimed in behind her. "Phoebe? She left an hour ago."

Right. It was past seven. Of course Phoebe wasn't here.

"Plague Saint," Dr. Liang began, her tone cautious. "The new hospital director showed up an hour ago. He said you had a new project and that you wouldn't be working with patients anymore."

Shock spread through the lobby. Anyone who hadn't already been watching the commotion turned their eyes on Winter. Their expressions brimmed with confusion. Fear. Grief.

Of course Marcus didn't want Winter working with patients anymore. She'd cured too many people for his liking, already.

"A lot has happened today," Winter said. "I'm still coming to an agreement with the new director, but at the moment I am working under his instructions. I do have a new project, and I promise it will be worth it." Her gaze swept across the lobby. Across the crowd of anxious, terrified people. "But please, I need space tonight to do my work."

Winter turned to Dr. Liang and continued. "Keep doing your work, doctor. It is difficult, but the people need you and the others doctors now more than ever. I am not a saint. I am one man, and you can go on with or without me by your side."

Dr. Liang nodded, albeit reluctantly. "Thank you for everything you've done, Plague Saint."

The crowd dispersed, and quiet chatter filled the space. Winter hurried into the halls beyond the lobby and walked to River's room.

He was fast asleep, but he looked healthy. This cure stuff was a goddamn miracle. Winter added more to the IV line. Marcus's dosage recommendations weren't as specific as they'd been for previous treatments, but he had some rough guidelines based on his testing of the cure. Winter used half of the bottle she'd made and tucked the rest back into her bag.

Hunger still gnawed at her stomach. Winter went to a bathroom to change, then returned to the night. She paused just outside the hospital to tip her head back and study the dark sky. Amidst the thick clouds, there were sparse patches through which she could see stars glittering.

How many people were out there across the Earth, looking up at the same space? What were lives like in the other cities and territories? Were they all as rotten as Devil's Pass, or were there places where people took better care of each other?

Chapter Twenty-Two
Caught

Winter fell asleep waiting for a sandwich in a diner, and then again after she'd finished the thing. At ten p.m. the waitress gently shook her awake and informed her they were closing. Winter numbly made her way to the nearest trolley stop and rode home, drifting off a couple more times on the journey.

Her parents had been at the back of her mind throughout the day, but she hadn't actually had a moment to think about what she was going to say to them. She blankly climbed the icy steps up to her apartment and wondered if they were even home. Or awake.

Unfortunately, the answer to both of those questions was yes.

"Winter! Where have you been all day?" Dad demanded as soon as she opened the door. "We didn't see you once! No call! No mention of work—speaking of, I called the hospital, and the lady who answered the phone hadn't heard of you! Care to explain?"

"A lot of people work there. I don't know all of them and they definitely don't all know me." Winter adjusted her bag. "I left early this morning because I had a shift and—"

Dad interrupted her rambling explanation. "What's in that bag?"

"It's my work bag! You've seen it!" Winter's defensive tone wasn't doing much to help her case, but she didn't have the capacity to force calm right now.

"What do you even put in there, anyway?" Dad pointed to the table. "Come on. Show us what's inside, if you have nothing to hide."

"I've had it for weeks," Winter tried again.

Mom stepped in. "Winter, if you have nothing to hide, just open the bag. Please. We're worried about you." She shot Dad a concerned look that he didn't notice.

All right. It might be a hard sell, but if it worked, Winter could kill two birds with one stone: show that she had nothing suspicious in her bag, and prove she was working at the hospital. She grabbed the zipper and pulled. "Okay, okay, it's not a big deal. Most of the stuff in here right now isn't mine, it's the Plague Saint's." The beaked mask came out. Winter held it up to the light.

"He had an emergency today and asked me to hold onto a few things for him," she continued. "Apparently, someone broke into his lab, and he's been worried about security."

"So, he asked some new hire to take his stuff?" Dad still sounded skeptical, but his tone had calmed considerably.

Winter shrugged. "I thought it was weird, too, but he's a weird guy. I guess he figured no one would think to check my bag. And none of it is actually that important. Just a couple of extra masks and uniforms and an old notebook." She held out the mask to her father, an unspoken offer to take a closer look.

He shook his head. "We didn't hear from you once today. What the hell were you thinking?"

Winter set the mask back in the bag. "I'm—I'm so sorry. You're right. I didn't sleep well last night, and I was out of it all day."

"This is still unacceptable," Dad said.

Mom stepped forward and rested a hand on Winter's shoulder. Winter grimaced.

"We were worried sick," Mom said. "We were afraid you caught a plague or something, Winter. We kept waiting for the hospital to call us."

Winter forced herself to meet her mother's gaze. "I'm so sorry. It won't happen again. I swear I'll call next time." She dared to look at her father. "I do have another shift tomorrow, and if you guys aren't up before I leave, I'll leave a note, or—"

"That would be fine!" Dad exclaimed. "You just can't disappear for an entire day. Especially after lying to us for two weeks about your job and getting arrested!"

Winter nodded. What else could she say, anyway? "I'm going to go to bed," she said softly.

"Good idea," Dad replied.

"It's been a rough few days. I'm sure you could use some rest," Mom agreed.

Winter picked up her bag and went to her room. She was looking forward to getting some real sleep. Tomorrow would undoubtedly be another long day, and she still had no idea how to prevent Marcus from giving cure to the mayor and the council without having her identity revealed. Or getting River killed.

Once she was lying down, it didn't take her long to drift into unconsciousness. But it wasn't a full night's sleep that waited for her. The next thing Winter knew, she was jolting awake in the dark, her senses having picked up...something.

What had triggered her mind to wake her up? Winter laid in the dark for a moment, listening. Nearly a minute passed before a distant thud echoed through the apartment, so faint that she thought she might have imagined it. She jumped to her feet anyway and crept to her bedroom door. The thud came again as she stepped into the hall. It was coming from the direction of the kitchen. She glanced the other way, at the door to her parents' room. Silence.

Another thud drew her out to the kitchen in time to see a rock hit the window. Winter darted to the window and peered down at the street.

Standing under the streetlight was Phoebe.

Winter glanced at the clock. Nearly four a.m. The hell? She turned on a lamp on a table near the window and waved a hand to show Phoebe she'd seen her. Then, she ran to her room to get dressed.

After a moment's hesitation, Winter decided to grab the bag, just in case. Thinking ahead for once, she also scribbled down a note on a piece of paper saying that she'd left for the hospital and that she'd call her parents when she had lunch.

She left the note on the table, crept out the front door as quietly as possible, and carefully made her way down the icy stairs.

"What are you doing here?" Winter asked as she approached Phoebe.

"Sorry." Phoebe stood with her arms folded, her expression as cold as the night. "I couldn't sleep."

She did look tired. Exhausted, actually. Those bags under her eyes bordered on alarming.

"And what were you going to do if I didn't wake up? Wait out here until morning?" Winter glanced around the empty street. "How did you even know I lived here? And which window was mine?"

"I went to the station this afternoon, after what you said about getting arrested. I know you didn't actually do anything." Phoebe's eyes narrowed. Winter never thought she'd see intensity like this in her expression. "But they said that you quit the station weeks ago. So,

I got your address there and figured out which window matched your apartment number."

Surprising as it was, Winter couldn't fault her for good investigative work.

"Why did you lie to me?" Phoebe pressed when Winter didn't offer an explanation. "And why did the Plague Saint think you still worked there?"

"I can explain," Winter said. "I will. But did you talk to your uncle?"

"I did." Phoebe glanced at the ground. "He said that he moved to the boat because his other lab was compromised. He's working for the mayor now."

"Yes! I know!" Winter exclaimed. "But you saw the decoded notes. He made a white plague."

"Oh, like the decoded notes in the journal you stole from our apartment?"

Marcus had figured that out. Great. Winter flung up her arms. "So what? That doesn't change what he did!"

"What do you mean 'so what?'" Phoebe demanded, her gaze shooting back up to meet Winter's. Her voice was hoarse enough to make Winter grimace. "You broke into my family's home!"

"Because I knew what Marcus was doing and I needed proof!"

"And how did you know what he was doing?" Phoebe's expression softened abruptly. The anger dropped out of her voice, and the difference was startling. "Please. I'm scared. I don't want to believe my uncle is hurting people. But he told me he knew you'd stolen the journals, and he didn't seem surprised that you found the boat. It's like you two are enemies, but he won't tell me why!"

Winter swallowed. The streetlight above them flickered.

"How did you find out all this about my uncle, Winter?" Phoebe asked. "And if you haven't been working at the station, what have you been doing the past few weeks?"

"Phoebe, Marcus was—Marcus was the Plague Saint," Winter began, nearly choking on the words.

"Was?"

"And I—" Winter shrugged off her bag and held it out. "I've been the Plague Saint since just before you started working at the hospital." Her left hand found the zipper, pulled it open, and drew out the mask.

Phoebe stared at it. "I've known you—this entire time. It's been you."

Winter nodded.

"Why did you take over for Marcus?" Phoebe frowned. "Wait, those weeks he was missing, that was right after—"

"He was going to kill my mom," Winter blurted. "I didn't know his name or who he was. But I overheard him talking to Adams about how they were deliberately letting certain people die. Saving their rich friends, killing the poor who wouldn't be able to pay for the treatment. And their enemies."

Phoebe's gaze lifted to the apartment building behind Winter. "Your mother's still alive."

Winter nodded.

"What did you do?"

Winter couldn't force out anything more than a whisper. "It was an accident."

"*What did you do?*"

"I thought I killed him!" The bag slipped from Winter's hand, and the mask fell on top of it. She squeezed her hands into fists. "I thought he was dead, so I threw him in the river. And he left all these notes and journals, and the uniform fit, and I thought I could take his place! At least long enough to do some good."

Phoebe staggered backwards until her back was pressed to the streetlight post.

The heartbeat of silence that followed was too much. All Winter could do was continue rambling. "And then my brother was sick, and Adams wanted him dead, and I went to your house and your uncle was alive and he knew I tried to kill him and—"

"Wait. Go back," Phoebe interrupted.

"What?"

"Go back. Adams. His death." Phoebe trembled. "Did you...?"

Winter didn't answer. Couldn't answer. Phoebe pressed a shaking hand over her mouth.

"And then—then George Gordon died the same way—!"

"They were killing people, Phoebe!" Winter winced at her volume, praying she hadn't woken anyone up. Quieter, but her tone just as harsh, she continued. "And they plan to let more die. Devil's Pass is better off without them. Look, at first, I was just trying to save my mom and River. But then I realized I could save everyone. I *have* to save everyone!"

"By killing off the people running the city?" Phoebe wrapped her arms around herself. God, she looked like she was on the verge of collapse.

Winter didn't dwell on her concern for long. She just had to make Phoebe understand. "Yes!" She took a few steps forward, ignoring the terror that widened Phoebe's eyes. "If we kill them, we can replace them with better people. People who will do better or face the same fate."

"Do you have any idea how much chaos that would cause? Devil's Pass is struggling as it is. If our entire government collapsed at once—"

"I can't let them keep killing people!" Winter paused, desperately searching for the right words. There had to be some way to make her understand. "It's the trolley problem!"

"What?" Phoebe shook her head. "That wasn't—you're not supposed to take that seriously!"

"Why not?"

"It's not that simple! It never is!" Phoebe sank to the ground. Even the support of the post wasn't enough to keep her upright now. "What, are you going to kill the mayor next? He has children!"

"And he's passing a law that will kill countless children that aren't his!"

"There are better ways!"

"What ways? Voting in someone better? There's no time," Winter told her. "There are never good candidates, anyway."

"You're—you can't be serious."

"I am." Winter took a step forward and was surprised to see fear flicker across Phoebe's face. Phoebe couldn't possibly think Winter would hurt her, could she? "Seriously. Jonathan Forrest owns the city council, the financial advisor only gives money to people on her side, and the mayor's going to work the sick people to death instead of giving them a cure that we have!"

"You can't just—" Phoebe burst into a fit of coughing.

Winter frowned. "Phoebe?" Another step forward. "Are you—?"

"Stay—!" More coughing. Drops of blood on the sidewalk. "Stay back!" Phoebe pulled her knees to her chest and buried her face in her hands.

"You're sick." Winter closed the rest of the gap between them and dropped to one knee. She was stupid not to see it sooner. *Or just sleep-deprived as hell.* "Really sick. Come with me, I can—"

"No!"

Winter grabbed the bag and dove in. She had cure left, but it would take time to start working and Phoebe needed help now. "How long have you been feeling sick?" she demanded.

"I don't know. I thought I was just tired at first," Phoebe admitted. "I guess it was a few hours after the boat…"

The boat. Could she have been exposed to something there? There was a chance of catching plague everywhere, Winter supposed. But generally, if you kept your distance from strangers on the street, you were fine. It was the workers stuck in confined spaces with others who were most at risk.

"The rat cages," Winter remembered. "You were bleeding—did you put a hand through the bars? Did one of them bite you?" She looked up from her bag at Phoebe.

Phoebe looked up too, desperation in her eyes. "I didn't think it was a big deal," she whispered.

Oh God. She could have white plague. Actually, given the quick amount of time it took for symptoms to appear, she probably had some nasty combination. Winter found the bottle of cure as Phoebe dropped her head again.

Directly into the blood would be faster, but Winter had no way of doing that out here. Phoebe needed the hospital.

Half now, half later, Winter decided. She found an empty bottle in the bag that hadn't been used for anything yet and poured half the remaining cure in. She held it out to Phoebe. "Drink. Now. Come on."

"What is it," Phoebe mumbled.

"Cure, you idiot."

"You're not going to kill me for knowing your secret?" She was getting worse, fast.

"If I wanted you dead, I'd leave you out here alone," Winter said. "Come on. Please."

Phoebe lifted her chin and held out a shaking hand. Winter handed her the bottle. "Try not to spill it."

Thankfully, Phoebe managed to get all of the liquid down before the bottle slipped from her grasp. It clattered against the sidewalk and rolled into the empty street.

Winter pulled out the Plague Saint uniform.

Chapter Twenty-Three
Devil's Bridge

Winter stumbled into the hospital, struggling to keep a near-unconscious Phoebe upright at her side. The lobby was empty except for the receptionist, which wasn't unusual for four-thirty in the morning.

"I need a room. Now," Winter told the woman working.

"Plague Saint? What are you doing here this early?" The woman looked at Phoebe. "Let me call one of the doctors—"

"I'm a doctor, and my assistant is sick. Get me a bed and send down any nurse that's available."

"Of course." She leaned over and pressed a button on the radio sitting on her desk. "We need a team in the lobby immediately, we have a—" Her hesitant gaze darted up to where Winter's eyes were hidden behind the mask. "Code red?"

"Code white."

Her eyes widened. "Code white. We need a room right away. Thank you."

A team of nurses showed up within minutes and moved Phoebe onto a rolling bed. Winter followed them to the tower, barking orders. "Get her hydrated. I need the IV bag prepped as fast as possible. I have medicine for her. Make sure she's closely monitored. I don't want her alone for more than ten minutes at a time." Winter didn't want her left alone at all, but that simply wasn't possible.

As soon as the IV bag was ready, Winter added the cure herself, ignoring the watchful eyes of the nurses.

Finally, Phoebe was settled, but Winter didn't feel any relief. She was completely out of it now and had a high fever.

"I'll be back in ten minutes, then," the last nurse said before leaving. He paused by the door. It sounded more like a question than a statement.

Winter nodded. "Yes. Good. Do that."

"Will you still be here?"

Would she? She had other things to deal with. "Probably not," she told him.

The nurse disappeared into the hall. The door clicked shut behind him.

Winter had given the rest of the cure she'd made to Phoebe. Hopefully it would be enough. But Phoebe was Marcus's niece, after all. He'd probably be happy to spare some cure to save her. *Hypocrite.*

It was River that Winter should be worrying about now. She had enough leftover ingredients to mix together a little more cure for him, but it would take hours, and she was expected to start working on the big batch for the city council—

The door opened. Winter turned around, expecting a nurse.

Marcus Blackburn entered the room.

Winter stumbled back a few steps. Her back hit the wall. "What are you doing here?"

"I'm the new hospital director, remember?"

He certainly looked the part, now. He was dressed in a white suit, his hair had been slicked back, and he appeared to have covered up the worst of his bruises and scratches with makeup.

"Adams never hung out here at four in the morning, as far as I know," Winter said.

"Adams wasn't dealing with what I'm dealing with." Marcus drew his revolver. "I warned you, Winter. I gave you a chance." He gestured with the gun. "Take the mask off."

Winter did as he asked. The piece that covered her eyes, then the beak. Clutching the two parts in her hands, she asked, "Are you going to kill me?"

"I'm not letting you off that easy. Everyone's going to know who you are and what you've done. Come on." He nodded toward the door.

Winter shoved the mask into the bag, removed the hat to throw it in too, and crossed the room. "There's not a lot of people here right now," she said. "If you're so set on exposing me, you should wait—"

"Oh, word will spread," Marcus cut her off. "But I appreciate the concern. Now move. I don't want you dead, but I won't hesitate to shoot you in the foot."

Winter reached the door. Turned the handle. Paused. "How are you going to make enough cure for your friends?"

"I'll just have to take the time to teach someone else to do it. I've brought quite a few people into my employment this week."

"You're going to save Phoebe, right?"

"Stop trying to buy yourself time. Of course I am." Marcus snapped. "And set the bag down by the door. You don't need it anymore."

Winter glanced at the bag she held in one hand. At the door she held open with the other. Now or never. She bent over, acting as if she were going to set the bag down and stepping through the door as she did.

At the last possible second, she yanked the bag up and slammed the door shut.

The gunshot echoed through the hallway. The bullet that left a hole in the door missed Winter by several feet. *Idiot.* Half the hospital would have heard the sound.

Then again, it might benefit Marcus to have people come rushing over here. Regardless, Winter had to act fast. She stepped back from the door while plunging a hand into the bag to fish around for the staff. The door handle turned.

She wrapped both hands tight around the staff, letting the bag fall to the ground. As soon as the gap between the door and the wall was wide enough, she swung in an overhead arc.

The staff connected with the side of Marcus's face. Not as solid a blow as she'd wanted, but she supposed it was pretty good, considering the circumstances. It was enough to throw him off balance for a few moments. That was all she needed.

Winter grabbed the door to keep it from closing and swung again, this time hitting the hand holding the gun. It clattered to the floor. She bent down to scoop it up with her free hand.

Marcus grabbed her arm as she straightened up. Winter struggled, but she didn't have a chance of breaking free from his iron grip. His other hand moved to grab the gun back. Winter stomped on his foot. He hissed in pain but didn't relent.

Winter's thumb found the button on the top of the staff. There was a click, and then the end was sliding off, freeing the blade. Winter slashed blindly.

The blade sliced through Marcus's pristine white suit jacket and left a gash in his upper arm. He didn't let go entirely, but his grip loosened enough for Winter to yank her arm free. She staggered backwards and pointed the gun at him.

Marcus held up his hands. "Have you ever even fired a gun?"

Winter didn't respond, but her shaking hand gave her away. She didn't have a prayer of hitting anything she aimed at. And the first gunshot had already drawn attention, if the distant yelling and approaching footsteps from every direction were anything to go by.

The mask was off, but the rest of the uniform was still very clearly the Plague Saint's. Anyone who saw her would know she was the Saint. Would that be a bad thing? Marcus could easily twist her into the bad guy, maybe even blame her for the deaths he'd caused. Or he could tell part of the truth and reveal she'd tried to kill him, the real Saint.

Best not to let anyone see her.

Winter kept the gun pointed at Marcus as she backed away, eyes darting around for some path of escape. A door to her left opened into a narrow hallway that, according to a sign overhead, led to a pair of elevators.

As Winter moved to the door, Marcus lowered his hands. "You can't run forever, Winter. I'll be right behind you."

"Whatever you say, asshole," Winter growled. She slipped into the hallway and sprinted toward the elevators. They waited on the left about halfway down the hall. Past them, at the far end of the corridor, was a stairwell.

As Winter passed the elevators, she slammed the up button. The ding of the doors opening echoed down the hall, undoubtedly loud enough for Marcus to hear. Winter kept going and flew into the stairwell.

She dared to slow her pace as she moved up the stairs, trying to find a balance between speed and silence. She was halfway up the first flight when she heard another ding from the elevators below. Marcus thought he was following her.

Winter emerged from the stairwell on the second floor and sprinted to the elevators. She hit the up button here, too. The second elevator's door opened. She hit the button again to ensure Marcus's elevator would stop before stepping into the other elevator and pressing the button for River's floor. As her elevator's door closed, she heard the other elevator opening.

She wouldn't have long. She shoved the gun into the bag and realized that she'd left the scabbard for the staff-slash-sword on the floor outside Phoebe's room. Well, nothing she could do about that now.

The elevator came to a jerky stop. The moment the door was open wide enough to let her through, she shot out and raced to River's room.

Someone was inside with him. Fear coursed through Winter when she heard the unfamiliar voice, but when she flung the door open, it was just a nurse talking to River.

"Winter!" River exclaimed. "Did you hear that gunshot? At least, that's what we think it was—"

"No time!" Winter gasped.

The nurse looked Winter up and down, her brow furrowing. "Why are you wearing the Saint's uniform?"

River frowned. "Hey, yeah, what—?"

"I said there's no time! River, can you walk?"

"Yeah, I feel great!" River replied, his enthusiasm returning. "The nurse was just saying I could probably check out this morning—"

"River, I love you, but you need to shut up and get out of here." Winter darted to the window and yanked it open.

"Uh, Winter?" River climbed out of bed. He looked a little weak, but not bad otherwise.

"Get on the fire escape," Winter ordered. She looked at the nurse. "Could you please go tell the hospital director that Phoebe Blackburn needs immediate attention? He's on his way here."

"I can't just take orders from visitors," the nurse protested. "And Phoebe Blackburn should have her own nurses—"

Winter held up the sword. "Go. Stop. Blackburn. *Please.*"

Wide-eyed, the nurse nodded and hurried out of the room.

"Winter?" River's voice was soft, now. Almost scared. That was a terrifying thing to hear. "What's happening?"

"I'm sorry." Winter swallowed and blinked back the tears that had taken her by surprise. "You're in danger and it's my fault. I need you to go home and tell Mom and Dad that you all have to stay hidden."

"What about you?"

"I'll—I'll come to you as soon as I can." Winter told him. "And explain everything. I swear. Just trust me. And if Marcus Blackburn tries to tell you anything about me, he's lying." She gestured out the window. "Now go!"

River nodded and climbed out onto the fire escape. Winter slammed the window shut and stormed to the door.

She stepped out of the room. A hand grabbed her arm. She swung with the sword but missed. Light glinted off a second blade. A smaller blade.

Marcus swiped across her stomach with his knife.

Winter cried out. He released his hold on her, and she staggered away from him, pressing a hand to the wound. While blood spilled over her fingers, Marcus stepped into River's room.

"Too late!" Despite the pain, Winter laughed. It was a welcome distraction. "He's long gone. Checked out hours ago."

Marcus stepped out of the room and threw the door shut behind him. "I'll find him. And your parents. Everyone you tried to protect will die to save this city." Blood still trickled from the gash Winter had left on his arm, but he wasn't letting his pain show on his face.

Winter backed away from him. The leather of the uniform had done a pretty good job of protecting her, she realized. The wound hurt, but she could still walk. Hopefully she could run, too.

"You're not saving Devil's Pass." Winter held up her weapon. She kept her other hand pressed to her stomach. Blackburn stalked toward her. She didn't have a prayer of overpowering him. And her chances of outrunning him for long were slim.

Maybe she could use his own move against him.

No, he wouldn't be stupid enough to fall for that. At least, not for long. But if she could make him think she was dead, she could buy herself some time. Enough time.

But it wouldn't work if she couldn't get out of here, first.

Winter lifted the sword and charged Marcus, screaming. He halted and lifted his knife in defense. At the last second, Winter veered to the left and dropped the blade. She swung and grazed his shin. He grunted in pain but swung in retaliation anyway. In her attempt to dodge, she stumbled and fell to the ground.

The sword clattered across the floor. She pushed herself up, grabbed it, and risked a glance back.

Marcus was on one knee, assessing the slice across his leg. "Go ahead, take your head start," he hissed. "I'll catch up."

Winter didn't doubt that. She didn't want to risk waiting for an elevator, nor did she want to take the stairs and find Marcus waiting at the bottom. So, she ran past both of them and headed for the second stairwell on the other side of the tower.

She stumbled down the stairs two at a time. At the first floor, she took a right and flew through the double doors labeled "Trauma Ward." A doctor in the hall on the other side watched her run past, mouth agape. Winter ignored him.

"Miss, you're bleeding!" he yelled.

"I'm well aware!" she shouted back. As she rounded the next corner, there was more yelling behind her. She swore she heard the words "Director Blackburn" leave the mouth of the doctor she'd just passed.

Winter staggered to the right and used the wall to support herself as she stumbled down the hall, eyes on a massive metal door up ahead. She reached it, twisted the handle, and pushed the door open with a grunt.

A wave of cold air washed over her. Blood storage.

"You can't hide forever!" Blackburn called. He was catching up. "I worked here for years. I know this place inside and out. You don't stand a chance!"

Winter limped across the room. She grabbed a bag of blood off a shelf as she passed, popped open the front of her coat, and shoved the bag into an inner pocket. It was near impossible to redo the buttons with one hand, but she managed. Her other hand tightened around the sword's handle.

On the other side of the frigid storage room, Winter pushed another door open. She could hear Blackburn entering as she pulled it shut.

She looked down at the blood dripping from her wound onto the white floor. An easy trail to follow. How far was the bridge from here? A five-minute walk from where she'd dumped Marcus's body, maybe?

Better move fast.

Winter broke into a run. She couldn't stop herself from letting out a cry of pain, but it didn't matter. Blackburn would follow her trail of blood, anyway, and she needed him to see her die.

She was painfully aware of Blackburn getting closer every inch of the forest she stumbled through. It wasn't far to the river itself, but finding the bridge took so long she truly feared she wouldn't make it. And she'd been stupid enough to let Marcus chase her into the woods, with no one around to save her. At least in the hospital, she could have called for help.

And then ended up in prison after Marcus told everyone what you did.

This was her best shot.

And there was the bridge. Winter paused at the edge. The damn thing looked like it would collapse under the slightest breeze. She set one foot on it. Then another. Rustling behind her told her Marcus was moments away. She moved to the center, where she pulled herself up onto the bridge's railing.

"Winter!" Blackburn was almost to the edge of the bridge.

"Don't come any closer," Winter warned. She pointed the blade at him, though it wasn't much of a threat in the condition she was in.

Blackburn slowed, to her relief, and stopped at the edge of the bridge. "What are you doing?"

"You want me dead? Well, I'm going to save you the trouble. You're welcome."

She held the blade up to her chest and pressed it to the edge of the bag of blood she'd stolen. "Kill them all. See what I care. But you know what will happen when you destroy the people beneath you?"

she asked. "The chain of command will shift. Leave only people with power, and they'll fight for what power is left. Once you've killed the people you've deemed useless, you'll see it's your elite who are the useless ones. And Devil's Pass will rot away."

"I'm not stupid, Winter." Marcus scowled. "I know the difference between valuable lower-class workers and the people who are poor because they do nothing. I know who to save and who to kill."

Winter didn't have the time nor the words to explain that no one wanted to be useless. No one was poor for lack of trying. How could Marcus not see that, with his family struggling?

She was running out of time. "You could save all of them, you—" She swayed, and frantically waved an arm to keep her balance. "—you greedy rat. But you won't. And I'm not sticking around to watch them die." The blade sank in, slicing through the coat. "I'd rather go out on my terms than yours, anyway."

The bag burst, and blood spilled. Winter pulled her hand away and held it up, feigning a dazed expression. More dazed than she really felt, anyway. At the edge of her vision, she could see Blackburn watching the blood spray from her body. Far more blood than any person could survive losing.

And now came the worst part. Winter swayed again. This was going to hurt. Like. Hell. And it might actually kill her.

She closed her eyes and fell from the bridge.

Chapter Twenty-Four
Six of Plagues

The river swallowed Winter, tore her blade and bag from her, and turned her blood to ice. She slammed against the bottom. Rocks scraped at every inch of exposed skin.

She resisted the urge to break the surface for as long as she could. Then, she realized she might not make it to the surface. She'd expected currents to whisk her down the river. She hadn't expected them to turn her upside down so quickly.

So, this was hell. Dark and frozen. No sense of direction, no air to breathe, no light to guide her.

It was hard to think about anything other than the cold. Winter instinctively pulled in her arms and legs, trying to bundle herself up as much as possible. But that left her drifting with no control.

She kicked her legs out. They struck something solid. The ground was gone an instant after she found it, but at least she knew which way to go now. She forced her arms out and fought against the water.

She broke the surface long enough to suck in a breath of air. Then the current was taking her back under. Her arms waved around desperation, trying to aim her up while also moving toward the shore. She found the surface again.

The shoreline was barely visible in the dark, but Winter could tell it was far away on both sides. She pushed herself in the direction of the city, slipping in and out of the water. It was getting harder to move. At least the pain of the freezing water distracted her from the string of the knife wound in her stomach.

A shadow loomed over the river up ahead. A fallen tree, stretched out over the water. Winter watched it grow closer every time she managed to break the surface.

She slammed into the trunk hard, and what little air she had left escaped her lungs. The current threatened to drag her under the tree. She reached out blindly and grabbed onto nearby branches, unfazed by the smaller ones that jabbed into her as the water knocked her against them.

It took all of her strength to hold on. She sucked in air again and again and still couldn't quite seem to catch her breath.

It took five minutes and over a dozen failed attempts to pull herself on top of the trunk. She collapsed face down onto the wet bark. Cold water sprayed her face and she felt nothing.

Winter propped herself up and leaned back against a branch. Her eyes drifted shut, and she forced them open. Again. And again. She couldn't bring herself to move any more, but she'd be damned if she let the darkness take her.

The sky turned from black to gray. The sun was coming, she told herself. She swore to herself that she'd feel the light again. She wasn't done yet.

The first rays of morning spilled over the mountains and into Devil's Pass. Night faded, revealing the sword caught in the branches beneath Winter, and the bag bobbing up and down a few feet away.

Pain returned to her stomach. Winter unbuttoned her coat and lifted her shirt enough to assess the wound. As if the gash weren't enough, she'd been underwater, and God knew what kind of filth in the river could have gotten in. She needed disinfectant and bandages.

She used to carry more medical supplies in the bag, but most of those had been replaced by notebooks and bottles over the past week. But there was a place nearby that had plenty of supplies Winter could use.

If she could make it that far.

She moved slowly, testing the muscles in her arm before fully extending it toward the nearest branch. Her body refused to let her forget that she was freezing and soaking and aching all at once. That added to the challenge of navigating the branches, but Winter eventually made it to the bag. She almost fell into the water trying to get the sword, but she managed to keep a tight grip on the branch over her head while she grabbed the handle. With the outer shell of the staff gone, she'd have to find something else to keep the blade in.

Winter secured the bag over her shoulder and scrambled to the top of the fallen tree. Keeping her body low, she awkwardly and painstakingly made her way to shore, taking her time to move around branches carefully, throwing frequent glances at the river racing below.

She followed the shoreline to Marcus's boat. Her pace slowed when she remembered the guards that had shown up last time, but there was no sign of life, and the forest was as quiet as it could be. Apprehension fading, she approached the boat.

Seeing as it took both hands and all her remaining strength to get her body up the ladder, Winter was forced to leave the bag and sword sitting on the dock. She barely made it onto the deck before collapsing in a heap of heavy clothes and numb limbs.

You have to get inside, she told herself. *You have to get warm or you're going to die.*

Winter pushed herself off the wet wood of the deck and staggered into the cabin. The boat's lab held a far different scene from when she'd last been there. A horrifying one.

Every last rat was dead. Their bodies had been moved to trays on the counter. A few bloody scalpels littered the space between them. Winter found herself fighting back nausea on top of the pain she was already battling.

A bloodstained letter also sat on the counter. Winter gingerly picked it up, not wanting to touch the blood even with her gloves on. It was another letter from the mayor, shorter than the last and hastily scrawled.

Still on for the meeting tonight at seven. Everyone will get their medicine and we'll arrange for it to be made available to selected workers. By Friday afternoon we will be ready to release your weapon.

Weapon. Marcus had called the plagues weapons. Winter was shaking from more than just cold, now. What did Atherton mean by "release?" How many people could they possibly infect at once? If they were planning to treat every worker they needed alive, then they were anticipating widespread exposure.

Winter grabbed the counter to steady herself. She was still bleeding, she reminded herself. But before she could deal with anything else, she needed to get out of her wet clothes and get warm. Then she could handle the knife wound.

She pulled off her coat and tossed it onto the counter. As she peeled off more layers, she dug through cupboards. Scattered among the lab equipment and medical supplies were a few more lanterns and some blankets. She lit all of the lanterns, arranged them in a circle, and plopped herself down in the middle. The blanket she'd wrapped herself in was a bit scratchy, but it was thick and warm. Good enough.

Once some feeling had returned to her fingers, Winter rose to her feet and went back to searching, this time for bandages and disinfectant.

She tried a few cupboards she thought she recalled seeing first aid items in. One of them turned out to be a mini freezer containing a rack filled with vials that, judging by the red stains, had been filled with blood not long ago.

Winter grabbed one and squinted at the label. Then another. Each blood sample had been infected with a different plague. Comprehension dawned on her, making her stomach churn. The rats had been kept alive as vessels to store the various plagues until Marcus was ready. And now he'd used them to make God-knew-how-much of a serum that could kill within a day.

Bleeding. You're bleeding. Winter moved onto a set of drawers and found a bandage roll. The drawer beneath that one contained a bottle of hydrogen peroxide. She popped open the cap, adjusted the blanket to expose her bleeding stomach, and poured. The ensuing pain made Winter's eyes sting. She bit back a cry of distress and kept going.

Once she was satisfied the wound was clean, she wrapped the length of bandage around her abdomen until it seemed it would be enough to stop the bleeding, and then she went around a few more times.

Winter continued her search and found painkillers, which she swallowed eagerly. She took the bottle with her. Sleep would be nice, too, but that wasn't something she could afford right now. And she certainly couldn't risk it on Marcus's boat.

Another cupboard, one Winter hadn't touched yet, held several large bottles. The dark liquid inside definitely wasn't medicine. Winter leaned forward and squinted at the small text scrawled on the label. Her jaw clenched. This was it. A combination of all six plagues. As if the horrific white plague Marcus had created wasn't enough.

She grabbed one of the bottles.

Winter also grabbed a towel when she found where the clean ones were stored. The best she could do for now was wrap the sword in something that would allow her to keep it hidden, hopefully without causing damage to either the blade or anything else in the bag.

One last thing. The copy of the cure recipe she'd made had undoubtedly been ruined by the bag's dip in the river. Winter picked up one of the notebooks littering the counters, tore out a page, and sifted through journals until she found the written procedure for making cure. She copied it down.

Her clothes were still damp. A little warmer now from their time laid out by the lanterns, but that would change when they met the outside air again. Winter reluctantly pulled them back on. Once dressed, she gathered up everything that would be coming with her and left the boat. She loaded up the bag on the dock, including the now towel-wrapped sword.

She turned and scanned the river before setting off. It looked surprisingly calm on the surface, considering the violent currents she knew lay underneath. Something about the sight of all that water moving so quickly gave her pause. There was a thought, an idea, just out of reach. Like the surface of the river when she was tumbling across the bottom.

Oh. God. The river. The canal. It was a guaranteed path to every person in the city.

And that explained all of the bottled water in Forrest's basement.

But the boat couldn't be the dispersal point; it was downstream of the canals. And what about the water filtration system? Marcus had noted that the bacteria that caused the plagues were resilient, but did he really believe they could make it all the way through the water supply to people's homes?

Well, if he believed it, Winter wasn't exactly one to argue.

She crossed the dock to the shoreline. She couldn't keep pushing herself, the aches in her body warned. And if she spent any longer in these clothes that were practically frozen again already, she was going to lose her mind, and quite possibly a few extremities.

The sky was beginning to lighten in the east, advertising the sun's imminent arrival. Hopefully, by the time Winter made it back into the city, at least a few shops would be open.

The Saint's coat was too recognizable, so she shoved that in the bag when she reached the paved streets. Minutes later, she was hurrying into an open clothing store. The wad of emergency cash in her pocket was damp, but usable. And there were enough bills to pay for her new outfit—completely black, similar to the clothes she already had on.

"You fall in the river or something?" the girl ringing her up asked.

"Something like that." Winter grabbed the pile of clothes. "Mind if I change in the dressing room?"

"Go ahead."

Her purchase included a thick, hooded coat. Winter pulled the hood up as she stepped outside. It looked like it was going to be a clear day. Maybe the wind would stay away, too.

There was a building opposite the hospital—next to the restaurant Winter changed in before work—that housed a few shops on the first floor and a diner on the second. Winter requested a seat by the diner's window and strategically divided what remained of her cash to spend throughout the day so that the waiters wouldn't kick her out. With a steady stream of coffees and the occasional pastry coming her way, she took stock.

The notebook and papers that had been in the bag during her trip down the river were completely ruined. A few of the smaller vials of cure ingredients had broken and spilled, adding to the mess, but everything else was salvageable. Winter laid out the uniform and her other clothes on the bench across from her in hopes they would finish drying.

She copied down the cure recipe about a dozen times. She also dozed off a dozen times, and no amount of reprimanding herself stopped it. As much as she wanted to sleep, she was running out of time. The assembly meeting was tonight, Marcus would be releasing the white plague soon, and she had no idea what to do about it.

There had to be something. She could go up the river to where the city's canal began and come up with a way to prevent Marcus from dumping his death serum in the river. She could kill anyone who showed up. No, that wouldn't work. How would she make them drink poison?

Well, she could always kill them some other way. She did still have the revolver, although she wasn't confident in her ability to use it, nor was she entirely sure it would work after being waterlogged.

Maybe she'd finally have to use the sword for its intended purpose.

Winter laid her head down in her arms. She was so goddamn tired. She didn't want to do this. She turned to stare out the window at the hospital bathed in afternoon sunlight. She watched the front doors, her mind empty, for maybe an hour or so. People came and went, and she didn't care until Marcus emerged, Phoebe at his side.

She straightened up, her surprise gifting her a surge of energy. Phoebe was walking. Good. Marcus must have done everything in his power to save her. He really did care about her, despite his willingness to let so many others die.

The two turned at the sidewalk and walked in the opposite direction of the trolley stop. Winter frowned. Where were they going?

The church. Of course. But why was Phoebe going with Marcus? Because she worked as a church maiden? Did she know what was going to happen tonight? Did any of the maidens?

Winter glanced at the diner's clock. The meeting wouldn't start for over an hour, if that last letter she'd seen from the mayor was still accurate. That would give her some time to investigate the canal for any signs that Marcus did plan to dump serum there.

Winter swallowed four more painkillers and set out.

Chapter Twenty-Five
Hallowed Ground

The canal branched off from the river north of the bridge. Winter gave the bridge an anxious glance as she walked by, shuddering at the memory of standing on it that morning. The bloodstained wood revealed where she'd stumbled across. Where she'd climbed onto the railing. How long had Marcus waited there after she went in the river? Did he really believe she was dead? Had he told Phoebe?

Just past that was the massive pipe that drew in water for the city. But there was nothing out of place in the area around it. Winter crossed over the pipe and continued north.

Nearly ten minutes later, she spotted a figure in the forest ahead. She ducked behind a tree and peered around the trunk.

Jonathan Forrest stood with his back to her, assessing some metal contraption that sat on the side of the river. It was difficult to make out details from here. She needed a closer look.

Winter glanced down at her clothes. They were all black, but noticeably different from the Saint's uniform. Well, if Forrest pointed it out, she could spout any number of believable lies. She grabbed the mask and hat from the bag and put them on.

"Forrest!" Winter called as she approached. But her eyes were on the contraption, not him. The main body was a cylinder, with a pipe opening into the river, and a ladder leading to a hatch in the top that allowed access to the space inside.

"Plague Saint!" Forrest turned and waved. "I assume you're coming to the assembly meeting tonight?"

"Of course. I just came to give this a look." Winter gestured to the—*thing.*

Forrest walked toward her, swaying as he did. "Impressive right?" He lowered his voice and leaned in. "Engineers did pretty good, even though they didn't really know what it was for. Even set it on a timer so we don't have to be here. Slow, steady dispersal over the course of a few days." His words slurred into each other at the end of that last sentence. He laughed.

Slow, steady dispersal. Marcus's poison would creep into every last corner of the city.

Winter frowned. "Why bring in more outsiders than necessary? I thought you were an engineer, anyway."

"I'm just a businessman." More laughter, as if that statement were hilarious.

"But you designed the trolley system."

"Oh, no, I just bought the idea. Steal of a price, too. The idiots who actually came up with the thing—well, I don't know what they're doing these days. Probably begging for scraps on the street." Forrest took a swig from the bottle in his hand. Surprising, considering how composed he'd been at the last assembly meeting. Was he planning on sobering up before attending tonight's dinner?

Regardless, he was happy to keep spilling secrets. "Mayor told me I had to make the trolleys free to ride. Swore the financial advisor would compensate me for it, but factory owners and other businesses needed easy transportation for their workers," he explained. "This whole plague mess is perfect. Now I have some leverage, you know?"

"I don't think I quite follow," Winter told him. Her hand hovered over her bag, still open from when she'd grabbed the mask. Her fingers twitched.

"To force a fare. I'll go to the council and say, 'the trolleys are too crowded, the plagues will spread like wildfire. If we charge people to use 'em, we reduce that.'"

"And the people who need them to work?"

Forrest shrugged. "Guess they better save their money."

Okay, he didn't care about people, but he cared about himself and his money. And his money didn't just come from other rich people attending his clubs anymore. "You own some of the factories now. If your workers can't get to the building, you'll lose money..."

"Trust me, people will find ways to get to work when it comes down to it. They can walk if they have to." Another swig of the drink. "And there's no shortage of people looking for jobs. Even once the weakest start dying, there will always be more teenagers looking to support their families."

Winter's eyes narrowed. "Okay. Well. Good luck with that. I'm actually glad you're here, they sent me to find you." Her gaze flickered to the cylinder hanging over the river. "Has that thing been filled yet?"

"Uh, yeah. Blackburn wanted everything ready to go by tomorrow morning. Once we've all been treated with his new medicine, well..." Forrest made a vague motion with his hand. "Bombs away."

"There's actually been a change in plans. We need to postpone the dispersal and move this thing—"

Forrest chuckled, interrupting the lie she'd hoped would be convincing to a drunk fraud. "Sorry, Saint, but I'm going to need confirmation from Atherton and Blackburn. You're useful, but you're not exactly like the rest of us."

"And Marcus Blackburn is?" Winter snapped.

"Woah." Forrest held up his hands. Dark alcohol sloshed out of the bottle and splattered on the thin layer of snow beneath them. "Don't take it personally. It's just that the hierarchy here is more like you work for us but not really with us, you know?"

Winter yanked out the sword and angrily tossed the bag onto the ground. She pointed the blade at Forrest, the tip coming dangerously close to his neck. "Can you or can you not shut down this contraption, you fucking fraud?"

"What the hell?" The bottle slipped from his hands. "Look, I told you, I didn't design it! I have no idea how it works. Please don't—"

Winter swung.

She left Forrest bleeding out from his neck on the ground while she made her way to the contraption and up the ladder to investigate the hatch. The damn thing was locked. She examined the padlock, wondering who had the key. Marcus? Atherton? Maybe it was hidden somewhere safe.

No matter. There were ways to break a lock, and as Forrest had so kindly mentioned, she had until tomorrow morning.

Winter walked back to where her bag lay on the ground, wrapped the sword back up, and slid the weapon inside. Occasionally, her gaze moved to Forrest, and the sight of his body did nothing to wipe away the odd, detached numbness that had settled over her after she'd swung the sword.

Cold logic guided her now. She couldn't leave him here where another council member might stumble across him. Throwing him into the river above the canal could contaminate the water supply— the filtration system could only handle so much—and moving him below the canal intake would take too long.

The meeting started soon. She'd have to deal with him later. For now, she'd hide him. There was more than enough overgrowth to do the trick, and he easily vanished into the shadows of a thorny bush.

Winter's next stop was the church.

She smashed the lock on the church's rarely used back door with a large rock and crept inside. Distant noise warned her that there were plenty of people in the building, but she didn't run into any of them on her way down the corridor. She tried doors until she found a storage room.

Racks of church maiden gowns took up most of the room's space, with bins of masks balanced on top of them. Winter changed into one of the gowns. She tucked all of her hair under the hood. Then, she put on the church maiden mask.

The gown didn't have pockets. Winter lifted the skirt and made an incision in the inner lining with her pocketknife. She wouldn't be able to carry much without anyone noticing, and there was no way she could make the sword fit. She settled on shoving the bottle of liquid death into the inner lining of the gown and hid her bag behind the grate of an air vent.

She left the room and continued down the hall to an intersection. The faint drone of conversation came from the direction of the chapel ahead, but closer, clearer voices were audible to the left. A woman's voice barking orders was particularly distinct.

Winter went left and stopped in front of an open door. Church maidens filled the room on the other side, swarming around tables filled with platters of food. A table at the back wall—next to some rows of shelves packed with bottles and boxes—caught Winter's attention. On it, empty glasses surrounded a large jug.

A maiden stood in front of the table, emptying bottles of wine into the jug. Strange to combine so many bottles together if they were just going to be poured into glasses afterward. Unless something else needed to be added. Something everyone at the assembly meeting needed to drink.

Winter cut across the room, unnoticed among the dozens of other identical girls. Phoebe might be here. Winter scanned for girls who looked to be about the right height as she walked, but she wasn't certain any of them were Phoebe.

The girl at the drink table poured the last of the wine and reached for something new: a bottle of clear liquid.

Winter stopped next to her. "What are you doing?" she demanded before the girl could get the cap off.

The girl froze. "Um, the priestess told me to combine this with all of the drinks."

"No, I'm supposed to do that. It has to be a certain ratio. Go help that group over there get food platters ready." Winter gestured toward the tables in the middle of the room.

The girl set the bottle down and darted off. Winter picked it up. Clear liquid cure sloshed around inside. Winter glanced to her right at the crowded shelves. It was the best hiding spot within reach. She took a few steps to the closest shelf and shoved the bottle of cure into a dark corner behind a box of plates.

As she turned back around, someone shouted, "Hey!"

A priestess stormed toward her, and Winter wondered if she'd seen her hide the cure. She could run, but she couldn't just let them add the stuff to the drinks. And if they knew she stole it—

"These glasses aren't going to fill themselves," the priestess said, pointing at the jug and the empty glasses around it. "Drinks are supposed to go out in five minutes. Get going."

Might as well, Winter decided. She could keep searching for Phoebe while she worked. And with the cure out of the picture, the last big thing she had to do was shut down the contraption on the river.

While Winter returned to the table with the jug, the priestess wandered off to lecture a group of maidens standing around on the other side of the room. No one was paying Winter much attention. She knocked a glass off the table onto the carpet. When she knelt down to pick up, she was definitely hidden from view. Perfect.

She had no luck finding Phoebe while she worked, and after a few minutes she decided the task was impossible. It wasn't something she should be focused on right now, anyway, though part of her couldn't help but worry over whether Phoebe had really made a full recovery.

Maidens began to gather at Winter's table, bringing empty platters with them. They took drinks as Winter filled them. Excellent. Marcus and the rest of the city's elite would think they were drinking medicine that would save them from the death they wanted to unleash on their people.

"You get out there too," the priestess said.

It took a moment for Winter to realize the priestess was speaking to her. She hadn't noticed her approach. "Huh?"

"Take a platter. We have more than enough drinks poured for now. We need to get them out there." The priestess snapped her fingers. "Today, please."

Damn it. Winter took one of the trays and joined a line of maidens leaving the room. *They won't recognize you,* she reminded herself. *You have the mask.*

The thought didn't do much to slow her heart or stop her chest from constricting, but Winter managed to keep her hands steady as she entered the chapel and surveyed the tables. City council members, business managers, dozens of people she didn't recognize.

But there was a table of familiar faces. Mayor Atherton, Ellen Bates, and Marcus, along with a few other council members. Winter moved toward them without thinking. By the time she had the sense to reconsider, to keep herself as far from the one man who knew her identity as possible, she was too close.

"Is the Plague Saint coming tonight?" Atherton asked.

"Haven't seen him," Marcus said. "Maybe he's working on something in his lab. He doesn't really need to be here, anyway."

"Sure, sure." Atherton looked over at Winter expectantly. "Those drinks for us?" he asked.

"Oh, uh, yes," Winter mumbled. She closed the gap between her and the table and held out the platter.

As Atherton took his drink, he asked, "What about Forrest? You hear from him?"

"I saw him drinking earlier." Marcus took a drink for himself. Winter watched the glass move toward his mouth. "Probably got caught up partying somewhere. I'll go look for him later if he doesn't show up and take him a drink if I have to." The dark wine touched his lips.

Beneath Winter's mask, the barest smile crept onto her face.

Instead of returning to the food prep room with the other maidens, she took a different turn through the halls. Once she was around a corner and out of sight of anyone moving between the back room and the chapel, she abandoned the platter on the ground.

She opened the door to the storage room and walked to the vent where the grate she'd loosened still hid her bag. It was a comforting presence as it slid over her shoulder. She reached inside to check that the sword was still there.

A shadow passed over her. Winter glanced back at the figure blocking the light from the hall. The church maiden stood still, their mask looking down on Winter with something that felt a hell of a lot like judgement.

"Can I help you?" Winter asked as she straightened up.

"It is you." A hand moved up to remove the mask.

Phoebe.

"Oh." Winter's heart slammed against her ribcage. "You look well, considering, you know…"

Winter couldn't quite place all of the emotions warring on Phoebe's face, but they were certainly strong ones. Phoebe gestured wildly as she half-whispered, half-shouted at Winter. "You're supposed to be dead! What are you doing here?"

Winter removed her own mask. "Dead?"

"Mark said you stabbed yourself and jumped off a bridge into the river."

"That is technically true," Winter admitted. "Well, not the stabbing part. I stabbed a bag of blood. It wasn't my blood though. I mean, I did lose a lot of blood, but also—"

"Are you here to kill him?" Phoebe demanded, and Winter was grateful to have her rambling cut off. "Because I won't let you."

"I'm not here to stab Marcus, or whatever." Also technically true. Technically. Winter ignored the stab of guilt she felt at the relief on Phoebe's face and scrambled for a different reason for coming to the church. "I came here to—" She swallowed. "I came here to find you."

"How did you know I would be here?"

"I've been following you. Sort of. Look, I came here because I wanted to talk to you first, after Marcus forced me to fake my death," Winter said. "He pulled a gun on me, Phoebe! And attacked me with a knife! And he's already killed…God knows how many other people."

"What do you want me to do, huh? Trust you over him? He's my uncle."

"And I'm your—" Winter swallowed.

"My what? Friend?" Phoebe shook her head. "You killed—"

"I know."

"You tried to kill—"

"I know."

"You lied to everyone!"

"I know." Winter rubbed her forehead. "But even if you don't want your uncle hurt, you can't just stand aside while he and the council go through with their plans. Marcus is going to unleash the white plague on the city. Along with a mix of the other plagues." She locked her eyes with Phoebe's, mentally begging her to listen. To understand.

"I saw the contraption they're going to use, by the river," Winter continued. "They're only going to use the cure to save themselves, the rich, and people who are capable of working. They'll kill off the weakest in our population in a last resort to wipe out the plagues, because they don't think their lives are worth fighting for. Or paying for."

The muscles in Phoebe's jaw clenched. "Kill them, then, since you're so good at it."

"Phoebe, we have to do something. It doesn't have to involve killing them." Winter couldn't imagine a world where the people who planned this survived and didn't continue to find other ways to punish and kill innocents in Devil's Pass, but that wasn't what Phoebe needed to hear right now.

The anger and hurt in Phoebe's expression was fading to uncertainty. She knew better than to let her uncle get away with this, even if she loved him.

"Marcus has a strong plan and everyone in the chapel is on his side. I can't stop him alone," Winter continued. "I have a new plan. I want to get the cure to everyone." After a moment's hesitation, she added, "And I need your help."

There was still apprehension on Phoebe's face. She chewed her lip a moment before saying, "Me? Really?"

"I swear, I'm not asking you to do anything crazy," Winter said. "And I promise I won't do anything else to Marcus. No stabbing or fighting. Unless it's self-defense."

Phoebe folded her arms. "Not just him. You can't kill anyone else if you want me to even consider helping you." She took a step forward. "And if—if I help you, it's only because I don't want to watch this city fall to a plague. I don't want to see anyone else die."

Phoebe was more naïve than Winter had thought if she believed this could end without death. What did she think would happen at the end of this? Justice for the city council? A trial? Prison? They ran the city. If they were all in on this together, nothing could stop them.

Nothing but retribution.

"Of course." Winter swallowed. If anything ever were to actually drive Phoebe to murder, it would probably be tomorrow's events. And at this point, Winter just might let the girl kill her. "I swear that I won't harm anyone else from this point forward."

Phoebe sighed. "What do you need me to do?"

"First, don't tell Marcus that I'm still alive."

"Fine."

"Next, we're going to need River's help." Winter grimaced. "Could you...not tell him what I've done?"

Phoebe's eyes narrowed. "I thought you believed in what you were doing."

"I do, but—" Winter shook her head. "He deserves to know, but he deserves to hear it from me. I have to tell him everything myself."

"You're really going to tell him?" Phoebe sounded skeptical.

"I will," Winter promised. "But first, we have to save the city."

Chapter Twenty-Six
Medicine

While Phoebe went to tell Marcus that she was going to go home and rest, Winter changed back into plain clothes. She removed the now-empty bottle from the lining of the church maiden gown, left the gown in a pile on the floor, and put the bottle back in her bag.

Phoebe returned, and together, they headed back to Winter's apartment. They made the journey in silence—no point in Winter explaining the plan only to have to explain it again when they met up with River.

When the wound in Winter's stomach started throbbing again, she swallowed more painkillers. Phoebe watched and said nothing, her face displaying no hint of emotion.

After disembarking the trolley, Winter led the way up the stairs to her apartment, and Phoebe trailed a few feet behind her. Winter pounded on the front door. "River? It's me!"

The silence that followed was brief, but every second was excruciating.

"Secret code?" River called.

"Daisy."

Phoebe gave her a questioning glance. "Name of the dog we had when we were kids," Winter explained.

The door swung open. "Thank God you're okay," River said, pulling her into a hug.

Winter grimaced at the pain that flared in her abdomen. "We should probably sit down," she said as he pulled back, seeming to sense her discomfort. "I don't think any of us are in great condition."

"Right. Come in." River waved for the two to follow him into the apartment. He led them to the dining room.

Winter glanced around as they all settled into chairs around the table. "Where are Mom and Dad?"

"They, uh, went out looking for you."

Great. "Did you tell them they were in danger?"

"Trust me, I begged them not to go." River lowered his gaze. "I'm sorry. I told them what you told me, but I guess it wasn't good enough."

He hesitated, and Winter got the feeling there was more he wanted to say. "Did they tell you anything else?" she prodded.

"They said you've been acting really weird lately. And that you lied about your job, or something?" River's blue eyes lifted to meet Winter's. "I don't know. They didn't stick around long after I got back."

"They've been gone all day?" Winter's hands tightened into fists on the table. What the hell were they doing?

River nodded. "They called about half an hour ago, though, so I think they're okay."

"Where did they call from?"

"The hospital. They said if they didn't find you soon, they'd come home."

Winter couldn't deal with their parents right now. And if they came back in the middle of this, it would be over. She rose to her feet. "Then we have to get moving. I'll explain the plan on the way."

"Where are we going?" River asked, brow furrowing. He followed her lead and stood up though.

"First to Forrest's house—"

"Jonathan Forrest?"

Winter nodded. "Then to the factory you work at. If we swapped out some ingredients, could you use the equipment there to produce medicine?"

"Uh, I guess?" River said. "I'd probably have to change some settings—"

"But you know how to do that?"

"Yes."

"Great. Grab your coat."

River looked at Phoebe, apparently hoping to get answers from her, but she simply shrugged.

On the way to Forrest's, Winter briefed River on the existence of white plague and the plague cure, as well as the council's plan to hide the cure and infect the city.

The lights were on at Forrest's house, and there was no shortage of guests enjoying the music and food. Winter ignored River and Phoebe's hesitation and marched up to the open front door.

"Uh, won't we get thrown out?" Phoebe called.

Winter paused in front of the door to let them catch up. "No. None of these people care. And the host isn't here." And if anyone tried to make them leave, she had weapons.

"Never been in this part of town," River commented as he reached her side. "What are we here for?"

"Forrest is storing the stuff we need to make more plague cure." Winter led the two inside and through the crowd of dancers, raising her voice so they could hear her. "Some of it should have been moved to the hospital already, but there were a lot of boxes. I'm sure there's still some left here." At the very least, it was worth checking a dead man's house before risking a trip to the hospital where Marcus had posted guards.

Thankfully, Winter's guess was correct. About half of the supplies she'd seen during her last trip here remained. She instructed the other two on what to grab and began to empty one of the boxes so that they could carry what they needed in it.

"River, is anyone going to be at the factory this late?" Winter asked.

River paused, a bottle in each hand. "Uh, what time is it? Eight?"

"Eight-thirty."

"The regular workers should be gone, but supervisors are probably still finishing up paperwork. From what I've heard, they usually lock the place up around midnight."

Winter groaned. "I'd like to have a big batch of cure made by morning, ideally, and it's quite a process. And we'll need to get out before the morning shift starts showing up." Six hours would be enough, but they'd have to move fast.

"So, what's the plan?" River asked.

Winter sighed. "We'll have to camp out by the factory and wait for the supervisors to leave. It's going to be a late night."

The three carried their boxes out of the house without trouble. River had more questions, and Winter answered them as best she could without giving away the worst details of what she'd done. She confirmed what their parents had told him about her quitting the station for a position at the hospital and kept the lie about it being a paperwork job. From there, she managed a vague story about figuring out what was going on behind the scenes after River got sick.

Phoebe listened in silence.

They entered an alleyway next to the factory and settled onto a platform halfway up a fire escape, just high enough to give them a view of the factory's entrance.

"So, we're taking the cure to the hospital after we make it?" River asked quietly as they got comfortable. As comfortable as one could get on a metal platform, anyway.

Winter nodded. "But we're going to be very public about it. If we take it to the doctors, it'll be easy for the hospital director to step in and say it's fake. Prevent the public from ever hearing about it?"

"Couldn't he still say it's fake, anyway?"

"Not if we can treat some people with it before he gets the chance." Winter looked out at the nearby street, at the lights of the city glowing in the dark, occasionally blinking out as businesses shut down and people went to bed.

"They're desperate," she added, quieter. "They'll try anything. And this should give us some credibility." She opened her bag and pulled out the mask for River to see.

River's eyes went wide. "How'd you get that?"

"Long story."

His brow furrowed. "Where *does* the Plague Saint fit into all of this? You were wearing his uniform at the hospital this morning."

"It's...complicated," Winter responded with a grimace. "He did a lot of valuable research, but he was misusing it. When he joined the council to release the white plague he created, he sort of...stepped away from his position, you could say. I saw an opportunity to help people and took his place." She took a deep breath. "I'm the Plague Saint now."

Phoebe shifted abruptly and climbed to her feet. "There's a diner across the street that's still open. I'm going to go get us some coffees."

"Oh, uh, sounds great," River said. "Thank you."

"Be careful," Winter added.

Phoebe left without a word.

After a few minutes of quiet, River started up his questioning again. "So, I didn't actually have red plague, I had this new white plague? Which is something the old Saint made himself?"

Winter nodded, her gaze still resting on a streetlamp at the end of the alley. "I'm sorry it took me so long to figure out how to cure you. It must have been awful."

"You did your best." River shrugged. "More than most people would have done. And I think I was unconscious during the worst bits. Or hallucinating."

"I remember one of the nurses mentioning that." Winter turned her head toward River. "What did you see?"

"You or Mom or Dad, mostly, but you would all just stand there and stare at me. Sometimes you looked really young." River frowned. "I think I saw Daisy one time, too. As a puppy. Oh, and lots of spiders on the walls."

Winter shuddered. "Sounds awful."

"Well, I'm much better now." River reached into his coat. "I brought the card deck with me, in case we had down time like this." He surveyed the small space around them. "I don't think we have enough light or room for a game, though."

"Yeah, probably not," Winter agreed. "I bet we could manage a quick draw, though."

River slid the cards from their box and shuffled them around.

"Oh. One last thing," Winter said as she watched him.

"Hm?"

"Just in case...I don't know, in case something happens, there's an old jewelry box sitting on the roof outside my bedroom window. It's full of cash. I just want you to know it's there."

"Winter, everything's going to be okay." River continued shuffling as he looked up from the cards to meet her eyes. "But thank you." He fanned out the cards and held them toward her. Winter picked one and kept it facedown. River picked his, glanced at it, and held it up triumphantly.

"Ten of jewels," he announced.

Before Winter could reveal hers, Phoebe reappeared, holding a tray of coffees. "I just saw a guy leave the factory and lock the door behind him," she said.

River glanced at Winter. "You wanna go now?"

Winter nodded.

They quickly gathered their belongings and picked up the boxes. Phoebe climbed back down first, followed by River. Winter realized she was still holding her card. Not wanting to delay things any further, she shoved it in her pocket to deal with later and followed them down.

River tried the door's handle. "Yep, place is locked up for the night. How are we going to get in?"

"Get me something big and heavy," Winter ordered.

They scoured the alleyway until Phoebe found a broken pipe in a dumpster and handed it to Winter. Winter swung at the door handle as hard as she could. Something cracked, and the door drifted open.

Winter gave River and Phoebe their own copies of the cure recipe. "River, start getting the equipment ready. Get clean containers to put the final product in, too. Phoebe, set timers for the instructions that require waiting, and then do the math on how much we need to make ten gallons."

Winter, meanwhile, started on the first few steps, which mainly involved pre-measuring and mixing a few liquids and powders. While she worked, something still nagged at her.

"I don't think the hospital is the way to go," she finally said.

"What? But that's where the sick are," Phoebe replied with a frown.

"I know. I'm just concerned by how many people could intervene. And while the Plague Saint handing over the cure would be enough to get the doctors started, Atherton and Blackburn could step in and stop it." Winter sighed. "It might not be an issue, but I think we need to do both."

Phoebe rested a hand on her hip. "Both, meaning...?"

"I have a backup plan. I just need to figure out the most efficient way to split this up." Winter paced back and forth in front of the various chemicals she'd laid out as part of her prep work. It would take a lot of force to break into the contraption on the river, but that was something that had to be done anyway. If they could replace the plague mix inside with cure, even better.

While she worked through ideas, Phoebe and River started to mix together the cure ingredients. Winter watched closely and helped where she could. But her main focus for most of the night was making paper copies of the cure recipe.

During the longest waiting period, she encouraged them to sleep. She should have gotten some rest, too, but her mind was racing too fast and too hard. She kept pacing. With everything going on, she hadn't had much time for thinking long term. Now, she wondered what would happen to her when this was all over. What might happen to the city. She was torn between believing what she was doing was right and fearing she was making a terrible mistake.

No. Letting Atherton and Blackburn and the rest of them go through with their plan would be the mistake. This was the only way. Winter could only hope the people who took their places would do better.

Besides, she couldn't undo what she'd done at the church.

Winter moved on from pacing to digging around the supervisors' offices. She came across a few things that might come in use for the scattered semblance of a plan forming in her mind. A lighter. Spray paint.

Before long, she was back on the factory floor again, back to pacing.

One of the timers went off. River and Phoebe stirred while Winter checked on the final product.

"You guys should each have some," she told them as they came over to look at the clear liquid brewing in the vat. "I know you're feeling fine now, but better safe than sorry."

"Maybe you should, too," River said. "You mentioned it can be preventative, right? You never know when you might run into someone who's sick."

Winter nodded. "Good idea."

After setting aside a little for themselves, they were able to fill five large jugs with the cure they'd made. "So, what now?" Phoebe asked as she screwed a cap onto one of them.

"Follow the river north to the contraption the council had built. You can't miss it," Winter instructed as she tucked her bottle of cure into her bag. "There's a hatch with a padlock. I need you guys to find a way to get it open, get the stuff inside out, and put the cure in." She picked up two of the jugs. "I'll take these to the hospital, along with the recipe, and meet you guys at the river afterwards."

River nodded. "I'll grab some tools they keep around here. I bet there's something we can use."

"Great." Winter's hand tightened around the handles of the jugs. "Let's hope this works."

Chapter Twenty-Seven
Control

The sun hadn't touched the sky yet, but it was close. Winter walked with Phoebe and River to the western side of Devil's Pass. She directed them to find the river and follow it, while she circled the edge of the city up to the hospital.

Once she was a block from the hospital, Winter threw on the Saint's uniform. Bag slung over her shoulder, weighed down by the jugs of cure, she marched to the hospital's front doors.

"Is Director Blackburn here?" Winter asked the receptionist.

"He hasn't come in yet," the receptionist replied. "I think he has some meetings this morning."

"Good. I need you to send any available doctors to his office. Tell them the Plague Saint is waiting." Winter handed her one of the cure recipes. "And hold onto this. It's important."

As she entered the halls beyond the lobby, Winter pulled out the can of spray paint she'd taken from the factory and popped the cap off. She could hand out every copy of the recipe and they might disappear by the end of the day. But it would take longer for Marcus to get rid of this.

A press of her finger unleashed a spray of black paint that dripped down the white walls. Winter spelled out each ingredient, each step of the process, exactly as Marcus had written them.

"Plague Saint?" The voice came from Dr. Morrison, who watched her with shock plastered across his face as he came down the hall. "I heard the call to go to the director's office over the radio. What—what are you doing?"

"I came to this hospital to save patients. But it's not plagues you need saving from, it's people." Winter finished the last letter and took a step back. "Come with me."

Dr. Morrison walked with her to where other doctors were gathering around Blackburn's office door. The very same office Winter had killed Adams in.

"I have the cure," Winter announced.

Dr. Liang frowned. "For which plague?"

"All of them. Including white." Winter removed the jugs from her bag and held them out to the closest doctors. They looked confused, but they accepted the containers. "Divide this up. Start with the sickest patients and use the same dosage as you would if it were Red-X. Some of your red plague patients actually have white plague."

Winter reached back into bag and drew out her stack of recipe copies. "Here are instructions to make more. It's a bit complicated, especially with the timing, but follow the directions and you'll be fine. You can use my lab. There should be ingredients waiting, and there are more at Jonathan Forrest's house—"

"Sorry to interrupt, Plague Saint, but how are we supposed to get into your lab?" Dr. Liang asked.

Winter froze. "What do you mean?"

Another doctor chimed in. "There are city guards posted around your office and lab. They've only been letting Blackburn go in and out, and they wouldn't tell us anything when we asked about you."

"I am no longer associated with the hospital or Marcus Blackburn." Winter adjusted her bag and turned around. "I'll clear the path to the lab. Start getting the cure out. Make sure everyone knows it exists and raise hell if they try to take it from you."

She kept going, spraying steps of the recipe on every wall she passed until she turned into the hallway that held her office. Two city guards, both wearing their helmets, stood outside the door. Winter drew the sword out and tossed her bag aside. Her other hand still held the can of spray paint.

"Your presence is no longer needed," Winter told them.

"Plague Saint," the guard on the left greeted her coolly. "Director Blackburn said you weren't using this office anymore."

"Well, I'm back, and I'm granting access to my lab to every doctor in this hospital."

The second guard chimed in. "The director said—"

"You think Marcus Blackburn has any authority over the Plague Saint?" Winter raised the sword. "Get back to the station and do something useful."

The left guard drew his gun, and after a moment's hesitation, the other followed suit. They were far nicer weapons than Marcus's old revolver.

Winter cocked her head. "You've chosen your allegiance, then?"

"We're just following orders, sir," the left guard said.

"Okay, fine." Winter slowly lifted both hands, still holding the paint and sword, but relaxing her grip and extending what fingers she could in a gesture of surrender. "You're saying you won't move unless Blackburn tells you to?"

"Correct."

"That's a shame."

Winter pressed down the nozzle and swung her arm in a wide arc. Black paint coated the guards' visors. While they frantically tried to rub it off, she swiped at their hands with the sword. Their guns clattered to the floor. Tears opened in their gloves.

She stabbed next, driving the sword into the left guard's shoulder. His cry of pain went in one ear and out the other. The blade came free with a spray of blood. Winter didn't miss a beat before slashing at the right guard's upper arm.

"Better go get that looked at." Winter's voice was ice. "Trauma ward's just down the hall."

The guards staggered off, and she didn't care whether they were taking her advice or just trying to get away. She tossed aside the emptied spray paint can and threw open the office door.

More guards stood inside. Five of them. Their heads turned in near unison, and they took in the Plague Saint and her sword dripping with blood. Winter lifted the weapon. Five guns came out in response.

"I'm taking back this lab," she told them. "You can leave in peace, or we can do this the hard way."

One of the guards stepped forward. "Plague Saint. You saved my daughter from death last week. We're grateful for all you've done. But the hospital director ordered—"

"The hospital director is a killer and a liar. I am trying to save you and your families from death." Winter wished she could read their expressions under their helmets. "I have a cure, and I am giving it to the people. Not to a greedy director who only wants to sell it to his friends."

Uncertainty was a heavy weight in the air. Finally, the guard who had spoken made his choice. His gun lowered. "Clear out," he ordered.

While three of the others lowered their weapons, one man at the back of the room piped up. "Blackburn's the one paying us, not the Saint."

"You're an idiot if you think this is about money," the first guard said. "Let's go."

"You can go. I'm not leaving my post until Blackburn says otherwise."

"So easily bought?" Winter asked as the other four guards walked past her. "You shouldn't be serving any one man. You work for the city."

"The city's run by money. So am I."

"I don't want to kill you." Winter wasn't sure she believed her own words. The door clicked shut behind her. "Last chance."

"A gun against a sword? I'll take those odds." He took aim.

Winter dove and barely made it behind the desk. The gun went off, but the bullet didn't come anywhere near her. She rolled, pulled herself into a crouch, and circled around to the other side of the desk. When she peered around the corner, the guard was moving forward slowly, still aiming at the opposite end where he'd seen her dive.

Winter crawled forward a few feet. Then, sprang up and lunged. Her blade sliced the back of the guard's leg, but not deep enough to stop him. He spun around. The end of his gun struck the side of her head.

The mask probably helped soften the blow, but it still hit hard enough to send stars dancing across her vision. Winter collapsed onto her side. The guard took aim again. She rolled onto her back and realized her sword had slipped from her grasp. Her hand blindly searched the carpet while her heart pounded wildly.

"Who the hell are you, anyway?" the guard asked. "You're not some magical saint. But what kind of man would do all this?"

Winter didn't care to answer the question. Her hand found the sword. She grabbed the handle and scooted backwards, making herself a more difficult target. The guard stalked forward, keeping pace. Her back hit a chair. Phoebe's chair.

With her free hand, she grabbed the chair's leg. "You want to know who I am?" The Plague Saint's mask was just visible in the guard's visor, staring back at her.

"I'm not giving you a choice. You're under arrest. Put down the weapon, take off your mask, and put up your hands."

Winter pulled on the chair and swung as hard as she could. It didn't lift off the ground much, but it tipped and crashed down in front of the guard, tripping him. While he tried to regain his balance, Winter slashed at his hands with the sword.

A nasty gash opened up on the back of the guard's right hand. His gun slipped from his grasp. Winter frantically pushed herself out of his path and stumbled to her feet. The effort sent pain shooting through her abdomen. And blood leaking through the bandage. Gritting her teeth, Winter forced herself to focus on the guard reaching for his gun. It took a few more swings to make him back away and finally run out the door.

Once he was gone and the office had fallen quiet, she unbuttoned enough of her coat to lift her shirt and get a look at her stomach wound. Oh, God, that was a lot of blood.

Winter staggered into the lab and located bandages and disinfectant. She barely felt the sting this time. Once she had applied the new bandages, her head feeling a little clearer, she assessed the lab.

Jars of liquids were lined up on the center counter. Powders were measured out in trays. And a large bottle sitting in the middle of the table was full of clear cure. Winter inspected it closer. Sure enough, it looked ready to use.

She grabbed a rack of empty vials and distributed the cure among them. Once they were full, she tracked down more vials, continuing until the liquid was completely distributed into roughly fifty of them. She loaded them into her bag.

One last thing to do before she left the hospital.

Sword at the ready, Winter hurried down the hall, taking frequent turns and struggling to recall where the financial records room was. The halls were unsettlingly empty now.

Winter had finally figured out where she was when the receptionist spoke over the intercom. "We are asking all patients, visitors, and staff to stay in their rooms and out of the halls. The city guard is searching for someone. Please be patient."

Ah. That explained the lack of nurses milling about.

Another corner brought Winter to the hallway she needed. She picked up her pace and stumbled into the door when she reached it. She fumbled awkwardly with the handle and flung it open. The records room was empty.

She traced a finger up and down the drawers as she strolled past them, barely noticing the spots of blood left behind. Her eyes were focused on the letters labeling each drawer. She found the one marked "Pa—Pr" and yanked it open. More blood stained the pale file folders as she searched for River and Marissa Pierce.

She drew out the bills and studied the amounts. Mom's was a finalized bill, a copy of the letter they'd received in the mail last week with a payment plan laid out. River's still needed the director's signature before the bill could be sent out.

Now, it never would.

Winter fished the lighter from the factory out of the bag and held it to the bottom corner of River's bill. The watched the fire flicker and spread with eager eyes. Flames inched toward her fingers. She waited, waited, waited until the last possible second to let go of the paper. Ashes and embers drifted to the floor as the fire consumed the last of the page.

Winter moved on to her mother's bill. When the last piece hit the ground, still burning, she crushed the flame with the toe of her boot.

Well, that wasn't fair to everyone else, was it? Why should only River and Mom be freed from their debts?

There was no telling what changes to the system might come with a change of management. Maybe patient debts would be reduced or relived, maybe not. But at this point, Winter was all but doomed. May as well help as many as she could, right?

There wasn't much time, though, and she still had cure to distribute.

Winter opened the drawers one by one and set the files inside aflame. The fire might die out before they could all burn, but at least she could do some damage before she left.

The gloves, as she'd expected, weren't enough to keep the fire from biting her here and there. Once she was done setting her fires, she risked peeling one off to assess the burns. They didn't look too bad, but the gloves rubbing against them would be painful. She'd see what she could do about that later.

The fire roared in front of her, and she took one last moment to savor its warmth. Sparks jumped at her. Smoke drifted past her, clouding her vision.

Winter turned and left the fire behind. The door clicked shut behind her, and the sound was followed by distant shouting. Guards, getting closer. Undoubtedly, they'd see the smoke and put out the fire, but it was too late to salvage everything.

It was time to take the cure to the people.

Chapter Twenty-Eight
The Plagues and the People

Sunlight breached the horizon and flooded the city. It didn't take long for people to notice the blood splattered, limping, sword-wielding Saint smelling of smoke and death making her way toward the town square. When they called her name, asked for her help, she gestured for them to follow her. Her voice was getting hoarse, and she needed to save it.

The warm glow of the sun bathed City Hall, gleaming off the building's bronze dome. Across the square in front of the shining symbol of the city council's power, Winter climbed over the edge of the empty fountain and pulled herself up to the top. People gathered around the fountain's edge. A few chanted "Plague Saint" until she lifted a hand to silence them.

Despite her bleeding and shaking and uncertainty, for a moment, she felt more in control than ever before in her life. She raised her voice.

"I have come to save you from a new plague. White plague. There is a cure for it, and this cure will treat the other five plagues as well." Winter drew the first vial from her bag. "I've taken it to the hospital and given it to the doctors there."

A few concerned whispers reached her ears. A woman directly below Winter, leaning over the fountain's edge, raised her voice. "Plague Saint, please, my son is dying—" Her outstretched hand trembled.

"There's more to the story. Please, hear me out." Winter tossed the vial into the woman's hand and reached for another. "I've brought you the cure, but there are people who oppose me. People who want to keep it for themselves. Your leaders, your city council, your hospital director—they are ready to poison you for their own gain. They will let you die so that they can live and stay rich."

And this would be Marcus's biggest mistake. Whether he'd made himself into the Saint for glory, or the money, or purely to put himself in a position to experiment for his future plans, he'd created a figure outside of his control. Winter had never liked the people's worship of the Saint, but now she was going to use it to save them.

For a moment, clutching the vial in one hand and the sword in the other, looking down at the desperate faces that thought they were standing beneath some kind of savior, Winter felt a pang. Of hesitation, of disgust, of guilt, the wave of every terrible thing she'd done hitting her at once.

You're saving them. You're saving them. You have to do this.

She tossed another vial into the crowd. "Please, don't panic. You have nothing to fear anymore. The doctors at the hospital have the cure and the means to make more." Her resolve hardened. "And the people who wronged you will drop dead for their sins."

More vials went out into the crowd.

"Anyone who tries to work you to death, to use you for their gain, anyone who—"

"Plague Saint!" Ellen Bates's sharp voice cut through the air.

The crowd shifted, and Winter glimpsed the doors of the city hall swinging shut behind the financial advisor. Bates was accompanied by two city guards. In fact, she appeared to be leaning on them for support.

"Clear a path," Winter ordered the crowd. "I'd like to speak to her."

Bates reached the foot of the fountain. Pale. Bruised. Jaundiced. Even worse than Winter had imagined the serum's victims would look. "Plague Saint, what's happening? Everyone who took the cure is—"

"Where's Mayor Atherton?" Winter demanded.

"He's in his office, with a doctor he called. He's in even worse condition than I am. Please, do you have any idea what's happening?"

"Did you really think I'd let you all go through with your plans?" Winter demanded.

Bates's eyes widened. After a fit of coughing that sprayed blood on the fountain's edge, she asked, "What do you mean? Director Blackburn said—you were helping Adams—"

"Adams is dead because he hurt people. Same with George Gordon. And Jonathan Forrest. You will all face the same fate."

Bates tried to climb into the empty fountain but collapsed against it instead. The guards reached out to help her. To Winter's surprise, the crowd moved forward to grab them. To stop them. One of the guards managed to get out his gun.

"Stop!" Winter shouted. "It's already too late for her."

She'd hoped the crowd would have the sense to back off at the sight of the guard's gun, but they continued pressing in. He aimed, but he had to know things weren't going to end well for him if he fired, right? He was outnumbered.

Bates pushed herself up but couldn't bring herself back to a standing position. "Why me?" she asked weakly.

Winter lifted her chin. "How many here know friends, family, neighbors who couldn't pay their hospital bills and were removed from their homes? Thrown in prison?"

People in the crowd shouted and raised their fists.

"Do you know where the money goes?" Winter pointed her blade at Bates. "The money that belongs to the people the city locked up? It goes to her. And with all that extra money sitting around, the money paying for food and wine at assembly meetings and maintaining the extravagant homes on the east side, I find it funny that the hospital feels the need to charge hundreds of times the amount it spent failing to cure patients it had the means to save!"

The crowd was growing more and more agitated by the second. The guard, who'd lowered his gun, spoke into a radio, calling for backup.

"And most of that money's not going to staff. The doctors and nurses are hardly more well off than the rest of us. It's mostly been going to the director—"

"This has gone on long enough!"

Marcus Blackburn pushed his way to the front of the crowd. He held out a hand to help up Bates, but she was beyond saving now. She weakly sank to the ground, ignoring the offered hand, and Marcus didn't give her a second glance after that. His attention was solely focused on Winter.

Winter assessed him as well as she could from where she stood, perched at the top of the fountain. He wasn't in nearly as bad of shape as Bates, but Winter couldn't help thinking he didn't look great either. Maybe that was just her hoping. He likely would have taken more cure the moment he started feeling unwell.

"Speak of the devil," Winter said. "I've taken your cure and given it to the people, Blackburn. And I won't let you poison them, either."

The crowd was rabid now, moments from turning on Marcus. Winter held up a hand to stall them. "What do you have to say for yourself?"

"You're making a mistake," Marcus said. "You don't understand everything that's in motion. If all of the city elite drop dead of the plague—"

"That ship has sailed." Winter nodded at Bates. "She's not the first to succumb to the poison you made, and she won't be the last."

"Even you can't poison us all one by one," Marcus hissed. *One by one.* He hadn't figured it out then, had he? "You may have stolen our cure, but you're just one girl."

Winter's hand tightened around her blade's handle. "Are you going to expose my identity?"

"Nothing you can do will stop me. I've got city guards on their way to arrest you. All you've done is made a mess."

"I've saved lives. If I go to prison or even hell for that, that's fine by me."

Marcus climbed up onto the edge of the fountain. "I suggest you all disperse, before the city guard gets here and starts making arrests for rioting." His hand rested on a dagger hanging from his belt. "That person up there isn't a saint or a savior, she's just a foolish teenage girl named—"

"Sorry, Blackburn," Winter cut him off. Her hand moved up the edge of her mask. "You're not getting any more victories, if I can help it. Besides, don't you know a person can be more than one thing?"

She removed the mask.

"My name is Winter Pierce, I am your Plague Saint, and I am going to save Devil's Pass."

Chapter Twenty-Nine
Blades

The crowd was beyond control now. The shock on Marcus's face made Winter grin as she tucked the mask into her bag. The people were chanting "Plague Saint" again. Behind them, the doors to city hall flew open, and a group dragged Mayor Atherton out into the center of the crowd.

Marcus knelt down and said something inaudible to Bates. No response. No movement. Was she dead? Marcus's gaze moved up to Winter, and her racing heart was ready to give out.

"Winter." He spoke with a tone that might have scared her, once. "This has gone too far."

"You took things too far when you tried to kill my mother," Winter hissed.

Marcus shook his head. "You cannot let the crowd kill the mayor. This is a mob, Winter. Mobs are stupid. Reckless. Dangerous." He gestured to the screaming faces behind him. "You're insane if you don't think innocent people are going to get killed."

"Innocent people have already been dying!" The abrupt shift in volume made Marcus flinch. That surprised her. Despite the protest in her throat, the growing hoarseness, she kept yelling. "Who are you to lecture me? You think you're better than me? Smarter?"

He did have one good point, though. Angry people were dangerous. Winter knew that firsthand.

She gritted her teeth and addressed the crowd again. "The plague already has the mayor," she shouted, pointing with her blade. "Look at him. He's as good as dead. Leave him be and tend to your sick."

The crowd took a few steps back from Atherton, but no one was going anywhere yet. Atherton coughed and looked around, desperation in his eyes. When they found Marcus, relief flickered across his face. "Blackburn! What's going on? Your cure was supposed to save us."

"I'm afraid the cure was stolen from us before it reached our drinks." Marcus's fingers grazed his dagger's handle, but it seemed to be an absentminded gesture.

Atherton looked up. "Is that the Plague Saint? A teenaged girl?"

"She's not—"

"I am," Winter cut Marcus off. "And your days of taking lives have come to an end, mayor."

"Blackburn, you have more cure somewhere, right?" Atherton asked. "Please, I—" His words were drowned out in the crowd's rising anger.

"You haven't won yet, Winter," Marcus said. "I can make cure too, and I can still make sure my contraption doesn't fail." He hopped off the edge of the fountain and started into the crowd.

"Blackburn?" Atherton yelled after him. "Blackburn? Hello?"

Without thinking, Winter leapt off the top of the fountain. Her feet hit the edge at an awkward angle, and she stumbled forward, barely catching herself before she could hit the ground. Her cry of pain was lost in the voices of the mob.

She ran after Marcus, blade at the ready. She nearly lost him a few times in the crowd but managed to keep an eye on him until they emerged at the edge of the square. Free of the crowd, Marcus stopped and whirled around. His dagger cut through the air and barely missed Winter's face.

Winter swung back. Marcus dodged easily, and his next strike grazed her upper arm. She staggered back out of his reach, tightening her grip on the sword and biting back a cry of pain.

Marcus laughed. "You can't beat me in combat."

"At your best, maybe," Winter said, feigning confidence. "But you don't look great. You feeling all right?"

Marcus glared at her. "Ideally, I would have taken more cure before coming to check on the council. Unfortunately, the last batch I started isn't quite ready."

"You might want to go check on that, then." Winter kept her blade pointed at him and her eyes glued to his dagger, bracing herself for his next move.

"And let you wreak havoc across the city? I think not. I'll be fine." Despite that statement, Marcus coughed into his arm. Once he recovered, he took a step toward Winter. She took a step back.

"I am assuming it was you who stole our cure last night, after all," Marcus pressed.

Winter responded with a cold laugh. "It was easy. All I had to do was disguise myself as a church maiden."

Marcus shook his head. "When did you poison Bates and Atherton? And the other council members? Or did you just poison one and got lucky when it spread through the council?" His eyes narrowed. "If you used similar combinations to what you used on Adams and Gordon, then it must have been—"

"Oh, I didn't use my own combination. I used your own poison against you. The ultimate death serum." Winter laughed again.

Marcus hadn't figured out the extent of what she'd done last night. He might have been able to hold off the physical symptoms a little longer than the others—likely a result of taking more cure—but his brain was clearly rattled. Or maybe he was simply as sleep deprived as she was.

Marcus swung. Winter yelped in surprise and jumped back.

"The only other completed serum I had was on my boat—the river. You jumped in the river." Marcus hissed and swung the dagger again. "And the assembly meeting was probably a perfect opportunity for you to, what, break into the mayor's office? His home? Poison something there?"

Winter could hardly believe that he was still missing the obvious. She gleefully continued her taunts. "How many people have you talked to this morning? How many calls have you gotten from your friends crying about how sick they are? Because I promise you're going to get more." She lunged forward and aimed her blade at Marcus's hand. He yanked it back and she missed, but her next swing left a light gash in his side.

"Oh, wait." Winter moved backward before he could retaliate. "The dead can't make phone calls. My bad."

"How many people did you—?" More coughing. Marcus wiped blood from the side of his mouth.

Winter smirked. She couldn't help herself, no matter how loud some part of her screamed that this was too much, too far, too unhinged. "You know, I didn't take the cure with me. I just hid it in the prep room at the church."

Surprise flashed across Marcus's face. Then, his eyes narrowed. "You think you can trick me?"

"I'm not lying." Winter shrugged. "I couldn't sneak it out with all those maidens and priestesses running around. It was awkward enough was hiding the other bottle in my gown."

"What other bottle?"

All Winter offered in response was a cold smile.

Marcus glanced back over his shoulder, toward the church in the distance, clearly weighing his options and trying to trace Winter's thinking. If he went after the cure she'd left there, that would give Winter more time to help Phoebe and River replace the poison in the contraption with cure.

He broke into a run toward the church, just as Winter had hoped.

She began her sprint to the edge of the city, and another thought crossed her mind. If Marcus found the cure and saved himself, she might lose her only chance to put a real stop to his plans. The rest of the council dying might prevent him from attempting the poisoning city again any time soon. But he wasn't going to quit his mission as long as he was breathing.

Running was harder than Winter thought it would be. She tried not to let it worry her, reminding herself that she hadn't had much sleep and that she'd been racing around the city all morning. But there was an ache creeping into her body that felt like more than just exhaustion.

To her surprise, the sounds of the angry mob she'd stirred up weren't fading. In fact, they seemed to be getting louder. Were they going to the hospital? Or were they trying to follow her?

She kept going, kept thinking, until she was forced to make a choice. *Stop Marcus. Join Phoebe and River.*

She veered toward the church.

Chapter Thirty
Hellfire

Marcus was faster than Winter. Enough so that by the time she staggered into the church, he'd already found the prep room.

When she entered, he was searching the wrong shelf. Tables and chairs were overturned behind him, and every cupboard door was open.

"What the hell did you follow me here for?" Marcus pulled a box off the shelf and, when he didn't find what he was looking for, tossed it to the ground. "I was starting to think you were smart."

"I could say the same about you," Winter replied, coming to a halt in the middle of the room. "I really thought you'd figure out what I'd done by this morning."

"You mean besides stealing the cure I made?" Marcus tried another box. He was getting closer to the right spot.

"I'm also surprised you didn't save more cure for yourself."

"I'll admit I miscalculated in a few aspects. Is that what you wanted to hear?" Marcus threw aside the next box with more force. The glasses inside shattered.

His desperation made it clear that he was sicker than Winter had dared to hope when she'd first seen him. "I took a fair amount to the hospital," she told him. "You could try there. Assuming word hasn't spread far enough for the people inside to want to kill you."

Marcus whirled around. "You came here to taunt me? To watch me die?" Still, he couldn't stop his eyes from flickering to the door behind Winter. He had to be seriously considering the hospital. "This is beyond saving lives, Winter. Wanting to kill me like this?"

"As long as you live, you're a threat to Devil's Pass."

"If you're really as good and noble as you act, would you be so eager to see me suffer like this?" Marcus drew his dagger and gestured toward her with it.

"You really don't have time for this," Winter told him. "Are you going to fight me for the cure here and hope you find it before you're weak enough for me to kill you, or will you give the hospital a try?"

"Giving you more time to put a stop to my carefully laid plans?" Marcus managed a weak chuckle. "For an idiot, you've gotten pretty lucky."

Just end this now. Winter raised her sword and flew at Marcus.

He sidestepped and shot past her. Within seconds he was out the door. Gone.

"You're not even going to fight me?" Winter yelled after him. No response. Her ragged breathing was the only sound. Her legs refused to let her go after him, and she was forced to admit her body was beginning to fail her. Damn it, she didn't have time for this.

Winter stalked to the shelves and grabbed the box hiding the cure. She shoved the bottle in her bag. Her fingers grazed another bottle, the smaller bottle of cure she'd set aside for herself at the factory.

Winter didn't want to believe she was getting sick, but it would be stupid not to take precautions. She should have taken the cure as soon as they'd left the factory. Her trembling fingers unscrewed the cap and she chugged the clear liquid inside.

Ugh. The taste wasn't the worst thing she'd ever had, but the medicine burned her throat on its way down and made her eyes water. Winter wiped her mouth with her arm, tossed the empty bottle to the floor, and left the prep room.

Now to reunite with River and Phoebe and end this.

Winter casually swung the sword as she walked the halls. When her hands tired of that, she slashed at the walls.

Time to end this.

Doors to the chapel approached on her left.

End this.

Winter's free hand moved to her bag. Her fingers twitched.

River and Phoebe are waiting.

Out came the mask. Winter separated the two parts, returned the upper faceplate to the bag, and slid the beak over her jaw. She peeled her gloves off, slid them into the bag with the sword, and entered the chapel.

The priest looked up from the passage he was reading, his voice faltering. The few people gathered in the pews turned their gazes to Winter. A lone church maiden holding a donation basket froze.

One last thing. *One last thing.*

"It's about time you all left," Winter said, her hoarse voice echoing through the chapel. In the silence that followed, distant chanting and yelling drifted in from outside. The mob was approaching, after all. Maybe they'd get their hands on Marcus.

"What's happening out there?" The priest asked, glancing toward the stained-glass windows that failed to offer much of a few. His attention shifted back to Winter. He took in her clothing, her mask, and frowned. "And who—?"

"I am the Plague Saint." Winter had some smaller vials of cure left, so she pulled a few out. "Who here has sick loved ones?"

Nearly every single person rose to their feet. One woman in a pew just a few feet from Winter spoke up. "My brother is at the hospital with red plague." Her voice quivered. "They told me yesterday morning they've done all they can, but they don't think he'll—"

"If the hospital does not have enough cure to treat him now, give him this." Winter tossed a vial to the woman. "I gave them as much as I could, but there are so many who are sick."

A younger man stepped into the aisle and took a few steps toward her. "My mother's at home with green. We were hoping since it's less severe she could fight it off on her own, because we can't afford what they'd charge us."

Winter handed him a vial. "She can drink this if you don't have the proper syringes to inject it into her blood."

More people approached, one by one, and she handed out most of what she had left. Some left immediately after receiving medicine, while many remained gathered around her. Watching her with a mix of gratitude and curiosity.

"Go now," she said to those who still lingered once she'd finished her administrations. "You all need to leave this place. Nothing here will save you. Go to your loved ones instead."

The priest, who'd watched her in appalled silence until now, stormed away from the alter and down the aisle. "The Plague Saint works for the hospital!" he exclaimed to the dispersing crowd. "He doesn't march around the city handing out strange vials, and he's certainly not a young girl with no knowledge of medicine."

"I'm not a man who works at a hospital saving only those who can afford it." Winter gestured to the beak hiding the bottom of her face. "But I am the Plague Saint. I've spent weeks learning to make medicine and saving as many as I can. And as far as strange vials go…" She popped the cap off one of the vials, pulled down the beak, and took a swig to prove she thought it was safe.

"This really is a cure," she continued as she slid the beak back into place. She glanced around at the last stragglers. "Now like I said, I suggest you all leave."

The people listened, despite the priest's continued protests.

"What are you really here for?" he hissed to Winter.

"To save people," Winter repeated. With everyone else gone, she dared to pull out the sword. Candlelight glinted off the unspoken threat. "Now, I think you should go, too."

"I'm calling the city guard," the priest muttered. He scurried out of the chapel.

One last thing.

Winter let the tip of the blade sink into the wood floor and dragged it behind her as she walked. The scratch in the floor traced her path between the pews up to the altar. The altar that was draped in cloth and covered with burning candles. Winter tapped one of the candles with the side of the blade. It tipped over easily, and the cloth beneath it ignited in an instant.

The warmth was almost irresistible. The ache in Winter's bones was accompanied by a cold that no amount of heat would banish. She pressed a hand to the side of her face. Her skin was feverishly warm. What would win the race: whichever plague had taken hold of her, or the cure racing through her body?

Winter grabbed another candle and held the flame to the cloth at the other end of the altar. While the new blaze spread, she reached for a third.

As she moved the candle toward another corner of the altar, she misjudged the distance between her hand and the first fire she'd started. Its flames licked her hand. She hissed and dropped the candle.

The candle rolled to the edge of the altar, hung in precarious balance for a moment, and fell to the floor. Fire jumped to wood. The old, dry wood that had been salvaged from some other building, some other life. It burned quickly.

Winter stepped back, still clutching the other candle. She backed into a pew, and the flames spread further, eager to swallow the old bench. Fire found her fingers before she could pull them out of the way.

This stupid old place had been one giant fire hazard for years, just waiting for something like this to happen. Sure, if a candle had been knocked over by accident during service, someone could have put it out quickly. But Winter had no intention of stopping the flames.

The fire of the candle she still held flickered and died out, unable to keep up with Winter swinging it through the air as she backed away from the altar. She cautiously held it out to the growing blaze in front of her to relight it.

Candle reignited, she moved on down the aisle, starting fires on more pews. Wax melted in her hand, but Winter held out until the burning became unbearable. When that happened, she tossed the candle to the floor and dug around in her bag for the lighter.

Smoke formed into a cloud around her. She coughed under its embrace, but she wasn't ready to stop yet. She continued adding to the flames with the lighter, so lost in her task that she didn't realize how quickly the first fire had spread until she was completely surrounded.

Winter stood alone in the center of the burning chapel and turned in a slow circle. After all she'd been through—being arrested, being attacked by Marcus, almost drowning, bleeding, killing—she didn't think she'd feel fear like this again.

One last thing. One last stupid detour to get her killed.

No, it wasn't going to end here. Not yet. She desperately searched the growing wall of fire for a gap. For anything to give her hope. Smoke clouded her vision. Where was it the least intense? Where did she have a prayer of making it though alive?

She thought about putting the rest of the mask on for some protection, but she needed every second she had. *Run.*

She picked a spot, forced every thought and fear from her mind, and ran.

Chapter Thirty-One
Choke

Every step toward the river was hell. Shooting pain through every bone, bitter cold, burning skin.

When Winter heard River and Phoebe's voices, she checked that both parts of the mask were secured correctly to her face and tugged on her gloves. God, that hurt.

"Winter, there you are!" River exclaimed with relief when he spotted her. He was sitting on top of the contraption, which didn't look any different than it had when Winter first found it. Hopefully they'd managed to break the lock already. There was no telling how much time they had before someone confronted them.

"What's happening?" Phoebe demanded. "We've heard that yelling in the distance for a while now, and it seems like it's getting closer. And—what's that smoke over there?"

Winter didn't bother looking back. "Not important. Have you two made any progress?"

"We broke the lock," River said. He lifted the hatch to prove his point. "Still no ideas on how to get out the poison and replace it."

Phoebe frowned at a point in the distance, where smoke met the sky. The mob was getting louder. "Uh, Winter, what—?"

"We need to focus on this right now," Winter snapped. "Hospital's probably got buckets we can use. Maybe some tubing for siphoning." She walked to the contraption and climbed the ladder to get a better look.

River regarded her with concern as she popped up next to him. "Uh, wouldn't you be more comfortable taking the mask off now? It's just us here…"

He must have found the mask's distortion of her voice disconcerting, Winter realized. But she didn't want to deal with removing it right now. "Again, not exactly a pressing issue. Besides, I have to go get supplies." Winter assessed the amount of liquid inside. They'd have to be careful where they disposed of it when they were done. She climbed back down, fighting to hide how much pain she was in, how badly her hands were shaking.

"Even if we get it all out, the inside will still be contaminated!" River called as Winter walked away.

"I'll get disinfectant!" she replied.

"Do you want me to come with you?"

Winter paused. "No. You two need to stay here and guard this. I'll be right back." Getting to the hospital and back shouldn't take more than fifteen minutes, as long as she was able to find what they needed quickly.

Oh, how she wanted to send someone else. She should have thought of this before coming all the way out, but she could barely think more than a few moments ahead now. A disconcerting fog had overtaken her mind.

She approached the hospital from the back. The mob had to be just out front, judging by the volume of the chanting. Oh, God, what if they were inside? They could easily disrupt the careful routine of the doctors, the only thing keeping dozens of patients from death.

The inside of the building was quiet enough for Winter to relax. Maybe the mob wasn't planning on coming in, or maybe the city guard was actually succeeding at keeping them out. She shoved the thought aside.

Winter stopped the first doctor she passed. "Is Marcus Blackburn here?"

The man nodded. "He came in looking pretty sick about ten minutes ago."

"Did he say anything about me?" Winter asked.

"Not that I know of."

"But you're treating him?"

The doctor frowned. "Yes. That is our job."

"And do you know anything about the mob outside?"

"The entire staff is focused on treating people right now. We have no idea what's going on. I assume the city guard's handling it."

Winter nodded and kept going. She tracked down a supply room near her lab and tried a few shelves before she found what would hopefully be enough buckets, along with several jugs of disinfectant, plastic tubing, and some sponges and towels. She divided the buckets into two stacks, piled everything else in, and set out.

She'd almost made it back outside when Marcus yelled her name. "Winter!"

Groaning, Winter stopped and glanced over her shoulder. "Shouldn't you be in a hospital bed somewhere?"

Marcus didn't look much better than he had when she'd last seen him. Still, he ignored her question. "So, you've handed out the most valuable thing in this city. Not just the cure, but the instructions to make it. I spent months developing that! I *own* the cure!"

"Seriously," Winter hissed. "Even if you got them to give you a dose, if you don't rest, your body's going to have a hard time fighting off—"

"I'm not stupid. Don't recite my own research to me."

Winter turned around and continued toward the door. She couldn't let Marcus distract her, no matter how badly she wanted to make him shut up once and for all.

"You still won't save everyone!" Marcus yelled behind her. "The hospital's going to run out of supplies before long. And who on earth is going to pay for more? Who's going to buy lives?"

Winter ignored him and kicked open the door.

"You'll pay for this. You think you've ruined my plans? You've ruined your own life. You—"

The door slammed shut behind Winter. Was he going to come after her? Didn't matter. If she made it back to River and Phoebe, they could handle him easily, weak as he was.

If. Winter had barely passed the tree line when she collapsed to her knees. The fever, the cold, the ache, the burns; it all came together in a hellish combination, a nightmare she couldn't wake up from.

Thankfully, Marcus had apparently decided not to follow. That was the only bit of good luck she had. She forced herself to take in a deep breath and look up.

The buckets and cleaning supplies lay on the ground a few feet in front of her. She reached out for them. Her other hand slipped, and she fell face first into the snow.

Come on, come on, come on. Tears stung Winter's eyes. She couldn't stop now. She lifted her head and watched the world blur and spin in front of her. A shadow crossed the ground, moving toward her. Something emerged from the trees ahead. Winter lifted her chin a few more inches.

An animal. A dog.

Daisy.

The Saint Bernard padded forward. A sob racked Winter's body. She was dying. This was it, this was—

More shadows, more blurry figures. But these weren't dogs, these were men. Adams, Gordon, Forrest. The men she'd killed.

River's voice echoed in her head. *I think I was unconscious during the worst bits. Or hallucinating.*

"This isn't real," Winter choked. That seemed to stop the men's approach, but Daisy didn't stop until she was standing about a foot away, her eyes staring directly into Winter's, as if she could see every memory, every failure, every mistake—

Winter pushed herself up a few inches, tears coming faster now. "I don't regret it. They needed to die."

Her old dog sat down, pawns inches from Winter. One moved to rest on Winter's hand, but there was no accompanying sensation. No fur, no weight.

"I have to finish this. I have to save them." Winter shook her head. A sob racked her chest, making her choke. "I'm sorry." She squeezed her eyes shut and felt tears slide down her cheeks.

A heartbeat later, something cool was flooding her body. The cure? Was it finally doing its job? Or was she imagining the sensation racing through her blood? Maybe this was what death felt like.

Winter opened her eyes and lifted her gaze. The men she'd killed were gone. The world was spinning, and she was pretty sure the blood pooling on the ground around her wasn't supposed to be there. She blinked, and it vanished, too.

Daisy was still there, though. Shaking, Winter pushed herself up to her knees. She had to fight this. Marcus could still decide to follow her, Phoebe and River were waiting, and Devil's Pass wasn't safe yet.

"Go," Winter whispered. "I'm not done yet."

Daisy's form blurred with the rest of Winter's vision. Her mental haze was clearing, but she still couldn't force herself to walk away from the dog, hallucination or not. She closed her eyes and took a deep breath.

When she opened them again, Daisy was gone.

No, she was never here, Winter reminded herself. She looked down at her gloved hands. She felt a little better, but not by much. Even if she was on the verge of death, though, she couldn't stop yet.

She gathered up the supplies she'd dropped and kept going. Minutes later, she returned to the contraption, showing no outward sign of what she'd just experienced. She and River and Phoebe got to work.

River sat on top of the contraction and siphoned poison into the buckets. He handed them to Phoebe on the ladder, who traded Winter—face still hidden under the Plague Saint mask—for an empty one. Winter carefully lined up the full buckets a short walk from the river.

"All right, that's the last of it," River said as Phoebe handed Winter a half-full bucket.

"Great." Winter took the bucket. "Let's scrub it with disinfectant and rinse it as best we can."

She had one more empty bucket, which she filled with river water while Phoebe handed River the disinfectant and sponges. She brought bucket over to hand to Phoebe, but Phoebe didn't notice when Winter held it out.

"Uh, Winter?" Phoebe was staring past her. "We've got company."

Winter whirled around, still clutching the bucket's handle. Coming through the trees, led by Marcus, were nearly twenty city guards.

"Hand this to River," Winter hissed, shoving the bucket into Phoebe's arms. As her gaze settled on Marcus, she realized two people walking beside him weren't dressed in guard uniforms.

Her parents.

Chapter Thirty-Two
Playing With Fire

Marcus broke into his worst fit of coughing yet before he spoke. Phoebe watched his blood spray the snow with wide eyes.

"You're sick!" she protested. "How—?"

Marcus wiped his face with his arm. "Why don't you ask her." He glared at Winter.

Phoebe turned to look at Winter, her brow furrowing. "What?"

Winter didn't respond. She was too busy assessing Marcus's entourage of guards, their guns, and her confused and scared parents. She glanced at where River sat on the contraption, holding the bucket of water meant to rinse it. Winter gave him the slightest nod. He pressed his lips together and slowly added the water.

"If she won't confess to what she did, I'll tell you," Marcus said, apparently unconcerned with River's continued work, at least for the moment. "She stole my cure from me and poisoned the entire city leadership at the assembly meeting, leaving us defenseless and dooming most of us to death."

Stunned silence hung in the air for a long moment. Then, Phoebe turned her horrified gaze to Winter. "But she—"

"Last I saw, Ellen Bates was still on the ground on the verge of death," Marcus continued, cutting her off. "And Mayor Atherton didn't look any better. The entirety of the city council, various factory and business owners—"

"You swore you wouldn't hurt anyone else!" Phoebe exclaimed. She took a step toward Winter, jabbing a finger at her. "You said the last thing we would do would be to put the cure in the water!"

"I—" Winter started.

"You promised!"

"Technically, I made that promise after I poisoned the drinks at the assembly meeting." As soon as the words left Winter's mouth, she knew it was a mistake.

Phoebe's face twisted with anger. "They're all going to die! Winter, the mayor? I know he's done wrong, but he has kids—"

Winter's rage flared to life, burning brighter than Phoebe's ever could. "And he's passing laws that will get countless people killed! What about their kids?" Winter glared at Marcus—not that he could see it under the mask. "Besides, they weren't quite dead yet when we left. If Marcus wasn't wasting the city guard's time, maybe they could focus on getting them to the hospital. You left them lying in the town square just as much as I did."

Marcus glared back, but the bags under his eyes and the fatigue on his face undercut the expression. "These guards are under my employment, and I'm paying with something much more valuable than money: cure."

"You said yourself it doesn't have any value anymore," Winter pointed out. "I took that from you."

"There's still benefit in not having to wait at the hospital. But this isn't about me, it's about you. I'm not done exposing your crimes." Marcus nodded to the guard at his right. "Bring him out."

The guard walked into the undergrowth. A jolt of horror shot through Winter. How could she have forgotten about—?

"Jonathan Forrest," Marcus said as the guard dragged out the body.

"What makes you think I killed him?" Winter demanded.

"Oh, please. Who else would have done it?"

Winter stared at the blood stains on his clothes, so much worse than she'd remembered. "I..." What other defense did she have? More lies? What would be the point?

"Come on, it's over," Marcus growled. "You're outnumbered. Take the mask off and let's make this official."

Winter shook her head, a new idea forming. "You're dying. I'd bet you didn't take enough cure for how sick you are," she said. "You might not last long enough to make more, but I have some in my bag ready to go. We can make a deal."

"I tried to help you time and time again. I've made you more offers than you deserve. It's too late for you." Marcus laughed. The sound quickly trailed off into more coughing. Once he'd recovered, he added, "Besides, I'm just going to take that cure over there from you after I arrest you. You've brought me right to it, and now I don't have to wait at the hospital or fight anyone for it." He looked up. "You may as well give up now, River."

River straightened up, clutching the towel he'd been using to wipe disinfectant off the inside of the contraption.

His and Winter's parents were still silent, probably in too much shock to speak. Maybe they hadn't even fully processed what was happening. How much had Marcus told them?

"Phoebe, please," Winter said, glancing at her. "You have to make him understand—"

"I don't think *you* understand!" Phoebe exclaimed. "I mean, did you have to kill Forrest? Why did you—?" She glanced at the body and paled. "Why—?"

"Phoebe, you know I had to—"

"Stop! Stop. I can't hear you, Winter," Phoebe said. "All I can hear is some faceless killer. Take off the mask!"

Winter hesitated. Her gaze flickered to River, watching her with clear concern, to the jugs of cure at the foot of the ladder. Marcus waited eagerly.

Phoebe's voice dropped to a hoarse plea. "Take off the mask and look at me."

Winter lifted her hands and removed the mask.

Phoebe pressed a hand over her mouth. River's eyes widened, his lips parted. Murmurs and gasps spread among the guards.

Marcus chuckled. "I guess that's what happens when you play with fire, Winter."

"Oh, *I* played with fire?" Winter tossed the mask onto the bag laying open on the ground a few feet away. "You invented an entirely new plague that you had no hope of controlling once you added it to the city's water!"

Winter ripped off her gloves, exposing the burns that matched the ones marring her face.

"You really thought you'd be able to kill and save everyone you wanted?" she continued. "The plague spreads. The cure doesn't. Even if you survive today, your creation will catch up with you eventually."

Every word she shouted burned her throat, still stinging from the smoke. Momentarily forgetting the guards, Winter picked up her sword. "You started this fire, Marcus."

She pointed the blade at him. A dozen guns lifted in response.

"Let them take you quietly, Winter. This has gone on long enough." Marcus sighed. "Grab River, too. Shame he let himself get caught up in this. See what you've done, Winter? You weren't thinking about your family, were you? You were only thinking about making yourself into some kind of saint."

Winter's hand trembled. Could she lunge forward and stab him before a shower of bullets reached her? Probably not. She let the sword fall from her hand. They needed to get the cure into the contraption. And all of that poison was still sitting there in buckets. It would be so easy for Marcus to throw it into the river before anyone could stop him.

The guards were moving toward the contraption, toward River, toward Phoebe.

Marcus held up a hand to stop the two reaching for Phoebe. "I'll take her with me. I'm disappointed, Phoebe. We're going to have a long talk."

Winter tried to look at River. She wasn't sure what she was hoping to find, or what kind of message she was trying to send him, but it didn't matter. His gaze was on the ground, and he refused to meet her eyes as she shifted toward the ladder.

Phoebe walked toward Marcus, head lowered. She was giving up, too? Winter glared as guards surrounded her. Just like that, it was over. At least she'd accomplished something today. The cure was public. Even if Marcus poisoned everyone, at least there was a chance most would survive...

No, it wasn't enough. She could have saved all of them. *All* of them. Every person who died after this would be another failure on her part.

Phoebe slowed. Paused.

Marcus frowned. "Come on, Phoebe. I think if you get some rest, you'll feel better." Despite his earlier reprimand, he sounded like he was trying to comfort her now. But the strain in his voice was obvious.

Winter realized, moments before Marcus did, that Phoebe was only a few feet from the jugs of cure.

Phoebe darted forward and grabbed them. Guards rushed after her, but Marcus held up a hand to stop them. "Wait," he ordered.

"Smart choice." Phoebe held the jugs out over the river with trembling hands. "This is your best hope of survival, right?"

Oh, the look on Marcus's face was priceless. Even Winter had never managed to surprise him quite like this.

"Phoebe, wait," Marcus said. "You wouldn't—"

"Don't make me," Phoebe replied, voice trembling. "I *will* do it."

"You'll kill me." Marcus actually looked scared. "Phoebe, come on. You don't want that."

"I don't want anyone else to die!" There was a new fire in Phoebe's eyes. "I stand by helping River get your poison out of the contraption, and I won't let you put it back in." Her eyes narrowed. "If you want to live, you're going to make a few promises."

"Phoebe, this is more complicated than you could begin to understand," Marcus said. "I need you to trust me when I say I'm doing this for the good of Devil's Pass—"

"You think I'm an idiot," Phoebe said bluntly. "Both of you." She shifted her gaze from Marcus just long enough to shoot Winter a withering look. "You've lied to me and tried to use me as a weapon against each other. I'm not as stupid as you think I am."

Winter grimaced.

"You are going to let River finish cleaning the contraption, and then let him go home without arresting him. We're going to add most of the cure to the water, and you can have what's left."

Winter's shoulders sagged. "Thank you."

"I'm not doing this for you." Phoebe's cold gaze remained fixed on Marcus. "River goes free and the city gets the cure, in exchange for your life. And Winter's arrest."

"Fine." Marcus signaled for the guards to lower their guns. Except for the two standing on either side of Winter. "But I'm not going to just stand here and wait around. I have other matters to check on. I'll be back in twenty minutes for my portion of the cure."

As he walked past Winter, he barked orders to the guards. "Watch them to make sure they follow through on their word. A few of you should take care of Forrest's body. And escort her parents back to their apartment." To the pair guarding Winter, he added, "You two keep her here until I return."

"Did they have to be here for this?" Winter hissed. Mom and Dad hadn't said a word the entire time, and now they would probably never say another word to her again. They didn't even look her way as they were led off.

"I needed to be sure they knew the truth."

And with that, Marcus was walking away, following the river. Winter frowned.

"River?" Phoebe said as she set the jugs down on the ground. "How's it coming?"

"Good. I'm ready to add the cure, if you want to bring it up—"

"Wait!" Winter exclaimed. "Marcus is heading toward his boat."

Phoebe glanced in the direction Marcus had gone. "So?"

"He has more poison waiting there! We can't just let him—"

"How am I supposed to trust you?" Phoebe asked. "For all I know, you could be lying to try and escape."

"You think I'd do that? All I care about is saving you all!" Winter tried to keep her voice steady, acutely aware of the guards and guns surrounding her. "Why else would he walk away from the one thing that could save his life! What else could possibly be at his lab that's so important?"

"He knows we're adding cure to the water. Why would he bother?"

"The cure will be too diluted in the water system to do more than give people's immune systems a boost, if that," Winter explained. "If he infects the water, the plague bacteria will multiply and more than compensate for the cure!" She turned her attention to the guards surrounding her, hoping at least some of them would want to do the right thing. "Come on, you can't just let this happen!"

Nothing.

Phoebe's head turned toward the rising smoke in the distance. Her eyes narrowed. "What's been happening while we've been out here?"

River finished off a jug and tossed it aside. "Hey, yeah, shouldn't you guys be doing something about that fire?"

"Not our job," one of the guards said. "Besides, last I heard, there was a mob around the church making that difficult."

"You can hear them, if you're quiet," another added.

Winter's fists clenched at her sides. They didn't have time for this, no one was listening to her, and there was nothing she could do.

Distant chanting reached them. Phoebe's expression grew concerned. "It sounds like they're getting closer."

"What are they yelling?" River asked as he unscrewed the cap on the last jug.

"It doesn't matter," Winter said. "We need to stop Marcus before he—"

"They're yelling 'Plague Saint,'" Phoebe realized.

She was right. And the chanting was definitely getting louder. She spun to face Winter. "What did you do while we were waiting for you?"

Winter stared at her blankly. Nothing...nothing mattered anymore. Secrets, lies, every step Winter had taken in hopes she might salvage her life at the end of this. All for nothing.

"Seriously, Winter, how did you get those burns?" Phoebe pressed. "What's on fire? Why is a mob shouting—well, it's not your name, is it?"

Winter's thoughts were too fractured to answer her. Why *was* the mob coming this way? What had she said to them about the river, exactly? About Marcus's plan? She couldn't remember, really. The whole thing was a blur. But if they'd gotten bored of swarming the hospital and watching the church burn...

River held up a jug and assessed the remaining liquid. He put the cap back on, closed the hatch on the contraption, and started down the ladder.

The chanting grew. "Plague Saint! Plague Saint!"

Something flickered inside Winter. A chance. A final flicker of hope. She lifted her chin. Her lips parted. Phoebe's eyes widened, but there was nothing she could do to stop Winter from speaking.

"I won't let Marcus poison the water, and I won't let you take me," Winter said in as loud a voice as she could muster, praying it would carry the distance she needed it to.

Guards lifted their guns. "Don't try anything," one said. "We won't hesitate to shoot."

"Winter," Phoebe warned. "Don't do anything stupid. They'll kill you."

Winter let out a cold laugh. "What chance do I have? I'm screwed anyway. May as well fight until the end."

River looked at her, and his sad expression was the only thing that could actually hurt her, now. "Winter, please," he said softly. "I don't know everything that's happened to you these past few weeks, but you still have a chance."

"What chance? You heard Marcus. You saw what I did to Forrest. And the others I killed—" Winter shook her head. "Trust me, this is for the best."

The first members of the mob emerged from the trees.

Chapter Thirty-Three
Breaking

Winter lifted her hands as the mob swarmed the riverbank. "The poison in the contraption has been replaced with cure, but the threat isn't gone. We need to get rid of those buckets safely."

The guards not directly next to Winter moved to form a line in front of the contraption. The leader fired his gun into the sky. The warning shot was enough to make the mob pause and quiet down.

"Leave now," the guard ordered. "This is city guard business. Anyone attempting to intervene will be dealt with appropriately."

Winter lifted her chin. "If you fire at civilians, word will spread, and the guard stations will be destroyed within hours. And you'll all fall to the plague. The entire city will." She spoke the words as if she could make them come true through sheer willpower.

The guards hesitated. The mob hesitated. Even Winter felt a flicker of uncertainty. She'd thought she could overwhelm the guard with the mob and escape, but if even one guard fired and killed an innocent person—

But Marcus was still out there.

But...

Winter glanced at the sword and her bag lying on the ground a few feet away. She wanted to do the right thing. What the hell was the right thing? Could she even do right, anymore?

"Marcus can't save you," Winter told the guards. "If he lets the plague out, no one will be able to control it. Not even him."

"Didn't you let it out by poisoning everyone at the council meeting?" Phoebe asked bitterly. "You have no control over who they spread it to. You really think no one else will die?" She gestured toward the armed guards. "Tell the mob to back off before you make this worse."

"They wouldn't dare shoot innocent citizens," Winter tried.

The leader didn't lower his gun. "We don't want to, but we'll do whatever it takes to enforce the law."

Winter looked at the mob. *Whatever it takes.* Whatever it took to stop Marcus, whatever it took to—

To save herself. She'd gotten herself into this. She couldn't use these people to get herself out.

Winter lifted a burned hand. "Fine. This is over." She'd go to prison, a dozen or so council members and business owners would die, and Marcus Blackburn would get his cure. He'd keep running the hospital, keep doing what he could to enforce his vision. And people would rise up to take the places of Atherton and the other council members who died today. Would they do any better?

Not if they were selected from the elite, they wouldn't.

The mob still hung at the edges of the riverbank, all but frozen in time. No, it wasn't over yet, was it?

"I'm sorry," Winter said, quiet enough that only Phoebe and River could hear.

"That hardly makes up for what you've done—" Phoebe started.

"Not for everything else I've done. For breaking my promise."

"Bit late for that, too."

"No, this is an advanced apology." Winter dropped her hand. "Marcus Blackburn is still out there, and he won't stop as long as he lives."

Realization dawned on Phoebe's face. Her voice rose to a shriek. "Winter, no, please—"

"We won't let them take our lives," Winter said, her own voice lifting so the people could hear her again. "We won't let them poison us."

And then, somewhere in the crowd, someone screamed those two words that had twisted their way into the city's heart: *Plague Saint.*

The words spread through the crowd, the chanting returned, and the mob pressed forward.

Despite their earlier boldness, the guards quickly realized they were outnumbered and had no prayer of stopping the mob. They backed away from the approaching wave and quickly became divided. Now, if they fired, they risked hitting each other.

Winter grabbed the sword and bag and ran. She tried to push the shouting behind her from her mind, tried to focus only on reaching the boat and stopping Marcus.

She wasn't moving fast enough. Her pain was slowing her, her legs refused to cooperate. She struggled for each breath.

When the boat did finally come into view, it was far too soon. Winter stopped and stared, mouth agape. The roar of an engine cut through the air. The boat battled the current with surprising ease as it moved up the river.

Before Winter could even begin to figure out how she was going to get onto the boat, something moved in the undergrowth behind her. She spun around as Mayor Atherton emerged, brushing leaves off his tattered red suit and waving a gun.

"I'm going to kill you!" he growled.

"You idiot, you're going to drop dead any second." Still, Winter found it hard to swallow her fear. Even if he was weak, all Atherton had to do was fire once and get lucky with his aim. "I can save you. There's still leftover cure, just up the river." Winter hated herself for bargaining with him, but she just needed to keep him from shooting her.

"After everything you've done? I'm not going to let you trick me again!"

"Why kill me when you could just make me get you the cure—?"

"Shut up!" Atherton hissed. "Did you miss the part where I said I have a gun?"

Winter nearly laughed. "What are you going to do, shoot the plague out of yourself?"

That was a mistake. Atherton fired. The bullet missed Winter by a good ten feet. Oh, good, his aim was shit.

"Seriously, Atherton, are you stupid? I'm your only chance at survival," Winter told him. "I'm the Plague Saint."

His bruised hands shook violently. Blood stained the front of his jacket. "Really? Because I'm under the impression you're a fraud."

She had to take the risk and attack. No time for anything else.

"Well." Winter's voice shifted from pleading to icy in a heartbeat. "No one will ever know the difference."

She swung her sword.

She was running again before Atherton's body even hit the ground. She was barely faster than Marcus's boat. Barely. Up ahead, she could see a fallen tree lying halfway across the river, the same one she'd hit the night she'd fallen in.

She hurried out across the tree, navigating the branches with as much speed as she could muster without losing her balance. Marcus's shadow was just visible in the cabin of the boat. Winter stood at the edge of the tree and watched the vessel approach.

When the boat was in reach, she tossed her sword and bag onto the deck. She jumped and grabbed the railing. The cold of the metal was a shock to her skin, and the burns on her hands screamed as they twisted around the bars.

She slammed into the side of the boat and yelped in pain. For a moment, all she could think was that she was going to fall and drown and die. Sheer panic flooded her. Her first attempt to pull herself up failed, and she nearly slipped off, sending another jolt of fear through her. Body screaming from the effort, she tried again. Her foot found the edge of the deck, and she moved her hands up the railing to pull herself over.

She collapsed onto the deck with a painful thud. It only took a moment to regain her senses and push herself up, but that was all she could do. She couldn't even get a grip on the sword's handle she was shaking so bad.

The door to the cabin swung open, and Marcus stepped out.

Chapter Thirty-Four
The Devil in Devil's Pass

Marcus lunged at Winter before she could make another attempt at picking up the sword. The next thing she knew, her back was slamming against the railing. She gasped in a desperate attempt to reclaim the air that escaped her lungs.

"You never learn, do you?" Marcus released his grip on her shoulders and straightened up, looming over her. "I'm starting to think I can't let you live."

"Funny, I was just thinking the same thing," Winter wheezed. She grabbed the railing to steady herself but didn't attempt to stand yet. "Why'd you come back here? Why take the boat back up the river?"

"I think that's obvious."

"Phoebe would know."

"I don't give a damn." Marcus stepped away from Winter to pick up the sword. He was trembling, too.

"You're risking your life every second you're out here," Winter told him.

"So are you." Marcus said. "I think you understand the idea of putting your life on the line for the right thing. Even if you're going about it the wrong way."

The taste of copper filled Winter's mouth. She spat out blood. "Don't give me that."

"Give you what?"

"The 'we're not so different' speech."

"I wasn't. You may have ambition, but you're naïve and foolish." Marcus raised the sword.

Winter pushed herself off the ground and dove left. She awkwardly rolled across the deck and staggered to her feet. She stumbled into the cabin. The blade sliced through the air behind her.

Sure enough, bottle after bottle of dark liquid sat lined up on the center table, ready to be dumped. Winter grabbed one and turned around. Marcus came stumbling in, and she swung the bottle and struck the side of his head.

He stumbled into the nearest counter. A surprising amount of blood streamed down the side of his face. He swung the sword again. Another miss. The weapon slipped from his hands and clattered to the ground.

Instead of grabbing it again, Marcus lunged at Winter. In her attempt to dodge, she slammed into the table. Bottles tipped over and hit the floor, rolling in every direction. Waves rocked the boat. Two of the bottles rolled out the door and onto the deck.

Marcus collapsed to the floor. Winter looked down and met his gaze. The exhaustion in his eyes made her think he wasn't going to get back up.

She wasn't sure what surprised her more: the laughter that escaped her, or the fact that he joined in.

"I win," Winter told him. She knocked the last few standing bottles onto the floor and watched another roll out onto the deck. One passed between the bars of the railing, and a distance splash followed. "Hell, maybe I'll throw this all in the river. No one in Devil's Pass is going to drink it."

"Please do," Marcus said. He turned his head and chuckled as another bottle rolled off the deck.

Winter froze. "What?"

"Devil's Pass isn't the only city on this river." Marcus let out a sound somewhere between a laugh and the worst cough Winter had ever heard. Blood and saliva dripped from his mouth. "Hell, we trade with some of the communities south of the pass. And they all take water from the river farther down."

Winter darted forward to grab two bottles within reach before they could roll out the door. With her foot, she tried to stop a third from escaping, but she wasn't fast enough.

Oh, God.

Winter tried to think. "They're in the bottles—"

"You really think they won't break?" Marcus laughed again. "That glass won't last long banging against rocks."

"Why are you laughing! You haven't won!" Winter couldn't keep her hold on the bottles. They slipped from her hands. One survived the fall, the other shattered. Dark liquid sprayed the floor and her boots. "You're minutes from death and Devil's Pass is safe."

"Sure," Marcus gasped. "But that look on your face? The horror? The realization that you did all of this and still failed to save everyone you could? If you'd just let me do my work, Devil's Pass would be purged. Within a few years, it would be a better place for everyone."

Winter opened her mouth, then closed it. No point arguing with a dead man. She limped out onto the deck and grabbed the railing.

The water below was turbulent, and the bottles were long gone, probably already leaking poison. How long until it reached the first cities? How long until people started getting sick from something they had never seen before, something they didn't have the slightest chance of fighting?

The door thudded against the outer wall of the cabin. Winter glanced over her shoulder. Marcus had dragged himself across the floor and was clutching an uncapped bottle of poison in each hand. Before Winter could stop him, he tossed them both over the side of the ship.

"Stop!" Winter shrieked.

Another bottle went over the edge. Winter tried to walk. She fell to her knees instead.

"Are you happy now?" she demanded. "Knowing you spent your dying moments trying to kill as many people as possible?"

Marcus didn't answer. Maybe he didn't have the strength to do anything but let out one last laugh.

Phoebe's voice echoed in the distance. "Winter!"

Winter dragged herself along the railing toward the sound. Phoebe stood on the shoreline, waving her arms. River stood next to her. There was no sign of the city guard, or the mob.

"Is the cure still ready to be released?" Winter called hoarsely.

River nodded. "We already started it."

"What happened?" Phoebe demanded.

Winter glanced at Marcus. He was face down on the ground now, although he still seemed to be breathing. "He was bringing the boat back up to release poison. I was right."

"Oh, you were right?" Phoebe asked incredulously. "Are you happy now?"

"I don't have time for this." Winter stormed back into the cabin, to the steering wheel. She twisted it as far as she could. The boat veered in response.

Once she'd turned the boat all the way around, she returned to the deck. Phoebe was jogging alongside the river now, clearly not done yelling at Winter. River followed a few feet behind.

"Did you kill my uncle?" she demanded.

"We offered him the damn cure. It's not my fault he thought poisoning people was more important!"

"Winter, please, get off the boat!" River tried. "The guard ran off, and I think the mob dispersed, too."

"Yeah, right." Phoebe rolled her eyes. "They won't be happy until everyone Winter told them was evil is dead!"

"Maybe she can calm them down," River suggested.

"And why would she do that?"

Winter's hand tightened around the railing, the only thing keeping her upright. "I can't come back."

River shot her a desperate look that broke her heart. "What do you mean?"

"I am a criminal, River. There's nothing for me in Devil's Pass but prison."

"What? You can't just—you can't just leave us!"

The ache in his voice put cracks in her facade. But she couldn't let herself shatter. Not yet. "River, seriously, think about it. There's no way they let me go after all this."

"But you—" River's pace faltered. "You can't just...leave."

Winter swallowed. "I'm sorry." She thought of her parents. What was the last thing she'd said to them? In front of them? "And tell Mom and Dad I'm sorry, too. Even if they hate me now."

"And where will you go?" Phoebe demanded. "To ruin some other city?"

"You know what Marcus did before he died?" Winter snapped at her. "You know what the last thing he decided to do was? Dump the last of the poison in the river, so that he could tell me about all the cities south of the pass who are about to get hit with a wave of sickness they have no hope of dealing with."

Phoebe stumbled, nearly tripping, only saved by River's hand on her arm. "He—did he?" she stammered.

"What, you don't believe me?" Winter's gaze briefly darted down to her knuckles. White as bone.

Phoebe lowered her head, shaking it. When she looked up again, tears streamed down her face. "No, I do believe you. I just can't believe him. I thought I knew him."

"I'm sorry, Phoebe." It was hard to muster sympathy after Phoebe had fought her every step of the way, but it was also impossible to ignore that Phoebe's intentions had been good. She simply hadn't wanted anyone to die. Hopefully, she would learn something from this mess. Maybe even accept that some evil could only be stopped by death.

"So, what? You're following the river?" Phoebe asked as she wiped an arm across her face. She sounded like she was on the verge of sobbing.

Winter nodded. "There are supplies on the boat, and all of his records and journals. I have to hope it's enough for me to help them." She swallowed. "It's—it's what I have to do. Something that's purely good, for once. No more death."

"Let me come with you," River pleaded.

Winter shook her head. "We can't both abandon Mom and Dad. Not right now. And I need to know that there are people here working to make things better. Do what you can to undo the worst parts of my plan. Calm everyone down. Make sure the plague recipe doesn't get suppressed." She swallowed and added, "And do what you can to see that someone better gets elected in place of Atherton and the rest of the council."

The currents were getting stronger, the boat moving faster. River and Phoebe weren't going to be able to keep up much longer.

"One last thing!" Winter reached into her coat. "You won!"

"What?" River asked.

"Three of stars. You had ten of jewels." Winter held up the card she'd drawn the night before, along with the locket. "You won."

River stopped. "Wait, no, we didn't—"

"Catch!"

River's hands went up just in time to catch the locket.

"I'd throw you the card, too, but I don't think it would make it." Winter's eyes had begun to sting. She fought back the impending tears. River and Phoebe had both stopped running, and they were almost out of earshot.

Not that it mattered. What else was there to say?

Winter couldn't keep herself together any longer. She turned away and staggered inside. Once she'd collapsed onto a chair, she let it out. The fear. The anger. The ocean in her chest squeezing her lungs and crushing her heart.

Tears blurred her vision. Sobs wracked her chest.

If she spent the rest of her life undoing Marcus's mistakes—and maybe even her own—so be it.

Devil's Pass was behind her, and she could only hope that the people would pull through, that the hospital's doctors would triumph, that River and Phoebe and everyone she'd fought for would survive. No, not just survive. *Live.*

She needed to take care of her injuries and wounds. And then—

She had to deal with Marcus's body. Groaning, Winter stood up. Before that, she needed to make sure he was really dead this time.

He'd managed to roll onto his back and stared up at her as she approached. No anger, no triumph, nothing. Just an emptiness behind his eyes.

"Any last words?" Winter asked.

Nothing but a hint of a smile on his lips. He knew, didn't he? He knew she'd ruined her own life to stop him, and she'd keep working to stop him, even after his death.

Maybe he'd won, after all.

Winter picked up the sword. This was the easiest kill yet. Not just physically. Relief flooded Winter as the light finally left his eyes.

Right. Her injuries. Then deal with the body. And then…

While digging around looking for medical supplies, Winter found a familiar book. The first Plague Bible. The book that had helped her save countless patients, until Marcus had made her return it to him.

The hardest task in the foreseeable future would be figuring out which cities were at risk. Winter supposed she'd travel until she saw some sign of civilization and go from there.

She sank back into the chair and peeled off her coat. She pulled out the three of stars card—stained with her own blood— and set it on top of the Plague Bible.

Behind her, an empty jar tipped over and cracked. Winter glanced over her shoulder in time to see a small white rat dart to the edge of the counter. She took a slow step toward it. Blood stained its fur, and one of its legs appeared injured.

Winter held out a hand and let the rat sniff her cautiously before stepping into her palm. It must have been tougher than the rest to last this long.

"Just you and me, I guess," Winter murmured. "Mind if I call you Daisy?"

By the time the sun went down that night, she'd left the land of ice and cold behind. She sat on the boat's deck and watched the sky darken. Even as the last rays of sun disappeared, she could still feel their warmth on her skin.

Undoubtedly, it would drop to freezing temperatures again within a few hours, but this was a reminder that there could be something good for her in the south. Something more than self-inflicted punishment for the things she'd done.

Maybe there was still hope for her, in another time and place.

Thank you for reading
PLAGUE SAINT

To get updates and find out how you can be the first to read new books, find me at:

www.rorynorth.com

Enjoy the story?

Leave a review! Tell your friends!
Request the book at your local library!
Share on social media #plaguesaint

More by Rory North:

Be the first to know about new stories and upcoming releases! Sign up for my newsletter at:

rorynorth.com/Starchatter

Bonus Chapter: Aftermath

Sunlight glimmered off the locket as it sailed into River's hands. Phoebe barely saw it through the tears stinging her eyes. The boat blurred in her vision.

You know what Marcus did before he died? You know what the last thing he decided to do was? Dump the last of the poison in the river, so that he could tell me about all the cities south of the pass who are about to get hit with a wave of sickness they have no hope of dealing with.

Phoebe had seen it while she and River were running up to the boat. Seen her uncle throw a bottle over the deck. What else could it be, besides the death serum he'd created?

Winter had been right all along.

Phoebe squeezed her eyes shut. How could she have been so blind? She'd known the man her whole life.

But...

Maybe there had been signs. Maybe he'd talked a little too much about making sacrifices. Maybe he'd always liked playing devil's advocate when her parents discussed ways to end the plagues. *There's no way for everyone to survive. It's simply impossible. We need to be careful about how we save people.*

We need to be careful about who we save.

"She's gone," River said quietly.

Phoebe's eyes opened slowly. Her senses reminded her that this wasn't over. The sound of distant screaming. The smell of smoke. The bitter taste in her mouth.

Phoebe glanced at River. "Do you know what's to the south?"

It took him a moment to tear his gaze away from the water. From the last place they'd seen Winter. "No idea," he replied, his voice still weak. "I haven't exactly had a lot of education." Even when he'd been sick with white plague, he hadn't looked this...broken. "Do you know what's out there?"

"Not exactly," Phoebe told him. "But I know where we can find out."

River nodded. He gave the locket in his hand one last glance before sliding it into his pocket. "I think we have some work to do."

They set off into the woods, toward Devil's Pass. Phoebe had a million things she wanted to say but no idea where to start. She wasn't sure her voice would work, anyway.

She and River had just stepped onto the first city street when someone called River's name. The two turned in unison as his parents ran toward them. Isaac and Marissa Pierce. Isaac had been the one to shout River's name, and he called it again as he and his wife reached their son.

"Mom? Dad?" River frowned. "I thought the city guard was taking you home."

"They got distracted by the riots," Isaac replied. "We came to find you and Winter."

Silence settled between him and River. River's gaze lowered to the ground.

"She's gone," River said quietly. "She went to save people in the south from the plagues coming their way."

Marissa's mouth fell open. No words came out. The heartbreak in her eyes made Phoebe's chest constrict.

"Well, maybe we can send the city guard after her—" Isaac started.

"She left the city. They won't consider her their problem anymore," Phoebe interrupted him before she could stop herself. "Especially with everything else going on."

Isaac's expression hardened. "You're telling me my daughter just threw the city into chaos and ran away?"

"She was trying to stop—" River struggled to find the right words. "The council was going to—"

"She saved River's life," Phoebe cut in. Nodding toward Marissa, she added, "And yours."

Surprise flashed across River's face. Phoebe still needed to tell him the full story. All River knew now was the deaths Winter was responsible for.

Phoebe continued. "The original Plague Saint was going to let you die, Mrs. Pierce. Everything Winter did was to save your life, and then River's when caught the white plague my uncle created. And she saved dozens of other patients as well." She took a shaky breath. "Maybe her methods were extreme, but so were the original Plague Saint's actions. And the council's. They were going to poison the city to save themselves."

"It wasn't her place to question the council," Isaac said. "They're the ones with education and experience. They're the ones we voted for."

Phoebe exchanged a desperate glance with River. "Don't you understand we're trying to help you?" she asked, gaze turning back to his parents. "Why are you siding with the council when they were willing to let you die? Us turning against each other only benefits them."

"Look, it's a lot to take in," River chimed in. "We're shocked, too. But we don't have time right now to walk you through everything that's happened."

Right. Arguing with his parents was a waste of breath. There were more important things to deal with.

"River, wait—" Marissa started.

"There's something Phoebe and I need to take care of," River told her. "I'll try to make it home in time for dinner."

"But the city—"

"Lead the way, Phoebe," River said, already walking away from his parents. He gestured toward the buildings ahead. Toward the chaos. Toward the smoke rising on the horizon.

Phoebe quickly fell into step at his side. "We're headed to the college," she told him. She glanced back at his parents. The two stared in disbelief. They didn't move to follow.

Phoebe led River through side streets, a slightly longer path that helped them avoid the crowds. They did pass graffiti, but to Phoebe's relief, there wasn't much damage to the storefronts besides the paint. The graffiti voiced support for the Plague Saint, spelled out the council's plan, and announced that the cure was here.

St. Minerva's was completely deserted. Phoebe and River's footsteps echoed through the otherwise silent halls, tracing their path from the entrance to the library.

Phoebe led River to the west side of the library. "I haven't been in this section much, but there should be geographical information on these shelves," she explained to him as they entered one of the aisles.

"Got it." River scanned a row of book spines before selecting one and cracking it open. Phoebe began her search on the opposite shelf.

It didn't take long for something to turn up.

"This looks useful." River turned around, holding the book open to a map. "Devil's Pass is here at the top. The river passes by us here and flows down to these canyons." He traced the path with his finger. "There are multiple settlements marked in the area."

"The southern canyons," Phoebe muttered. "I learned about those in one of my classes. That part of the world was dried up for a long time, but the water eventually returned. People arrived in boats to make a living fishing and harvesting other resources in the area."

River's brow furrowed. "Sounds like the water is their main source of...everything."

"We'd better hope Winter's able to stop the plague from destroying it all." Phoebe wondered if it was as deadly to fish as it was to humans. Even if it weren't, though, a lot of people were in danger.

"It looks like this book has some more information on the communities down there." River closed it up and tucked it under his arm.

"What are you going to do?" Phoebe asked. *Follow Winter?* Would she need their help? Want it, even?

"Winter did ask us to stay here and make sure things get better." River glanced toward the windows. "My first priority is doing whatever I can to help get the city back in order."

Phoebe's eyes stung. Part of her couldn't believe Winter had left such a monumental task to them.

Then again, Winter had done so much work already. She had so much more work ahead of her.

And Phoebe had tried to stop her.

"I wish I could apologize to her," Phoebe muttered. "I was wrong about my uncle."

"I know Winter doesn't seem the type, but if you really want to help the city and save lives, I think she would forgive you," River said.

"I don't know if I deserve it."

"Maybe you can earn it, right?" River lifted his chin. "Let's start by making more copies of this plague cure. I'll spread word among my coworkers. We have friends in factories all over the city who could help us make another batch."

"What about the riots?" Phoebe asked.

"We need to give them a goal. A positive way to direct their anger." River started toward the library doors. Phoebe followed. "For example, helping the hospital."

"We also need to replace the council," Phoebe said as they returned to the college's halls. "I think the policy in a case like this is for the city guard to hold an election. But most of the people stepping up to run will be friends of the old council members."

"Then we'll just have to find people to run against them."

It was a relief to see River's confidence returning.

An idea popped into Phoebe's head. "I think I know where we could get some extra funds for the hospital to pay for treatment without charging patients."

River raised an eyebrow.

"Adams was taking most of the hospital budget for himself, right?" Phoebe asked. "And other rich people like Forrest and Gordon have died. Since they were all actively involved in a plot to poison the city, maybe we could convince the new council to seize their money and use it to fund cure production."

"Not a bad idea for a proposal. Let's spread that idea around," River said. "And even if we can't get a council of entirely good people, they've seen what the city is capable of if they don't start helping. Hopefully, even the greediest people in power will see that they can't get away with everything."

Phoebe and River turned a corner and found themselves facing the building's front doors. River paused, and Phoebe stopped next to him.

"It sounds like things are quieting down out there," River said after a moment. "Let's get people's attention and start planning our next moves."

Phoebe let out a small sigh. "They have a right to be angry, but I hope they're ready to listen to reason. This could get chaotic if people don't think things through."

"I don't know for sure if this was the best way to go about things, but the council wasn't going to change if we asked nicely," River said. "They didn't value our lives."

Phoebe nodded slowly. She'd heard hints of stories like this in one of her history classes. Stories of revolutions in the old world. When governments stopped serving the people and prioritized keeping the wealthy in power, they fell. They were outnumbered, after all, and people were only willing to put up with so much.

"The way other people in my factory talked, I kind of knew something like this was going to happen eventually," River continued. "Especially after I got sick."

Phoebe started toward the doors. Maybe she'd missed the obvious signs of brewing unrest. With all her time spent working and taking classes, it had been easy not to think too hard about how things were run. Sure, she knew the government wasn't perfect, but her classes had always emphasized the council's importance. The people had voted them in, and people wouldn't vote for liars and monsters, right?

But voting had never come with a lot of options, Phoebe realized. The only people who could afford the time and money to campaign were already wealthy.

Her jaw clenched. She wouldn't let her naivety blind her anymore. Marcus had taught her a valuable lesson.

Time to start paying attention.

River spoke again as Phoebe reached for the door handle. "I think we should start with the vote to replace dead council members. And hold a negotiation with those who are still alive," he said. "All of the rioting out there will hopefully have shown them that they can't manipulate us anymore. Even the city guard is outnumbered. They need us on their side to keep things running smoothly."

"Sounds good," Phoebe said. She pulled the door open.

"One last thing," River said.

Phoebe paused. "Yeah?"

"I don't think fixing things down south will be as easy as handing out cures." River spoke with a faraway look in his eyes. "Some people in the factories are recent transfers that moved up from the southern canyons. I've heard rumors that they're facing their own problems down there. There are still fights for resources going on."

River lifted the book he'd taken from the library to examine the cover. "If the new council moves the city in the right direction, and we're able to get plague treatment to everyone who needs it...will you come with me to look for Winter?"

Phoebe swallowed. That sounded completely and utterly terrifying. Leaving Devil's Pass for the first time in her life? Traveling through the wilderness? Visiting communities that might be at war with each other?

But Winter was doing it. And she deserved help.

Phoebe nodded. "Yes. I will."